GREAT
REALIZATIONS

Also by Hugh Hood

NOVELS

White Figure, White Ground 1964
The Camera Always Lies 1967
A Game of Touch 1970
You Cant Get There from Here 1972
Five New Facts about Giorgione 1987

THE NEW AGE/LE NOUVEAU SIÈCLE

I: *The Swing in the Garden* 1975
II: *A New Athens* 1977
III: *Reservoir Ravine* 1979
IV: *Black and White Keys* 1982
V: *The Scenic Art* 1984
VI: *The Motor Boys in Ottawa* 1986
VII: *Tony's Book* 1988
VIII: *Property and Value* 1990
IX: *Be Sure to Close Your Eyes* 1993
X: *Dead Men's Watches* 1995

STORIES

Flying a Red Kite 1962
Around the Mountain: Scenes from Montréal Life 1967
The Fruit Man, the Meat Man, and the Manager 1971
Dark Glasses 1976
Selected Stories 1978
None Genuine without This Signature 1980
August Nights 1985
A Short Walk in the Rain 1989
The Isolation Booth 1991
You'll Catch Your Death 1992

NONFICTION

Strength down Centre: The Jean Béliveau Story 1970
The Governor's Bridge Is Closed 1973
Scoring: Seymour Segal's Art of Hockey 1979
Trusting the Tale 1983
Unsupported Assertions 1991

The New Age/Le Noveau Siècle XI

GREAT REALIZATIONS

A Novel

HUGH HOOD

Published in 1997 by
House of Anansi Press Limited
1800 Steeles Avenue West, Concord, ON
Canada L4K 2P3

Distributed in Canada by
General Distribution Services Inc.
30 Lesmill Road
Toronto, Canada M3B 2T6
Tel. (416) 445-3333
Fax (416) 445-5967
e-mail: Customer.Service@ccmailgw.genpub.com

Distributed in the United States by
General Distribution Services Inc.
85 River Rock Drive, Suite 202
Buffalo, New York 14207
Toll free 1-800-805-1083
Fax (416) 445-5967
e-mail: Customer.Service@ccmailgw.genpub.com

01 00 99 98 97   1 2 3 4 5

CANADIAN CATALOGUING IN PUBLICATION DATA

Hood, Hugh, 1928–

Great realizations

(The new age = Le nouveau siecle ; pt. 11)
ISBN 0-88784-171-6

I. Title. II. Series: Hood, Hugh, 1928– .
The new age ; pt. 11.

PS8515.O49G73 1997   C813'.54   C97-931381-3
PR9199.3.H66G73 1997

Cover design: Pekoe Jones
Text design: Tannice Goddard
Printed and bound in Canada
Typesetting: ECW Type & Art, Oakville

*House of Anansi Press gratefully acknowledges the support
of the Canada Council and the Ontario Arts Council
in the development of writing and publishing in Canada.*

For Robert and Muriel Beckett
with love from Noreen and Hugh

CONTENTS

I
LAUNCH

"We have a launch. We have a clean departure. We are thirty seconds into the mission. This is the voice of Mission Control speaking from the permanent space station *Wayfarer*. You are watching and listening to the departure of the first manned flight to the planet Mars. You can see on your screens, in the top right quadrant of the picture, the spacecraft growing smaller as it leaves the space station behind. There, you can see, behind and above the vapour trails that are drifting away, the disappearing spacecraft manned by a crew of nine that includes three women and personnel from Russia, France, Britain, Canada and the United States, in an unprecedented example of international human cooperation in a great scientific venture.

"Our cameras are shifting now. Directly in the centre of your picture you can see the docking space from which *Visitor I* has just cleared. We are three minutes into the mission, the most difficult minutes of all, the initial application of immense power. There in the centre of your picture you can see the fuelling conduits and supply ramps that until minutes ago were linked directly to the spacecraft. Already it seems a long time since *Visitor I* got under way, though it is only four and a half minutes.

"We go now to our long-range tracking cameras to see if we can give our vast audience of viewers and listeners a sense of the present position of the cosmonauts and astronauts. Their ship is just within range of our trackers at five minutes, the vapour trails widening out behind. There at the very top of your screens to the extreme right we can make out the moving form of the spacecraft. Five minutes, the crucial period, have elapsed, and everything has gone as planned. The crew are too busy at this time with their individual duties, which are highly specific, to supply voiced messages or television images of the interior of the vessel. But we must state at once that this is a long-term space voyage unlike any other so far. In *Visitor I*, when it has cleared the gravitational field of Earth, there will be a functioning artificial gravity service, a completely new aspect of space travel, the yield of the most sophisticated technology, a great advance on previous missions. This service relies on very complex theoretical constructions in pure physics concerning the essential nature of weight, mass and gravitation. As the voyage progresses, there will be television pictures from the interior of the spacecraft showing an environment much like ours on Earth, in which the crew can move and stand and take their meals and rest without any of the inconvenience of weightlessness.

"Now back to our picture of the departing vessel, almost gone from sight. Can you spot her, up in the corner of your screens, seeming to move faster now as her course flattens slightly in the upper atmosphere? Nine minutes into the mission and we can all stop holding our breath. This broadcast originates in our internationally linked service from the permanent space station *Wayfarer*, and if you are monitoring our broadcast by video you are now seeing the interior of the space station. You are inspecting the main cargo bay, or grand lobby as the crew terms it. This is the part of the space station that seems most like living quarters on Earth itself. The temperature is maintained at an even seventy-two degrees Fahrenheit, or twenty-one Celsius, and crew members thrive on it. Here too are some of the experimental botanic reservoirs where studies are made of the life cycles and nutrition of the biological systems that the spacecraft has taken with it on its more than a year-long journey."

There is a brief pause in the transmission of picture and sound.

"Sorry about the interruption, everyone. We go now to a very sophisticated animation segment of our transmission, to show the enormous audience exactly how *Visitor I* will be supported and supplied during its long flight.

"Here you see a rendering of *CV I*, the cargo vehicle that left Earth's atmosphere in mid-October last year carrying the main supply base for the manned spacecraft which follows it from today. *CV I* carried everything the crew of *Visitor I* will need for its program of surface exploration, the Mars landing and reascent vehicle, the surface launcher and rover cars, together with the fuel supply for next year's return trip. *CV I* is now nearing its orbital position around Mars, with about three months to go on its transit. When it arrives it will go into a near-surface orbit, taking extensive photographs of the two tiny satellites Deimos and Phobos, prospecting them for useful landing sites for later exploration. And here is a likeness of the Mars landing and reascent vehicle which is stored in the main cargo bay of *CV I*. This unit will transport the four Mars walkers — three men and one woman — to the surface of the planet. When their stay has been completed after approximately three weeks they will return to the orbiting *Visitor I* and the final stage of the mission will begin.

"It is expected that *CV I* will be in a correct position to await the arrival of her manned consort in about ninety days. Then she will begin to deploy observation equipment, as you see here in our animation. The vanes you see on either side of the hull are designed to observe and record atmospheric conditions close to the surface of the planet, as well as details of the proto-atmospheres of Deimos and Phobos, during successive flypasts. By the time *Visitor I* arrives on the scene, now represented graphically on your screens, *CV I* will be ready for linkage, with enormous bodies of information ready for use by the astronauts and cosmonauts.

"All this time, of course, *Visitor I*'s crew will have been on a schedule of daily exercise, work assignments, tending the onboard modules for plant cultivation, the food-production and -preparation units, and management of the waste-disposal and recycling systems without which the mission would have no chance of success because of its length. The detoxification and decontamination of waste forms a procedure almost as vital as the new method of producing an artificial gravity aboard. These modifications of former practice have taken the technology of space travel forward in a giant leap. In later voyages a totally familiar environment will be sustainable, and as you can see in the onscreen simulation of the interior of *Visitor I* the systems for organic recycling have been given prominence in the layout of the vessel. In animation you can see a crew member repositioning a light source in the direction of a soil bed, to supply essential light and heat for the maturation of plant growth. It might be called a space garden. And in the same way the recovery of perfectly fresh sweet water from the crew's collected urine forms an essential part of the management of the onboard living conditions.

"At fifteen minutes into the voyage, the spacecraft is no longer trackable on our cameras. Later in our extended coverage of the mission we will furnish live communications from *Visitor I*. Radio voice transmission presents no difficulties, and picture transmission has become more and more reliable in the more than thirty years that humans have been in space. Today's departure time has been selected to provide the shortest and best-shaped Hohmann ellipse track towards the neighbouring planet. Here is a diagram of the course now being followed. At this moment the spacecraft is making for point A as shown in the diagram, the most favourable point of departure available for space travel in the last two years. The simulation on your screens at this moment shows the path chosen for this flight by the flight commanders, Colonel Miles Kinnick, USAF, and Colonel Serge Lebedev, of the Russian space program RSRI, in cooperation with experts from each of the participating nations. At this time Mars is in a highly favourable position for our venture. Not for a dozen years has the Red Planet been in closer proximity to us, or as well placed for approach and landing.

"Here we see film of the two colonels moments before boarding the spacecraft. Both are veterans of space flight. Either one could in the event of an accident successfully assume the other's functions. Militarily speaking, Colonel Kinnick has command of the vessel and its crew as well as of *CV I*. The crew will take orders from him for the duration of the voyage while at the same time retaining full responsibility for their own independent fields of specialization. The highest-ranking woman member of the crew is Canadian astronaut Captain Céline Hervieu, who will be one of four Mars walkers, remaining on the planet for some twenty-one days, together with her male companions. One of Captain Hervieu's special fields is her close knowledge of soil chemistry. She will be responsible for the collection of surface and core samples for return to Earth. Her geological knowledge will enable her to decide on these crucial matters.

"In this recent photograph we see Captain Hervieu with her fellow-Canadian Professor John Sleaford Goderich of Cambridge University. Professor Goderich, a Canadian by birth, has lived most of his life in Britain, where he was educated at Cambridge, specializing in theoretical astrophysics, from which he branched out into the mathematical description of non-atmospheric space structures, or, to put it more clearly, the description of space in which virtually no matter is to be found. Here is a picture of Professor Goderich in a lecture room at Cambridge, demonstrating physical models of purely empty space, or space as nearly empty as can be described in mathematical language. Space travel depends on the most economical expenditure of energy in extremely rarefied spaces and the attainment of what we must consider very high speeds. Sometimes during the flight of *Visitor I* speeds approaching eighty thousand miles per hour may be required in order to make the journey in a conveniently brief period of time. Professor Goderich will be available to advise the colonels about speed corrections essential for the maintenance of the flight schedule.

"Now we turn to an animation sequence that gives viewers and listeners an accurate impression of the departure from our atmosphere which will take place when the spacecraft has made three orbits of Earth at gradually increasing speeds. After three orbitings, *Visitor I* will have reached the point indicated at A in the animation. This will be at eleven A.M. Eastern Standard Time, or five P.M. in western Europe. At this point the spacecraft will accelerate to nearly her highest speed and the slingshot effect will be achieved, positioning the craft precisely at the start of the Hohmann ellipse path to Mars.

"Travel in rarefied spaces over very great distances is a technical possibility that will have to become an everyday reality if humankind are to extend their life-space to the limits of our planetary system and even, who can say, beyond it into deep outer space where the distances and the emptiness are very much greater than we can readily imagine. Today's thrust towards Mars is a great first, but only a first. The conquest of space starts here."

"Those beautiful aerial cars," well yes. I calculated that the best spot near the city from which to witness the slingshot effect would be at the extreme tip of the Leslie Street Spit as it curves way out into the lake, probably the most southerly point in the region, certainly the place with the widest sky and deepest horizons. What did I come out to see? A widening puff of grey-white vapour and nothing more. That at least would serve as a guide to the progress of the distant object. What I and millions like me hoped to witness was the final push at the tail of the craft. The bump-off into emptiness with nine lives definitely committed to the deep. This was our first serious try. In a decade the thing would be a matter of routine. Technical evolution includes a series of hazardous — no, risky — firsts. When Lindbergh flew the Atlantic solo he was taking the same risk as the first three men on the moon and the nine aboard *Visitor I*. He was hazarding all that he possessed. You can't offer more and might offer far less. Why did John want to be the first Goderich in space? Those beautiful aerial cars! That's what he'd called the Minirail at Expo 67 when he was four years old. He had pleaded to be allowed to emulate his brother and sister, who were disappearing along the elevated tracking. A technical first of a lesser order, not so very risky as this morning's departure, which must be as risky a venture as humanity has so far conceived.

I slept little and rose at eight, still a resident of Crescent Road in the heart of midtown Toronto. For some years I had owned a small car, the cheapest I'd been able to find. Living alone for most of any given year, with the occasional visit from Andrea and Josh and their children, I had let the terrible din of media attention focussed on me by the events of the beginning of the previous decade gradually die away. Now I could claim to be the least obtrusive individual on Crescent Road, with my little car and my quiet apartment and my few visitors. The sudden prominence in the media of my younger son might rub off on me to some extent. I hoped that it wouldn't, and wondered, as I drove downtown at nine, whether the spit would be packed with would-be observers of the morning's departure, in the way that people flock to favourable observation points to witness the occasional lunar or solar eclipse or the arrival of one of the comets that pass by our planet from time to time. There might be tens of thousands in attendance. I hoped not.

Parking at the foot of Leslie Street was easy, few cars in evidence. Had I been lucky in my choice of site? I had a second rendezvous in the same place, later in the day, with a person whose feet would be planted firmly on the ground, or at least on the landfill. There should be no unwelcome coincidence of arrival. I parked my little car just at that corner where the roadway onto the spit begins, meaning to walk out to the tip of the manmade peninsula for the exercise, to put in time and to calm myself. I did not want to witness a final departure, an historic aborting of purpose.

I kept a transistor radio in the glove compartment, and before setting out on the longish walk ahead of me I fished it out and tuned it to CBC. I didn't want to monitor the runup to eleven. The CBC would be full of chat about the spring into space, interviews with Canadian space scientists, Captain Céline Hervieu among others. Was "Captain" a courtesy title conferred by the media? My son John was continually referred to as "Professor" although he had never held that academic rank. Why did they have to have specific ranks anyway? At least a couple of lieutenant-commanders were going along for the ride, and one commandant, the French officer. Naturally space exploration had to be placed in the hands of the military establishments and government-sponsored research institutes at first, because of the immense cost of such undertakings. We would know for certain that Mars was fully accessible and safe for visitors when commercial flights became available, say in a decade. I wondered if I would ever take a commercial flight to our planetary neighbour and decided that, on the whole, no. Not very likely. I would probably miss the opportunity by a few years. But plenty of folks not much younger than me would respond to the blandishments of excursion posters and book themselves onto tourist cruises. In ten years the authorities would have regularized everything so as to be able to get you there and back in about fourteen months. The trip would be the equivalent in time elapsed of a round-the-world retirement voyage. Plenty of moderately well-to-do people would be lined up at the wickets to sign up for this popular vacation trip. "Fly now, pay later!" It would come to that fairly soon, and why not? If it came right down to it, I felt jealous of them.

As predicted, the weather was startlingly fine for early April, the skies an unmixed blue, no haze, nothing to obscure any sight that might be deployed in the spacious firmament on high. Excuse the language. Skies are a great natural subject for lyrical description, by prophets or poets or prose writers or hack songwriters. "My Blue Heaven," "Blue Skies," "The Spacious Firmament on High," what did the archaism mean, exactly? It had something to do with the shape of the sky, treated as an arch, with its keystone placed at the very centre of the structure, the topmost reach of heaven. Mythological thought dwells on the significance of the skies, as much as that of oceans or mountains, the other great symbolic properties of human life. Today's departure would doubtless be fraught with all sorts of symbolic narrative incident. Astronauts, colonels, captains, the French *commandant*. How would they manage among all these nine, each holding a fairly senior rank, excepting my son John, and him a professor? They might have been wiser to include a few private soldiers in the lineup, people used to receiving and acting upon orders. But such people wouldn't have the requisite technical qualifications. Astronauts. Argonauts. Cosmonauts. The syllable "naut" must mean voyager or sailor, I thought. The link with classical mythology clarified itself as I wandered along the south bank of the spit, occasionally turning on my radio as I proceeded. I hoped to catch a few words from Professor Goderich, taped earlier for broadcast. In this I was fortunate. When I'd come about halfway along my route I heard him talking to some interviewer about his birthplace and early upbringing.

"Yes, I was going to tell you, I was born in Stoverville, Ontario, in 1963. My brother and sister and I were all born in Canada. We were taken to Britain in 1973 when I was ten, and after preparing for university entrance and completing my undergraduate studies I studied at the Institute for Theoretical Physics at Cambridge, in a group that was working on some of the basic problems underlying the structures of space as we know them. We are a team, not a collection of individual theorists. I can't stress that too much; my work on weightlessness, space medicine and artificial gravity could not have been carried out without the fundamental investigations of the Cambridge group. I just happened to be the one who wrote it up and was selected for training in astronautics; that's why I'm here."

"And you must be in absolutely tip-top physical condition for a man in his late thirties."

"I'm in fairly good form, yes."

"Thank you, Professor Goderich. Have you a last word for our listeners?"

"Can I send my love to Emily, that's my wife?"

"Consider it done, sir."

I could hear the Canadian speech, learned in his first ten years, lurking under the precise Cambridge pronunciations. I wondered when they had made the tape. Just before departure yesterday, up at the space station, or perhaps much earlier? He sounded well and happy and calm, as hardly anybody else would be at the start of such an undertaking. He had been the calmest of the three of them. Anthony, now a department chairperson at Northern British Columbia University (as far from Britain as one could reasonably hope to be), unmarried, into his forties, said to have been hit hard by the sudden death of an admired woman, was only superficially calm. Andrea wasn't calm at all, not after what she'd been through with Adam and me some years ago. How does one approach a journey of more than a year in space with equanimity? What qualities are needed? I remembered the instant and long-lasting love that existed between John and his wife. It was characteristic of John that the last words of his message to listeners on Earth were "love to my wife."

I was getting there, nearing the west end of the spit. I might have another ambling forty minutes ahead of me, and so far there were very few people out here waiting for a glimpse of the historic departure. Nobody was carrying binoculars or toting a telescope; the spacecraft would after all be too high up to be seen clearly. It would at best be a tiny moving dot, some spreading vapour as trail. The thing to do was to stay tuned to the radio commentary, which would provide a guide to what to look for. Ten thirty-five. I speeded up, moving well over onto the south side of the roadway, where I could spot huge chunks of paving stone and other landfill still partly visible under the imperfectly tarred surface of the track. This manmade peninsula had not been here before the 1970s, nor so much as thought of when I was a child in Toronto in the 1930s. It had been conceived as part of a super-harbour installation for the Port of Toronto, serving the purposes of a mole or roadstead pier so as to create dockage and transport facilities appropriate to a world-class port. The spit had afterwards been converted first to the status of a conservation area designed to protect birdlife and the unusual botanical specimens to be found there, products of the movements of wind and water along the Lake Ontario shoreline, and then to an enormous shelter for pleasure craft of all sizes, a gigantic marina.

At one time the tens of thousands of seagulls to be found here had almost counted as an environmental danger. Now the numbers seemed much reduced. They used to come here in enormous flocks, I recalled. Where might they have gone? Had some mysterious pollutant been blown along the spit by an unwelcome new eddy in the prevailing winds? When first developed, the spit had turned without warning into a splendid bird sanctuary. I remembered a previous visit some twenty years back, when I'd turned up an overgrown path towards a seagull lagoon on the city side of the landfill, drawn by the honkings and whirrings of perhaps a thousand gulls. All at once I'd been attacked, positively dive-bombed, by a ferocious red-winged blackbird who wouldn't go away and wouldn't take no for an answer. I'd had to turn away from his nesting ground. Protecting the nestlings, of course. I wondered whether the red-winged blackbirds had survived the new pollutant. They are tough little creatures, but perhaps not so tough as all that.

I turned my transistor on, and sure enough CBC was on the spot with chatty newsy coverage, full of background anecdote. How would you feel, you son of a bitch, I said to the commentator in my thoughts, how would you feel if it was your boy who was about to be catapulted off into the most desperate, chancy voyage in history? Columbus, Lindbergh, Armstrong, the crew of *Apollo 13* simply weren't in it for danger. And I, standing on this almost deserted chunk of bald reclaimed land, had to hold still and watch him and his companions take their leave of us. A singular experience, one of the few in my life that I'd describe as unique.

I'd chosen the right place; the other strollers had not come so far out. The single park bench at the very end of the landfill was unoccupied, smeared with equivocal deposits of sandy mud, weed, bird dung. Just sittable on, I reckoned, and fortunately placed so as to look inwards towards Ward's Island, the Eastern Gap and the fantastic many-towered city skyline, an impressive sight and almost brand new.

The radio quacked on and on. I recognized the speaker, somebody who had been busy in harassment during the weeks that Adam had lain dying in my home so many years before. These people never die. At Armageddon or at the end of the apocalyptic thousand years, the commentators will still be running on about the end of all things, full of informed statistics and estimates of how much longer we have to go.

"Here with you at the Last Judgment, with round-the-clock radio and TV coverage . . ."

I squatted on the dungy bench, settled my bottom in the least-mired space, and listened to the uninterrupted flow of comment and bold interpretation.

". . . best view of the historical event of any observers on the planet. The American Northeast with clear skies and full light. In five minutes the spacecraft will appear in the topmost vault of the heavens, at the centre of the arch of the sky, as the end of this orbit brings her to point A, as shown on our TV transmission. It is just possible that the craft will be visible as a small black dot trailing a thin film of vapour that may resemble a wisp of cloud. As there is no cloud this morning, it will be identifiable as *Visitor I*. When it has been visible for about thirty seconds, it will suddenly accelerate and disappear, as full power is applied and the craft is boosted into orbit-quitting mode, attaining close to maximum power and speed for the first time. Those of us following the event on audio should prepare yourselves to scan the southwestern quarter of your view. Keep your position as steady as possible. The merest glance away from the area may cause loss of visual contact. Two minutes now."

I was the sole person at this spot. There were scattered groups of observers about a hundred yards away to my right but nobody intruded on my attempts to achieve a sighting. I wondered whether by any chance they had identified me as John's father.

"Thirty seconds . . . Keep your eyes fixed towards the southwest. Hold your positions . . . steady . . . steady . . . ten seconds . . . and here she comes."

I stood with my head craned back as far as possible between tensed shoulders, like an old turtle defying eagles and herons.

"Eleven A.M. and there she is, everyone."

This production had something of the Roman circus about it, a quality of violent excitement. My stomach heaved. I had eaten almost no breakfast and I was very thirsty. And here, as predicted, a filmy wisp of pale grey spread out somewhere a great distance above Niagara Falls. I narrowed my gaze and tracked the trail forwards to its source. And there was the black dot, almost invisible, seeming to drift lazily across the sky though it must have been moving faster than any previous human invention. A tiny black dot like a printed period, a full stop. I thought, this is an end to things, perhaps the first day of the new age, like the day of the Resurrection, the first Easter or the approaching days of wrath, when all things shall be made otherwise than they are. I rotated on my heels, feeling dizzy from the pressure on my neck. I kept the spacecraft well in sight; the radio babbled on for some moments. All at once the tiny dot vanished.

"Departure from point A perfectly accomplished. The Hohmann ellipse path is now being followed. All extrapolations for the first days of the mission have been met one hundred percent. The spacecraft is now leaving Earth's atmosphere behind and in eighty minutes the artificial gravity system will be activated. Then all the conditions of space flight will be in place and the crew will begin their day-by-day and hour-by-hour activities. We've just received a last message from the crew, from Professor Goderich who once again sends his love to Emily, and on this very human note we end our transmissions for this date, with the sense of a new era beginning from this moment."

Love to Emily. I wept briefly as I took this in. John had known Emily since he was seven years old and she was four. First cousins. I remembered his fascinated attention to the small girl from New York, not really more than a toddler but already the distinct and lovable, slender, leggy Emily Underwood of family legend, the queen of the new generation. At four she had been a mighty sweet child. Now she must be in her mid-thirties, a wife of six or seven years' standing. She and John had been married during one of his training courses under the NASA space program, now the ISA program. That was quite a while ago. An astronaut's training has to be exhaustive and protracted. He must have been preparing for this day for about eight years.

Married for seven years and no signs of any kids as yet; this might be the consequence of strict planning. John and Emily were first cousins, after all, "within the forbidden degrees of kindred." I could not remember whether any sort of permission had had to be obtained in order for an Episcopalian marriage service to take place, as it had, in New York. My brother-in-law, Tommy Underwood, wasn't the sort of man to insist on strict doctrinal regularity in the matter. Certainly the wedding had taken place without any editing of the language of the service. I remembered the wedding very well. An honourable estate, certainly, aimed towards the begetting of children. Perhaps they had decided quietly not to run the genetic risk. That would be a great pity, given John's predictable place in history. If ever a couple deserved to become parents, John and Emily did. Well, there would still be time for that when he came back from his wanderings. Love to Emily. How natural and how reassuring; he might have gone on a bus trip to Lake Placid. Familiarize! Take enormities for granted. The nine space voyagers — why deny it? — were for all practical purposes condemned to an isolated and dreadful extinction. That reality underlay the triumphant tones of the broadcasters and the space scientists at ISA. True enough, everything had so far gone according to plan. But this was only the beginning of the mission; by much the greatest risks were ahead.

The tiny black dot was now invisible. John sends his love to Emily, human attachment stretching and stretching across the widened gulf. The tears in my eyes were hot, genuine and heartfelt, in no way automatic. I turned to watch the few dozen others who had come to the end of the spit. I guessed again that some of them had identified me. They seemed reluctant to insist on intrusion into my private anxieties. None faced me; they melted away silently into the glorious April morning under the vast and empty sky, blue fiction, falsely splendid appearance.

I've never been able to believe in the blue of the skies since that morning; it's only a human illusion. I didn't believe at that moment that human love could bridge such a separation. Maybe John knew something I didn't, a scientist, a theoretical physicist, a believer. Married an Episcopalian. Believer in what? The stretch and reach of human affection, that surely, but what book of revelation might lie on the other side of the widening space? The sky was empty. Nothing more to be witnessed; the grey vapour had departed. Clouds began to form in the west, fleecy and innocent in appearance. I slumped onto the bench behind me and thought again of John's aching need to voyage on "those beautiful aerial cars." The little moving vehicles of the Minirail in that distant enchanted summer when for six months the nation seemed easy to manage. Expo 67. Furniture of myth.

I recalled John's exclamation of delight when we walked through the throng onto the grounds of the exposition, swarming with unfamiliar figures, peoples of all nations, in holiday dress, strangely polite in their enthusiasm for the spectacle displayed before them. What a great time that was! We came out from the Métro station into the tall light of a late spring day, me and my three kids, equipped with plenty of money — it was not by any means a cheap show — and with those passport-like documents whose holders were guaranteed unlimited access to the site. There was a kind of wide-open courtyard or plaza which spread out in front of you as you left the Métro station, with the first of a multitude of souvenir kiosks and sandwich bars sprawling to right and left. In the distance — not a great distance — the splendid silver sphere, Bucky Fuller's dymaxion creation, the pavilion of the U.S.A., swelled up in the sunshine like some heavenly body. You couldn't miss it. It dominated the site as it had certainly been meant to do. Of course Bucky Fuller was a genius of some sort. I had heard him speak to both popular and learned audiences, and he had never failed to arouse the strongest enthusiasm among both the learned and the casual for proposals that in my mouth of course would have seemed far-fetched, visionary. Here was living proof for everyone of his immense gifts, the splendid globe through which ran the rails of the neat little overhead railway that enchanted all visitors to the site. The Minirail. As it happens, the first working model of an overhead railway I'd ever seen, and a striking instance of the beauty and glamour of technology that really works, that embodies an idea in radiant metal.

Of our three children, it was the youngest who stood open-mouthed at the sight of the curving, leaning little trains as they swung around to the left and rolled away towards the Biosphere. The cars were coloured a sweet medium blue, darker than the blue of the heavens, almost marine blue, somewhere between the sky and the ocean. Anthony and Andrea darted across the plaza, keeping well in my sight as per previous agreement, and started to spend their pocket money lavishly on souvenirs, beanies, key chains, T-shirts, carryalls. It was great fun, a once-in-a-lifetime event for all of us, something to be cherished in the memory, a day on which fatigue never supervened.

When the question of Minirail voyaging surfaced among us, I was reluctant to let John take the round trip over the site. He was only four. I thought he might throw up from sheer excitement and self-induced vertigo upon the heads of unfortunates below. In the event, I need not have worried; this was the boy who grew up to conquer weightlessness in space. He must have known in his heart and guts the strange destiny that lay waiting for him thirty years down the road. Could he really have guessed at it? I remember his starry-eyed stare upwards at the shining blue trains as they crossed over us, making that sound with their little wheels that I've never heard since and could at once identify in a dream. I hear them now across the decades.

Never a frequent nor dedicated flier, I'd been reluctant to take the Minirail ride, which rose in some places more than fifty feet above ground, a distance that made me shut my eyes and hold on to my seat. Anthony and Andrea had been the first to take the leap into airspace, having bought tickets and found seats on a train that left before I realized where they'd gone. John then set up a wail of frustration.

"But I want to go on those beautiful aerial cars."

The astronaut at four! My guts are those of a groundling; they don't take readily to flight. But John, at four as at thirty-seven, was eager to ascend to the greatest heights. When you think of it, there isn't much difference between a first Minirail ride and a first flight to Mars. They both rise very high, in their scale. As I left the ground on that first Minirail ride I felt like a voyager in deep space and gazed backwards and down regretfully at the receding ground. And all this little voyage did was bring us back over our starting point about forty-five minutes after departure, having circumnavigated the Expo site. Epoch-making exploration! Perhaps all first voyages seem the same, trackless in some sense, although the Minirail ran on its fixed course of metal, and *Visitor I* had to find and follow the beginning of the Hohmann path into deep space. All aerial voyages presuppose heavy bumps after free fall, if there is any surface to land on. John and I after all had been able to look down upon swarms of holiday-makers from his first aerial car in 1967, only a year before the first Moon landing. In those days space travel had been a popular project. Then high costs and the persistence of certain political struggles had led governments to abandon the idea. Only when the outcome of the political struggles seemed to have been decided, the Cold War unrefrigerated, had space travel become respectable again. The period from 1967 to the present day and this morning's terrifying departure constituted a distinct historical movement, the windup of the second millennium after Christ and a turn in human affairs that clearly implies the dawn of a new day.

The trouble with primordial fall in deep space is that there is no stopping you after you drift free; you can fall forever unless you chance to come into a gravity field that draws you, unconscious, onto an alien surface. Otherwise you just fall and fall and fall . . . Weightlessness is actually alien to conscious human awareness. It is an insult to our bones and marrow and the trace metals they must contain if we are to remain human. Without the familiar pull of gravity we lose our humanity, gradually at first, then more quickly. The first cosmonauts stayed pretty sane for some weeks or months; eventually they began to lose control of their behaviour. Some of them came out of it in very poor shape mentally and muscularly; they couldn't throw a ball or mount steps after a year of weightlessness. Total biological disorientation might have been the next step in their decline. Our metabolism, our digestion, the bare ability to consume food and drink, depend on gravity for their continuance; you can only with difficulty swallow in a weightless state. You can't keep anything down, as we say carelessly, and careful chewing is of little help. This is a rooted physical condition in the lives of humans and other animals. You need to keep your feet on the ground, or if you're in flight you must have some sense of a bottom to things. Free empty space, void of gravitational pull, simply isn't livable. I'm certain that John's theoretical interest in and mathematical description of weightlessness and artificial weight came out of his first experience of being up off the ground, of being able to look down from the height of fifty feet at a surface on which he and I would go bump if the supports to the Mini-rail should give way. Free fall from fifty feet would damage you but would at least conform to gravity-oriented dynamics, with no chance of being lost in emptiness. His primordial perception of flight was the foundation of today's flight.

I don't understand the dynamics of artificial gravity. I understand that it is partly illusory, a conjuror's trick worked by the slow rotation of the entire space vehicle something like the spin of a football in a long forward pass. The spacecraft would be continuously rotating at a pace imperceptible to its passengers in much the way that Earth moves imperceptibly on its axis while simultaneously speeding forward on its orbit, adjusting its tilt as it moves, so that the entire sphere moves in three different ways at three different speeds. All the time the earthbound forms of life, human, animal, the very plants themselves, move, grow, decline as if we were in fact stationary.

Suppose the planet were to brake suddenly in its rotation or its orbit, or both, what would be the consequence? Would all things be launched off into space because of the cessation of gravity? Probably yes! There would no longer be any system of relations between Earth and the other force fields of the

solar system to keep us in place. While I don't make a habit
of brooding fearfully on this kind of catastrophe as the likely
end of life on earth, I can grasp that repugnance towards some
such event is built in to our biological structures; we exist on
the sufferance of gravity. Viewed from this angle, all gravity
is artificial. Earth is a large space vehicle much like *Visitor I*,
just as the Minirail cars of 1967 were a very small version of
the spacecraft and of Earth . . . I suddenly saw something I'd
never fully understood before, though John had often referred
to something of the kind. Aboard the spacecraft, working
under the conditions proposed by the Cambridge theorists,
the crew would record no impression of flight or rapid motion
at enormously high speeds towards a planned destination.
Nor would the ship's rotation on its axis be perceptible. The
crew would be living in or on a small planet with a dynamic
of its own.

According to the Cambridge calculations, the crew would
experience a force about ninety percent of Earth's gravity; you
would feel somewhat stronger and lighter than on Earth; you
would expend slightly less force and energy to perform a given
action than on the terrestrial surface. The differences would
not be so great as to cause atrophy or loss of muscle tone. The
medical consequences might even be beneficial, as effecting
a modest reduction of cardiac stresses. One's whole medical
picture would be conditioned by the environmental change.
Blood pressure, pulmonary efficiency, functions of the ali-
mentary canal, most bodily operations, including the feed of
blood to the brain, would all be modified by the subtle change
in the play of bodily forces. This system exists in every bodily
state, deep under water, on mountaintops, in flight, in space
travel. We are almost infinitely adaptable beings. When John
talked me into taking him on the Minirail, his small four-year-
old body must have sensed the change in environment that
comes of being lifted fifty feet above ground; in this there were
predictions of his present undertaking. Flight is flight; and
height is height; how far and how high we soar is matter for

private decisions, but we never outrun our natures. John's need for flight had lain in his limbs and heart for decades and was now taking him far away. Goodbye, John, I thought, and a safe return! There goes a generation of wishing and willing. Time to find out what he was made for, a generation, half a lifetime.

Taking a generation as something slightly over thirty years, I realized that my own identification with this place was a matter of fully two generations. I sat facing north, at the very tip of the reclaimed spit, looking directly towards the Eastern Gap, the old passage that divided the Toronto Islands from the mainland at Cherry Beach. On the island side of the passage I could see the crumbling concrete pierhead that had been my private land of meditation in August and September of 1939, more than sixty years ago now. From where I was seated now in early April at the beginning of an historical cycle — the age of interplanetary travel — the time of the great rollover into futurity, I was able to look back over two full generations of temporal evolution, to bear witness to the intolerable complexities of our age of moral confusion and anxiety, from 1939 to the present. What should I call it?

As I sat there looking northwards from the end of the land, I could see myself at the age of nine, in the summer of '39, perched sitting at the end of the Eastern Gap looking southwards at the very place where I sat now, about fifteen hundred yards from 1939, to mix together categories of space and time. I didn't have to strain my eyes to spot myself there at that age. There I was in the flesh, in a relaxed sitting posture, my back propped against the red-painted pole on which were hung two flotation rings and a boathook. I could see all that, the lifesavers and the brown paper bag that held my picnic lunch, two peanut-butter sandwiches on brown bread and a jelly doughnut. My childish existence was timing my morning today at a distance of sixty years and more, as actually as I am here now. My child self seemed to emanate from my present person like a wraith, a sending of spirit, and stream

across the dividing water to recompose itself in my favourite
spot with my favourite lunch at hand, even to the bottle of
cream soda, red, sticky and very fizzy, with which I would
regale myself later on, during those solitary sessions of meditation. I saw the form of the tall old girl's bicycle that I used
to pedal along the boulevard from Centre Island to Ward's,
lying on its side behind my child self, the slow tic-tic-tic of the
revolving back wheel perfectly imaginable at this distance. I
certainly heard it, and all those other sounds from September
1939, the wash/swish of water in the Gap, the sound of my
humming a popular tune of the day, the ticking of the well-
lubricated old bike, the calls of the seagulls of sixty and more
years back, in that place then as now. I felt as if the ground
on which I actually sat had still to be invented or projected
into space. I was still to be born, hanging in imaginary time,
myself a child lodged in the fearful expectations of September 1939, in that terrible year of suspicion, lies, diplomatic
tomfoolery, appeasement, political sin on the grandest scale,
political folly of the same proportions, Hitler, Stalin, Cham-
berlain, Daladier, all sitting over there with me as I sat
peacably propped against the lifesaving pole, eating my
jelly doughnut, drinking my sugary drink and thinking the
thoughts of a nine-year-old boy with a taste for solitude. What
had I retained of those childhood musings? What kept me
coming back at different times to gaze on the wide prospect
of the lake or the skyline of the new city? I used to wait for
ships that might or might not come in. Now I trailed *Visitor I*.
I tried to site myself in my childhood mind. God knows,
I could see my small body plainly enough, that haunting
apparition or *revenant*. Twice he stood up and bent peering
forwards as though looking out for my present self in a light
obscuring mist.

And I understood, as he or I or both looked forward and
back, that it was the distant future he was searching for, in
the light mist that in memory always seemed to swim around
Eastern Gap shipping arrivals. To my child self everything that

had brought me here today was inexistent futurity, an early dream. He already existed while I was lost in sixty years to come. I felt my aging self dissolving around me. I was a being in my 1939 dreams. There I stood, across fifteen hundred yards of gap water, leaning forwards into the distant future. And what I strained to see was my two-generations-on reality, where I'd gotten to now, all the terrible things that September 1939 seeded, then brought to full growth, the epoch that might now be ending or recycling itself. What is its name?

Pre-history, classical antiquity, the Dark Ages, the High Middle Ages, the Renaissance, the Enlightenment, Romanticism, the Modern Age, these factitious names for Western history would take us to the middle of the last century, the twentieth A.D. There remains a great and terrible age to be christened, and in naming it to make it real, in the invented story that we agree to call Western history. What are we going to call those years from 1939 onwards? That disastrous, ruinous experiment in the destruction of traditions and civilizations. What is the time we have made for ourselves to be called? The Age of Genocide? Can that be the name for our seven decades? I recall that little Matt Goderich — my child self — had said to his father on the morning of September 3rd, 1939, "If they're going to have a war, they'd better declare it now and get it over with." What I was asking for was World War II, the age of atomic weaponry, the Cold War, NATO, the Warsaw Pact, the death camps, the Gulag, the various other genocides that have given the special character of our age. King Genocide. Let's get started and get it over with!

The light mist in which I now seemed to be folded wasn't a true physical mist; the day of the grand departure continued as clear now as it had been at eleven; only a tiny cloud here and there in the west broke up the expanse of blue. All the same there was this mistiness of spirit that wrapped around me and clung. I and the ground under my feet had the status of pure unreality, something yet to be dreamed into existence, then realized over sixty and more years. This was a very disturbing state to find oneself in. That little boy over there was dreaming of a future in which I now existed. I saw him lean again, peering into the slight mist. What was he looking for? I used to sit there hoping for the arrival of certain ships that used Toronto as home port. I stirred uneasily, as if *Northumberland* or *Kingston* or *Cayuga* might be steaming up behind me out of the past. If I turned and faced south I might see two or three of these elegant swanlike vessels swimming gracefully towards me in a flotilla whose home port was not in a place but a year, 1939.

These reversals and involutions, these time-tricks, began to seed my imagination with terror. I felt inexistent, imprisoned in my own small head, trapped in the witness of a nine-year-old prophet. Just as my son John had predicted in his wishes at Expo 67 the long long flight entered into this morning, so I at nine years had dreamt and wished for the thing I am now, an old man at the end of the land. I felt the limits of the cranium around me, the pulsing brain of the child who was to create me in the here and now. I could not escape the limitations of the personal. The child across the water was me then, and I as I am now. We are really identical, calling across the gap to one another, across the span of a life. This has nothing to do with memory as we usually perceive it. I was not exactly remembering how I was then. I was being myself at nine and at my present age *simultaneously*. If I'd had the gift of prophecy, which is only experience rewound so that you see your lifetime in the future as though it has already happened to you, I could have foreseen in that deadly summer everything that was to happen, not just to me but to all my contemporaries. While I was scanning the surface of the beautiful lake with no manmade spit to bar my view, I might have read out and renarrated all that was to come.

For all those times coexist in the dreaming person, the striving scanning being that ranges through sequences and connects them into unities. Just as I was now imagining my child self, my young self was imagining myself to come, me

and my friends and my opponents and even my few enemies.
Even innocuous Matt Goderich can have enemies, you see.
The challenge is to keep their numbers down. Let me see, I
mused, what foes did I imagine and invent for myself in those
days? What friends? I already knew Adam Sinclair in 1939
and was afraid to be identified as his associate. Had I had any
idea at that time that fifty years afterwards I would live
through Adam's death? I seemed to recall that already in those
early times I had grave forebodings about Adam. I guessed
that nothing very fine would happen to him, and in some ways
I guessed right. Adam had certainly had his moments, but the
following fifty years hadn't revised his destiny.

What about sheer physical possibility, the possession of
posterity, if we can be said to possess our descendants? Did
I at nine suspect in my body a link to others to come? Does
the child suspect his or her children? I tried to recall early
suspicions of the kids that might come out of me and some
girl. I can't have done that at nine, can I? Does biological
suspicion precede the actual falling in love that biology later
presses upon us? I think that we all feel ourselves — all
without exception — to be little links in a very long chain,
from which we can partially extract ourselves only by the
exercise of a very strong will. At nine I must have longed for
a loving and pretty partner. Letty Millen? Alysoun Selkirk?
Ina-Mae Rae? Esther Bannon? Bea Skaithe? Claire Begin, or
her little sister Alanna, of the soft and rose-petal lips? What
a troop of feminine lovelies had wound through my infant
emotions by the time I was nine! Perhaps the children in
my body were also alive in imagination while I sat at the
end of the Eastern Gap looking at "*la mer, la mer, toujours
recommencée,*" in a solitary ecstasy of apartness. Looking
southwards then there was nothing to get in the way of my
quiet passionate search for the future.

It was precisely the future that I had *behind me* in those
solitary moments. Not so much in front of me on the lake, but
stowed on the reclaimed flats of Toronto Harbour where in

1939 the features of the skyline were the tallest building in
the British Empire, the Bank of Commerce at 24 King Street
West, and the Royal York Hotel, the largest hotel in the British
Empire as it then was, with the most rooms of any, and the
first accommodation-tunnel under a roadway from the north
side of Front Street to the south, so that travellers might pass
between the hotel and the railway station (largest railway
station in the British Empire) without getting wet. That tunnel
was the first serpentlike link in the maze of underground and
indoor passageways that mutates and ramifies itself every
year in what would be the largest underground city in the
British Empire if there was a British Empire. Nothing is now
the highest, largest, longest anything at all in the British
Empire. But in 1939, looming up behind young Matthew as
he ate his sandwiches, there was a vast weight of Empire
towering behind in August and September, red on the map of
the world (Mercator projection) and red all over the globe.
These imperial forms made a little boy think that we'd better
go ahead and get the war over with, maimed political thinking
that he at nine and I at my present age would disavow.

He saw no Leslie Street Spit curving across his vision in light
mist; he might just have predicted it. Occasionally a bucket
dredger would traverse the Gap, headed towards certain offshore sandbanks that needed to be lifted from the paths of
navigation. But the actual living present that moved little
Matthew in those times lay looming behind him, tallest,
widest, longest in the British Empire. The skyline of Toronto
in 1939, besides the station, the bank and the hotel, featured
the shapely spire of Saint James' Cathedral, seat of the Angli-
can metropolitan of Toronto and essential expression of kingly,
even imperial, ecclesiasticism.

If Matthew had turned his back and scanned the shore
from west to east in 1939 he'd have seen the Island Airport
and the Western Gap, with some of the buildings of the
Canadian National Exhibition faintly visible behind them,
and then the ballpark, Maple Leaf Stadium and the Tip Top

Tailors building, then the Master Feeds storage elevators and the Terminal Warehouse, the ferry docks, the excursion steamers' docks, and wharves and piers serving the lake freighter traffic, with the Royal York and the Bank of Commerce tall behind them. In the foreground some mudbanks where land reclamation was proceeding speedily, and behind them the spire of Saint James', and along again to the east the channel that led to the turning basin, the two bascule bridges that lay along the road to Cherry Beach, and finally certain great heaps of bituminous coal, the source of the gassy stink that overhung the district on damp days. That was the actuality of harbourfront and skyline, the true Toronto at the child's back in the given year. Now as I stared at the same harbourfront the first thing I saw was Harbourfront, equipped with fancy architecture, flags and banners, and acres and acres of condos for the entrepreneurial class, something that had not been visible sixty years ago except in dreams and prophecies, scarcely even there. If I could re-enact and re-create my nine-year-old self this morning, what prophecies would I find in my mind?

I could not have predicted Harbourfront. What did I look forward to in Toronto life? High school? The cadet corps? I don't believe that the first weeks of WW II endowed me with a wish to hurry into uniform. The Canada of 1939, population twelve million, was the Canada of colonial times in most aspects, an element of Empire, a dutiful daughter. Canada was in essence a colony of Britain when I sat alone on that corroded pierhead. I enjoyed the ideas of a colonial child. The best that could happen to me would happen in Britain, and I would not be there to see it. What did I imagine as the best of happenings? That I might grow into some sort of quasi-Briton? That little boy had grown into me. Was there nothing left of him?

Let me see. I knew no other language than English, and very colonial English at that. I could not have translated the simplest sentence of French, Italian, Latin, German. I might have mastered the emotional drift or tendency of about five hundred feature films, all very Hollywoodian in tone, and I had certainly read five hundred books, many of them rather grownup books. I had started to look at buildings with some appreciation of their design and their history. I had the beginnings of a sense of social structure, mostly from my callow observations of the differences in people's clothes from Eaton's, from Eaton's basement and from Eaton's Annex.

That left me an English colonial, untypically a Roman Catholic, with the pitiable rudiments of an education, no knowledge of any foreign tongue or culture beyond the random remarks of my grandmother Jeanne, no imaginative or emotional discipline or cultivation outside of family life, reading and constant moviegoing. I think what I was most in need of unconsciously was a music more complex and developed than the popular songs of the day. It would be another decade before contact with painting or serious music began to be important to me. I was still almost a savage, without anything more than impulse to direct my life. At the same time I was keenly and sometimes hurtfully aware of many warring impulses. I needed to belong to an interesting group, a street gang or a class in school, and was moving in that direction with hesitant steps. At the same time I badly needed regular doses of solitude. When alone, contemplating "the sea, the sea, always beginning again," and watching the lake vessels on the horizon, I began to construct the self that would finally bring me to the tip of the then imaginary landfill, the reclaimed peninsula on which I now found myself.

This construction went ahead unconsciously. I had no idea where I was going, no sense of the bearings of my emotional life, my affections, gender or sex. In 1939 I was still an imaginary person, a fictitious adult. Now my child self is in that predicament, relative to action, existing only in my historical imaginings; even so we are both in some sense real, a kind of reciprocity intrudes between us. He could have imagined me, and I can imagine him doing so. There is probably some year that connects and fuses all these realities, some age, say around thirty-five, in 1965, that links every-thing, the year John was to celebrate his second birthday, a year before little Emily Underwood was born. Now I began to see the events of this morning, the magnificent launch and the disappearance of the black dot in the middle of the heavens, in a new context. Between my youth and my age came the lifetime so far of my son. Everything I could guess about myself at nine came filtered and interpreted through the lives of all three of my children, Anthony Earl, Andrea and the far-wandering professor. I now began to see my life, and everybody's lives, as an infinite series of filmy layers, one on top of another like onionskin, through which a never-ending process of interpretation, references forward and backward, goes on. We see ourselves existing in the distant year, the long past, and our view is coloured by the likeness of our past selves to the realities of our children and their children. How was little Matt Goderich like his son John? They certainly share some purely familial resemblances. My sister Amanda, who heard me on the telephone at nine, swears that Anthony, John, her son Mark and I are almost indistinguishable on the phone. Our heads, mine at nine, Anthony's, Mark's, John's, are alarmingly similar in their modelling. The skulls beneath the skin are rounded here and flattened there in precisely the same conformation; our hairlines trace the same paths; none is threatened with baldness.

There is more in this than common sense allows. Some of these forms may descend through millennia. A child born from these lines of descent will have stored in genetic inheri-tance such a multitude of replications as to make the marriage of cousins very risky. John had married his first cousin. Should they conceive a child, we might have to face up to these genetic implications. My son John would not have undertaken this perilous voyage without calculating the risks of parenthood. Surely he would not have left Emily pregnant. But this was what rumour insistently declared, in New York and in Toronto, and we were all anxious to learn more. If Emily was indeed pregnant and gave birth to a healthy child, this would probably occur while its father was preparing for his Mars walk. If she was really carrying a child, it would come to term in about seven months, say around the middle of November. It would be several months old before its father returned to Earth, a unique historical instance of parenting, as it were, by remote control. I longed to know what truth there might be in the rumours. None of the other voyagers in *Visitor I* was in this curious position, so far as I knew. I felt that as the long flight evolved, the transmission of this happy news might form a regular feature of reports on the trip. "Astronaut's Wife Pregnant." People all over the world would begin to count months, just as I was doing, working backwards from the time of the announcement to the night of conception. Something to look forward to.

Coincidence of all happening, past, present, future; we seem to be systems for turning the future into the past by the digestive organs of presentness. My ghostly nine-year-old self had at his back a skyline that featured the head office of the Bank of Commerce, the Royal York, the notion of the British Empire. Now all that historical stuff has been superseded by a new skyline that defines itself in the image of SkyDome, the CN Tower, Roy Thomson Hall and four enormous bank head offices rising like high objects of worship from a cluster of lesser novelties at their feet. Skylines — heavens — change relentlessly from month to month, slower than the continual self-renewal of the sea but with similar restlessness. Looking back at the new skyline, I wondered how and when it would next be altered. By nuclear catastrophe?

The banks remain dominant on the skyline, have indeed multiplied, and the old building at 24 King Street West can scarcely be seen among the tall new slabs that dwarf its form. The Royal, the Commerce, TD Centre, First Canadian. Skylines seem to require banks to support them; finance forms history. I remembered, as the childlike form of young Matthew began to dissolve in my imagination, that the Canadian Bank of Commerce (nothing imperial about it then) used to issue annual calendars at New Year's as promotional devices. They came rolled up in light cardboard tubes, and when unwrapped proved to comprise a poster with a handsome illustration at the top, produced for the occasion by "the bank's artist," and below that the pages for each month. I vividly remembered the calendar for 1934, which involved its beholders in precisely the same effort of imaginative reconstruction that I had put forward this morning.

That year was the hundredth anniversary of the incorporation of the city under its new/old name of Toronto. The city had been Toronto before it was "muddy York," and after it had been York for a generation it reverted by popular choice to being Toronto. The citizens seemed pleased to see their new little community going back to its old and hallowed name. The youngest citizens, who remembered little of the city's past, were pleased with what they believed to be a new name for a new place that was going to create its own history. "Toronto" therefore satisfied most people, as both a new name and an old one, while getting rid of the imperial connotations of "York," which surfaced as soon as the ancient line of dukes was called to mind. The grand old duke of York then living was the second son of George III, the soldier who marched his ten thousand to the top of the hill, then marched them down again.

In exchanging York for Toronto, the new Torontonians were making an act of faith in their future as Taronto, or Toronto, "the place of meeting," while at the same moment recalling the earlier age of primeval forest trails that ended on the sandy flats of Toronto Bay where I was now posted. "It's never present till it turns to past," wrote Philip Larkin. He might have gone on to say that it's never future till it turns to present.

The Commerce calendar for 1934 illustrated this double process remarkably. The tasteful watercolour displayed above the monthly leaves was a portrayal of two skylines from my present viewpoint. I had been seeing *and* imagining the twinned skylines of 1939 and the present of Harbourfront and Commerce Court. The twin skylines of that calendar were those of 1834 and 1934, a montage of distant times and the same site, just like mine of this morning. At the bottom of the calendar picture was a really rather elegant depiction of the town of 1834 as it would have appeared from a point on the lake close to where I was standing now, a good mile and more offshore; the view must have been taken from some small boat or other. Much was made of the city's status as a busy little harbour, small trading schooners well represented; the water was an unpolluted blue-green. Trees onshore, churches, wharves, government buildings, the promising township, in its multiplicity, ran across the picture in the lower third of the space, the real 1834.

And then above it, coloured softly as if seen in a vision, rose the city of the future, the Toronto of 1934 with its magnificent tallests and biggests of Empire, tallest Bank of Commerce, biggest Royal York, the colonialist name brought back after a century as a promotional property. "Never till it turns to past," says Larkin, and he is right. Now I've got four skylines and four places of meeting to imagine and they merged and separated and merged and separated dizzyingly as my aging man's prescient memories began to assess and digest them. Today was a turning-point designed to reinterpret all the others, the beginning of the age of space exploration, something to surpass Columbus and the Wright brothers at Kitty Hawk, 1903. Truly a new age, an epoch-making undertaking. How do you make an epoch? Do you decide to do it consciously, or is it only much later, perhaps after a century or two, that we see the beginnings of epochs? I think we know already that the citizens were beginning an epoch when they re-called their city Toronto, failed to find Hitler's body in the ruins, set out for Mars.

Three or four times before, in my lifetime, I'd been involved in heady beginnings to *local* epochs, if there are such things.

The first season of the Stratford Festival, the closing night of the Dominion Drama Festival in Stoverville in 1967, the design and execution of the Canadian Pavilion at the Venice Biennial in 1980, the last illness and death of a popular idol at the ever-to-be-remembered last days of the 1980s. These four events, epoch-markers, were all part of the history of the arts and entertainment in Canada. Why were my little local epochs all involved with this kind of action, whereas my father's public actions, and even more his covert, secret activities, were political, ethical, even moral in their bearings? My son John's epoch-makings beginning from this day seemed to be scientific, military, social, in fact very multiform, in use and reference. My father cast his net very wide, my son wider still, and I, the middleman or entrepreneur, could only claim a foothold in the arts and entertainment.

A famous death remains a death, epoch-making for the decedent. Adam Sinclair's death had had little to do in itself with the arts and entertainment. It was the final fundamental human act, the definitive ender of epochs. So I conclude that the true epoch is the span of human life, birth and death being the makers adjunct to temporal sequences of every kind. We do nothing before we are conceived and cannot be seen to act after death, although human narrative usually insists on the reality of personal survival and personal action after the first death. Think how many movies involve some silly story of reincarnation where a funny man comes back as a gorilla, a car, a dog, or if he has been a rake, a beautiful girl, illustrating the permanent human need to treat imaginatively with the likelihood of existence in an afterlife.

Beginnings and endings, politics, ethics, art and entertainment and science, exploration, theoretical physics, space flight, all seem to imply the possibilities of death and rebirth, the oncoming of the age when all things sacred and profane shall be made new. The New Age. The millennium and the Second Coming of the gods and heroes. And heroines. Perhaps I should write "heroes" only, refusing to genderize the heroic.

Women are as often heroic as men. The heroic is a unifying, cross-gendered mode of action, erected over our impossible wish to know what we were up to before we were conceived, what we will be doing after we are dead. What was God doing before the Big Bang? Heroism seems to spring from nowhere and to defend and apologize for nonentity. We act our conceptions and we act out our deaths. Some of us act them in the heroic mode.

As the crew of *Visitor I* sets out this day for our nearest planetary neighbour, we are all aware of the extreme dangers of the mission. It is very likely that these heroes, three women and six men, must die in the course of the voyage. The odds are much against their safe return. Yet we continue to behave as if life were the readier option, routine, day-to-day business. We hide from them and ourselves the imminence of their deaths, and our own as well. Perhaps the truly epoch-making act is that which most powerfully proposes to conquer death. Every day that passes from now on, while their mission unrolls, is a day closer to its successful completion. Thirteen months, is it? Or fourteen. Days of this year's calendar, and next year's, to be ticked off daily till they return, with the odds changing from one hour to the next. Soldiers died in the last moments of both world wars; some died after the official cessation of hostilities, with the silence deepening after the guns stopped firing. Did such a victim "die in the war" or was he a peacetime casualty? Mortality is the justification of significance and indeed creates it. It is the imminent end of one phase of existence, to be followed by something indescribable, making everything new and different, that creates meaning. Without the epochs, everything would be stagnant; nothing would be in contrast to anything else, would always and only utter itself, like a bird with a single maddening cry. That isn't what we expect from life and consciousness, both of which require risk taking in the hope of discovery. That's why the nine visitors had left our atmosphere forty minutes ago, seeking something totally unlike what we have known before: this is how human experience wrings the new from the old.

Discovery and invention. Not the same but always found in close proximity, reciprocal expressions of an endless search. Discovery unwraps what is already in place without our knowledge of it — the relativity principle, distant galaxies. Invention comes from inside ourselves; we contemplate the world and think how much better it would be if only pigs had wings, or we were first cousins to the apes. And we proceed to create the poems of pig flight or evolutionary biology. These may not correspond to the facts discoverable in the world. It is perfectly possible to invent a reality and at the same time discover it. What is now proved was once only imagined, said Blake. Perhaps the poets are right. Perhaps we set out deliberately to create epochs. The first document to deal at great length with the exploration of space was *Buck Rogers in the Twenty-fifth Century.* It recorded that epoch more surely for its witnesses than King Edward VII created the Edwardian Age. Giving names to new things — sometimes to old and unknown things — is the most creative of things. Some scholar sat down with a pipe one day and mused, and suddenly there was Post-Modernism, 1958–2005. Sometimes I'm tempted to invent/discover/create Pre-Post-Post-Modernism. Only I could not bear the weight of the responsibility implied. When the name has been put into circulation, the thing itself will soon enough be found.

This very morning, following the departure for Mars, people all over the world will be trying to invent the name for this new epoch. Whoever does so will have fashioned an undying achievement. Who first saw that the Renaissance *was* the Renaissance? Who thought of the Romantic Movement, sometime round about 1840? We live in A.D., not in C.E., as some of us profess to believe.

" 'Tis well an old age is out, /And time to begin a new," wrote John Dryden, not very long before his death in 1700, a year that the poet seems to have regarded as specially significant in human history, no doubt for very good private reasons. We witnesses of the dawn of our new age have even better grounds than Dryden for self-congratulation. At the same time we aren't ready to abandon A.D. for C.E., or B.C.E. The destroyers, time and death, agents from the abyss, are always encroaching on our ambitions, undermining us, sapping our underpinnings. I felt the power of this fact as the hands on my wristwatch moved towards noon. My second appointment was about to come due. The great voyage of discovery and invention was now fully launched. *Visitor I* had already covered eighty thousand miles.

Now that an hour had passed and the midday April sun was high, I began to feel intimations of the arrival of my secret date for noon, creeping towards me from the northeast under the blaze of noon. My second mind, the mind of invention, glimpsed a spectral form, unseen for more than two decades, darkening the roadway from the foot of Leslie Street. Pluyshin. Gerda Kotecke Pluyshin, dressed in her characteristic iron-grey clothes, with hair of the same middle hue, moving slowly but dead on time along the reclaimed road, casting a broad shadow in the deepest black across the way as she came. I thought of Christian Hopeful pursuing the way in *Pilgrim's Progress*, finding it in its latest stages overcast by the terrible winged figure of Apollyon straddling the path, the demon-angel whose name means ruin, the Greek version of Abbadon, the dreaded strong wrestler who must be overcome if the end is to be gained.

Looking northeast I saw her come. By my watch she had thirty seconds in hand before beginning our contest. Gerda Kotecke Pluyshin from everywhere and nowhere, of unknown origins, to whom no tongue seems native. The dark-grey lady who had supplanted me at the Venice Biennial in 1980, when doubled disaster had made me return to Canada with all speed. True enough that another arts administrator of impeccably Canadian background had been deputed as my nominal substitute, but Pluyshin had taken the project in hand and refused to release it when my gentle replacement arrived on the scene. That was Pluyshin's launch as a figure to be reckoned with in the formation of official Canadian policies for arts administration. Perhaps in the country illegally, she took her slow way towards me on the reclaimed land in the last seconds before noon, wearing a look that seemed to me in the last degree malignant, but full of meaning. I must wrestle with her to persist in my way. Now she spoke.

"Aren't you glad you came?" she asked. "Aren't you glad?"

II

THE LAST TITIAN

"Mission Control back to you again. The video portion of this presentation consists of an animated rendering of the position and progress of *Visitor I*, providing a vivid commentary on the text of the daily radio transmissions available for relay to our worldwide audience. Listeners and viewers alike have deluged the space centre with indications that they accept the video renderings as equivalent to on-the-spot televised pictures of the spacecraft in flight, taken from positions outside the craft by the astronauts and cosmonauts in the course of the voyage. This is theoretically possible, but extremely hazardous at interplanetary speeds. Earlier televised footage of the crew at work on their various undertakings, botanical servicing, exercising to retain muscle tone, relaxing on various recreational assignments, taking meals together, all of this has been transmitted direct to our relay stations on Earth, and from there to viewers throughout the globe. But rather than risk the lives of crew members, we have decided to go the normal route of animated simulations of the exterior of the spacecraft in flight. We know that you will concur in our choice.

"The televised pictures will provide a running commentary on the radioed voice transmissions, which are sometimes imperfect or interrupted. When vocal comment is unintelligible, computers analyze almost immediately the contents of the message and restate it in clear phonemic patterns. In the unscrambling process the characteristic pitch and tone of the original speaker has usually been simulated accurately. What you hear will be more accurate even than what you see.

"You must also remember that these exchanges of vocal messages are going back and forth across distances that far exceed those of ordinary radio transmission. Messages from distant space, such as we are every day receiving from *Visitor I*, show a distinct time-lag in communication; they may take more than eight minutes to traverse the intervening distance. By the time the craft has been positioned around the target planet, depending on its orbital path, radio transmission may require more than eleven minutes to bridge the enormous distances involved. At that time there may be frequent interruptions of contact between the crew and ourselves on Earth. But on the whole, nearly continuous exchanges should be possible, as well as televised pictures of the tiny moons of Mars and the surface of the planet itself. It should even be possible for the four astronauts who do the Mars walk to send televised reports of their progress during their time on the planet's surface that will preserve essential records of the soil components, rock formations, atmospheric conditions, functioning of equipment and other matters. This report will be the first direct account of the state of another planet taken from positions on its surface. The human history of Mars will start henceforth from that point.

"Since its departure in early April the spacecraft has been in flight for over four months, a total of one hundred and thirty-two days. Here is a depiction of the positions of the two Martian moonlets, Phobos and Deimos, relative to that of the nearing cargo vehicle *CV I*, which is just about now reaching the position for its orbiting of Mars. There it will conduct automatic laser probes of the surfaces of the moonlets, to determine their composition, and to verify the ionic structures of matter lying on the surfaces of these small bodies. *CV I* will have accomplished much exploratory investigation before the manned craft arrives on the scene this coming November. And here you see the manned vessel entering your picture in animated reconstruction. At this point we find that only trivial course corrections have had to be made to the Lebedev/ Kinnick flight plan. Both officers are supremely qualified commanders; their cooperation during the voyage has been exemplary. Each day that passes illustrates the wisdom of ISA in its choice of these two veteran officers. With the voyage out halfway completed, we can say that the likelihood of a successful completion of the whole undertaking already has been immensely increased. Living conditions aboard *Visitor I* appear to have stabilized after some early confusion. Food supplies, and the problems of recycling or disposal of waste matter, are now under routine control. Living schedules are being carefully observed; the atmosphere of improvisation of the early days has been overcome. Radio contact and computer reconstruction of messages has become a settled, orderly procedure; today we are going to attempt transmission of a personal message from one of the astronauts' families to the crew's onboard quarters. This copies a transmission that occurred early this morning, Eastern Standard Time."

Badly distorted vocal transmission interrupted by cosmic ray bombardment. Heavy cracklings. Occasional blips of audible speech.

". . . uninterrupted darkness . . . hard . . . too dark . . ."

"That was a computer restoration of Colonel Kinnick's voice, as recorded this morning. We have something else for you."

Whistlings, then a strong, rhythmic roaring.

"We appear to be receiving radio signals of unknown origin, emitted in deep space from a transmitter of non-terrestrial source. Astrophysicists working on this question at Mission Control believe that these radio frequencies are characteristic of emissions from non-intelligent sources outside our solar system. They must originate at extreme distances from both *Visitor I* and Earth. They are surprisingly strong, given these conditions."

A long moment of near silence. Then some words from Colonel Lebedev in Russian, later translated by American broadcast authorities as assurance that the flight was proceeding routinely.

"Excellent. No interruptions. Cooperative flight team," said Colonel Lebedev.

Further interruptions. Then the attempt by Mission Control to message a crew member in space, an historical first.

"This is Mission Control messaging *Visitor I.*"

Crackling and whistling.

"Say again, Mission Control to *Visitor I.* Do you read me?"

Indistinct sound afterwards reconstructed as "Reading you. Over."

"Message is personal, addressed to crew member Goderich. Message begins here. 'It's what we thought.' Repeating message. 'It's what we thought.' Message signed 'Emily.' Repeating message and signature. 'It's what we thought. Emily.' Message ends. Do you read me?"

Noise reproduced on computer tape for authenticity.

"Mission Control says again, 'Do you read me? Over.'"

Almost distinguishable words in English. Then a sharp remark apparently in French. Not quite clear enough for translation. Then perfectly clear English words.

"Say again please, say again, over."

"Message begins. 'It's what we thought. Emily.' Message ends. Message is addressed to Professor Goderich. It's personal, but whole world listening. Second message begins here. 'Congratulations to Goderich.' Message ends. Over."

Then follows an extended period of interference noise and then a single phrase from the spacecraft.

"News and congratulations received. And out."

"There we have it, listeners, the first transmission in history of private personal information from Earth to a spacecraft on mission. This is a great moment forward of human culture in human history. We have authorization from the Goderich family in New York and in Toronto, Canada, to disclose the meaning of this first message. In mid-February, six weeks before *Visitor I* departed on its flight, the astronauts and cosmonauts all received departure leaves, taking their time in turns. Professor Goderich spent his brief leave in New York with his wife, Emily Underwood Goderich. It can now be publicly confirmed that Mrs. Goderich is expecting a child to be delivered about three months from now, about the middle of November. A child will be born to a mother safely under medical care on Earth and to a father approaching the time of his landing and Mars walk on the Red Planet's surface. By the time Professor Goderich returns to Earth the child will be halfway through its first year. The professor becomes the world's first space father. The hearts of human beings every-where on Earth will reach out to Emily Underwood Goderich at this time of risk and strain, wishing her only the very best of health and happiness at this time of special meaning and purpose in her life and that of her gallant husband.

"Now we go to an animation of *CV I*, the cargo vehicle of sumptuous layout and marvellous equipment that is of the first importance to the success of this mission. On your screens you can see detailed working drawings of the vessel that departed on its advance mission last year. In a few days we hope to bring you filmed coverage, direct from *CV I's* automated cameras, of the flypast of the two moonlets which will have been carried out before *Visitor I* arrives. We hope to be able to run colour films of the two moons, showing their surfaces, their shape and size and something of their composition. Then the cargo vehicle will move into its orbital path around Mars herself, taking weather observations and preparing for linkup with the manned craft. During this time of waiting, *CV I* will relay massive information-input to the cosmonauts and astronauts, who will therefore be fully briefed about what is happening on the target planet.

"On our screen you can see an exploded schematic drawing of the different components of the cargo vessel. You are seeing the aero-brake control system that directs and sometimes alters the angle and speed of the cargo ship's movements. And there you see the large cargo bays at the rear of the ship. Here is an artist's rendering of the interior of the rearmost bay, just forward of the linkages that will allow the two craft to form up into a single joined unit. Crew members will be able to pass freely from *Visitor I* to the sister ship. The work of assembling the powered vehicles that will take the Mars walkers down to the surface of the planet and bring them back again, plus the life-support module that will house them during their stay on the surface, will be accomplished by the crew while in the cargo vessel. Here you see a drawing of one of the main access routes between the vessels, lighted, even comfortably warm and high enough for crew members to make the transit comfortably without stooping.

"We can announce at this time that *CV I* has successfully arrived in Mars orbit and should very soon begin low-level surveillance of the satellites of the planet. We expect to bring you first reports on the nature and composition of Deimos and Phobos within a few days. That will be a significant first step towards completion of the mission's assignments. The chemical composition of the moonlets will provide essential information about their histories; it is very important to our scientists to be informed about these matters, as they look forward to the future colonization of Mars. Some theorists believe that Deimos and Phobos may eventually function as space platforms on which permanent stations may be established, assuming the function of observation points especially of Martian atmospheric conditions and meteorology. But this is a long look forward into the future of space technology. Meanwhile, this concludes our report for today, as we once more present our congratulations to Professor and Mrs. Goderich, the first space parents."

Here's the tale as Pluyshin pitched it to me long before the morning of the launch, on that morning itself, and in later meetings, all conducted in the most secure conditions. We met on the morning of the launch at the very end of the Leslie Street Spit because Pluyshin thought nobody could listen in on us there, firstly because we were two miles from any point where covert listening posts could be set up, and secondly because observers in the air would be readily distinguishable in that wide sky. And she was quite correct in this. There was nothing moving in the sky, no helicopters, no light aircraft from Toronto Island airport. No living persons on this end of the spit; the sightseers had all gone away, after the tiny black speck in the sky vanished. On the other side of Ward's Island on Toronto Bay proper, a few of the usual small sailing craft might be moving to and fro; but they were at a distance. Speaking as we were, in hushed tones covered by the sound of moving water, it seemed to us unlikely that a small craft at that distance might pick up the sense of our chat. This made me chuckle. We could send messages to *Visitor I* that were reasonably audible but we couldn't be picked up by surveillance two miles away. Or perhaps we could; the point may be purely academic.

I was satisfied that nobody was listening to us; our subject of conversation was secret and secure and not a threat to global peace, not a matter for weapons analysis or the department of war plans. What we were up to was for Pluyshin — I'm convinced of this in the light of later events — her chance to bring off a final great coup in the strange world of art sales, prices and valuations, that would earn her a record-breaking agent's commission or finder's fee. For me it seemed to be the definitive act of cultural maturation, for Canadians and for myself; there was certainly a personal motive for this hazardous and costly secret undertaking but it had absolutely nothing to do with war plans or political positionings. Oh, I can see that a captious critic could say that we were taking political positions all over the place. That is so if you consider the curatorship of the great monuments of the human spirit to be politically based, a political act. Certainly there were elements of secret diplomacy involved. I have always tried to remain aloof from specific, programmed political action, unlike my father and my son John. Does the brave space traveller take a political stance by his or her choice of a dangerous but at the same time brilliantly novel form of action? I can't recall offhand any comments to the press, from the crew of *Visitor I*, about ideology or political theoretics. Mind you, the choice of joint Russian and American commanders might be thought to have world-historical implications, especially in our period, the post–Cold War Age.

Two decades ago a briefly popular work of vulgar history and political theory had advanced the idea that history was over, finished, final, a completed story. There were no new political ideas to be advanced. All rationally conceivable forms of government had been essayed: monarchy, oligarchy, democracy, anarchy. And only democracy had proved useful and acceptable to humankind. Similarly, capitalism and socialism and all the other points of political dialectic had been long examined in practical day-to-day life. One and only one possible choice had emerged. Like most types of theory, political and historical thought could be seen to be at the terminus and no novelties need be expected in future reasoning on these matters.

"HISTORY IS OVER!"

How well I recall the open-mouthed awe and ready acceptance with which this slogan was greeted by world intelligentsia. The notion became current about 1988 or 1990; it held the field for two or three seasons of academic debate. Down came the Berlin Wall. Socialism seemed definitively superseded; one Eastern bloc state after another abandoned the controlled economy for the free-market system, usually with terrible shocks and withdrawal symptoms accompanying the move. Capitalism had won and no imaginable rival could now arise to oppose the free-market ideology, not in the 1990s nor the new millennium.

What nonsense! Within months of the coming-down of the wall that had been the emblem of ideological rivalry for a generation, new forms of political thought and behaviour began to appear; they drove out the hoary conceptions that had dominated social theory since World War II. The Cold War might be over indeed but history continued to unveil new mysteries, new dilemmas. Government in and of space. The beginnings of space law and space jurisprudence — in effect the politics and sociology of Mars to begin with — now sprang up to puzzle the theorists who five years earlier had been declaring that there was nothing left for them to theorize about.

Who owns Mars? Do the nations that have financed the building and the operation of *Visitor I* and *CV I* have something to say about that? Do Russia, the U.S., France, Britain and Canada have claims to bits of property, subdivisions, on Mars? Money spent on the project must confer some sort of property right! That was more or less what the discoverers of the New World had thought, while the aboriginal inhabitants had been there all the time, waiting to be "discovered." Queen Isabella pawns her jewels and buys the Americas with the proceeds! The classical act of the European colonizer. But the great red world that has hung in our sky since a time long before human existence isn't a New World like the Americas. It can't be bought and sold, subdivided; planets come too high in the real-estate market. Nobody owns the Earth, although one imperialist after another has put forward the claim: Alexander, Caesar, Bonaparte, Hitler. Who owns Mars? Not Miles Kinnick or Serge Lebedev, and certainly not John Sleaford Goderich.

Politics, in the sense of diplomacy at its widest scope, must be inseparable from undertakings like the voyage of *Visitor I* now under way. But electoral politics should not be. Space flight doesn't have much to do with running for office and getting elected, winning the hearts and minds of an electorate. Or does it? I can feel that itching at the back of my mind that always means I don't know what I'm talking about. Mission Control never says anything about upcoming elections in Canada, Britain, France or the U.S., and nothing whatsoever about the state of the present administration of Russia. It would be foolish and wrong of the space scientists to tie the success or failure of their enterprise to the results of a series of elections.

All the same, these missions cost enormous sums of money drawn from the public purses of the participating nations. Who budgets for these expenditures? Who decides whether the voyagers are to have steak on Saturday night and chicken on Sunday? Somebody does, and that somebody must wield enormous powers, for the public purse is suspended next to the throne. I can't even tell you how much my son was being paid for risking his life continually for fourteen or fifteen months. His salary and expenses would be trivial compared to the overall cost of the mission. I don't think the cosmonauts and astronauts have political ambitions or secrets. There are no elections aboard spacecraft.

And yet *Visitor I* had Russian and American co-commanders.

I guess I'm making too much of all this, but if ever there was an epoch in history when the outmoded and dangerous notions of international diplomatic rivalry or military competition might be seen to be worthless and superseded, this by gollies is the time. That's why I felt so double-minded when Pluyshin first reappeared from twenty years and more in the past, virtually unaltered in appearance, with the same unswerving dedication to her purposes, none of them accessible on the surface of her discourse. She had always liked to make mysteries of anything that had happened in her neighbourhood. Just as in 1980, so today her precise national origin was simply unknown and likewise her native tongue. She spoke more than ten languages, some more fluently than others. Her English had clearly improved since the last time I'd seen her in the spring of 1980 during the runup to the Biennial. Or maybe she had spoken it pretty well then but just wasn't letting on. Anyway she spoke English these days with not very much accent and with a wide and exact vocabulary. This might in itself constitute some sort of admission.

She might be letting on that she trusted me, which only meant that she wanted something big from me, some grand favour, support for some project of a disgraceful nature, so dubious that it couldn't be proposed or explained without a long preliminary course of indoctrination of her target, me!

This meant that some large amount of money would be involved in her explanations and obfuscations. Nothing in the amount of a space mission's budget. We weren't, God help us, going to be talking trillions or even billions. It's useless to come to me about billions. I don't understand them and I don't want to hear about them. I have a modest competence to live on, the yield of various pension investments and bits of inheritance, and sums paid to me by the new management of *Codrington Hardware and Builders' Supplies. Since 1867*, as fees for consultation services on the board. I had and have enough to live on but no influence over the economic plans of governments. Yet Pluyshin had come to me.

She hadn't come unrecommended. I'd had messages from the top functionaries of three distinct ministries. Nothing on paper, and not from the ministries I'd have expected, starting in September of the previous year, to the effect that this free-lance member of the international arts administration circuit needed to see me on urgent business. One of these ministries, the toughest and best-administered in my judgment, had consistently spoken about the woman as if she had to be listened to very acutely and carefully. None of these covert communications could have been shown in court to bind anybody to anything; no form of contract and no authority to negotiate existed among Pluyshin, the federal government and me. The whole matter required ventilation, in my opinion, and I had put off seeing her for some months on one pretext or another. This noon encounter was only the third in a series which, I could now predict, was going to continue for some time to come. We'd spent most of our first two meetings sparring with one another about the choice of a more settled place to get together. The first time we'd spoken together, just after New Year's, we'd met in the Grand Concourse of Union Station, an ideal place for such an appointment, with crowds swirling around and lots of strange unpatterned noise in the background to frustrate and confuse surveillance equipment.

We had not sat down. Pluyshin held a carryall made of an unattractive satiny plastic fabric, into which she kept sliding her right hand as if to produce documentation of an intimidating or even incriminating nature. She had nothing on me, I kept telling myself. Nobody has anything on me because I've never done anything. But she had the most remarkable power to make me feel enmeshed alongside her in some very questionable intrigue. That doesn't suit me. I've never really understood what she was doing beside me in Venice in 1980. Had she been put in place to keep an eye on me, to insure perhaps that I made no useful contacts with operatives from what were still the Warsaw Pact nations, in fact the Soviet power centre? Venice, traditionally an interface for covert intelligence operations between East and West, could well have been the place where innocent-appearing Matthew Goderich might run off the rails in misguided enthusiasm for some kind of socialist policy on the arts. Who could tell? His father had been an effective agent, but too independent-minded to be fully relied upon, and besides, he was dead. His brother was some sort of writer, novelist and dramatist, a very undesirable associate, perhaps not an associate at all. He was known to have run off with the subject's wife in the early 1970s. Not a persuasive or convincing personal history for one of our chief cultural representatives in Venice at such a time; might get up to all sorts of escapades. We'll set Pluyshin on him. We've got enough on her to keep her in line.

So might their reasoning have run. If you work for governments on matters that have to be kept secure, you are subject to that kind of watch and ward. When I was in Venice I knew that Pluyshin was spying on me on somebody's behalf. I never tried to establish just who her master was. Could have been any one of six or seven security authorities from the grade of deputy minister on down. Might have been RCMP. I couldn't be bothered to go into the matter. And anyway, my stay in Venice was abridged by disasters in my personal life that had no element of secrecy about them. When Linnet and my mother died almost simultaneously, even the meanest-minded spymaster would have sensed that his surveillance had become superfluous. As a covert agent I was from that point on well out of the running, and had never been a starter. That's why I'd been more tickled than anything when Pluyshin made contact with me after a good twenty years had passed, insisting that we meet first in Union Station. She kept me occupied for two hours, sauntering up and down beside her while she murmured, sometimes quite inaudibly, about the politics of the Adriatic basin, on either side of that always troubled sea.

"A particular point of interest to your Mr. Churchill," she mumbled, pausing in her agitated pacings.

"My Mr. Churchill?" For a moment I couldn't make out whom she was talking about, the events of World War II having receded over fifty years into relative obscurity in my memory. Mr. Churchill didn't seem like an agent in contemporary history to me. To Pluyshin he was obviously a living force, to be reckoned with in any review of European, if not world, power alignments.

"Trieste, Split, Dubrovnik, and their hinterland," she said, fumbling for papers in her holdall, then deciding not to produce them, "full of Nazis and Partisans jockeying for control of the *postes de commandement*, the ports, the main roads and the inland passes. A perennial trouble spot, still is today. Look at the defacing of the antiquities of Dubrovnik, the bombardment of the palace of Diocletian. In a campaign of irregulars, any enormity, any crime against civilization becomes possible. That is why Colonel Peniakoff is still so much revered in the Veneto and along the Adriatic Gold Coast."

That was the first time I'd ever heard of Colonel Peniakoff.

Pluyshin must have decided that she was letting me in on things too quickly for my earthbound imagination to grasp them. For this, for some other reason too, perhaps, she gave up all pretense of direct communication and started to chatter, half fearfully, about the currents of trade in the international art markets. Prices. Exchange rates. Import and export regulations in effect in various European capitals. We spent over two hours together that first time, and I didn't understand the bearing of half what she said, except that it all had to do with the presence of British and Canadian units of the Allied forces in Italy from 1943 through 1945. She seemed to me to be casting her net pretty wide if she expected me or many others to remember the strategic situation of the Italian campaign.

Once I threw off a remark that seemed to interest her, and even to throw some light on the matters she wanted to discuss with me.

"The west coast, then the focus of the advance, got all the press attention," I said. "Anzio, Cassino, Roma, even the campaign in Sicily, which only lasted for a few weeks; in North America we heard little or nothing about the Adriatic. The press handouts were long and diffuse and always emphasized the actions of American forces. That was only to be expected; that was the big expensive show. I don't remember hearing much about the Adriatic until long after the war was over. I've heard very little at any time since."

"Perhaps he was not truly your Mr. Churchill, if that is how matters were presented to you."

"Why are we discussing Mr. Churchill anyway? I don't have any idea what you're talking about."

She gave me a wary sidelong glance, then tugged at my arm, leading me out of the main concourse towards the west end of the complex, along the ramps that lead to SkyDome.

"Nobody baseballs in winter," she said gloomily, giving a little shiver. She wasn't getting any younger, I noticed, and I wondered, not for the first time, how old she was. Mystery about her age was positively the only thing she had in common with the *Mona Lisa*. Agelessness, or rather invisible aging, contributes greatly to an air of mystery in women. I'd have guessed that she was a year or two younger than I was, but I might have been very wide of the mark. She gave few signs of loss of energy, hauling me behind her up the slopes like the little engine that could.

When we got to the top of the ramps, we found ourselves faced by barred and padlocked doors and could go no further, the wonderland of SkyDome being closed for the season. This brought Pluyshin to an unwilling halt. She turned around, deciding on the spur of the moment to say no more that day.

"You'll hear from me when I get back," she said, giving no indication of where she was going or how long she'd be there or what we were supposed to be discussing. I heard no more from her for about six weeks, and then one night a poor-quality white envelope with some cheap sheets of writing paper enclosed was pushed under the door of the Crescent Road apartment, with a snakelike slithering sound that seemed appropriate. This was towards the beginning of March, at a time when I was growing preoccupied with the upcoming space voyage. It appointed — it did not suggest — a brief rendezvous in an even more bizarre meeting place. This was a coffee shop on Queen Street West, frequented almost exclusively by young artists, painters, muralists, workers in fresco, graphic designers, whose profuse shop talk was quite sufficient to cover our chat and render it unintelligible. I remembered it as a haunt, under another name, of Josh and Andrea's, maybe a decade earlier.

"You might ask yourself," said Pluyshin this time, "why the British and Canadian forces placed themselves at the east end of the line of battle . . ."

I'd never thought of asking myself any such question. All my thoughts in the 1943–45 period had been concentrated around my mother's loneliness and my father's absence on some secret mission. I just had no emotion to spare for the woes of Yugoslavia, as it then was. More properly, Croatia, Serbia, Bosnia-Hercegovina and the rest of that dog's breakfast. "Trouble in the Balkans." My God, yes. You could have all of Croatia, I thought then. Just bring back my father safe and sound.

"The vilest of reactionaries," said Pluyshin in the accents of warm approval, still with reference to Mr. Churchill, "but a man with serious commitments nevertheless. He sent his own son into the area during the worst of the intriguing to try to establish the correct lines for British policy."

I knew, as perhaps Pluyshin did not, that Randolph Churchill's junket to that much-contested district, in the strange company of Fitzroy Maclean, Evelyn Waugh and Freddy Birkenhead, had had more of Gilbert and Sullivan about it than of Churchill *père*. At the same time, Winston's plans for the alignment of postwar European political blocs laid much stress, as we now know, on occupation of Balkan territory by governments sympathetic to British aims. That is, not the Soviet Union. Put baldly, the reason the Brits and Canadians fought their way up the Adriatic coast of Italy was the anticipation and advancement of British political ambitions during the postwar period in the region. Mr. Churchill had a fondness for costly sideshows in the overall conduct of war on the grand scale, as his Dardanelles project — so misguided and so costly — in the First World War had shown. He deeply wished to mount a similar project in Greece and the Balkans in 1944 and 1945, and repeatedly tried to persuade Roosevelt, Eisenhower and other senior policy makers that a strike at the "soft underbelly" of the Balkan states would yield rich rewards after the war, in the form of exclusion of the Soviet power from the affairs of the region.

In this he was swimming against the tide of history. Russia, or her representatives, will always be a force to be reckoned with in the largely Slavic countries that lie east of Vienna and west of the Danubian estuary. Mr. Churchill could not by any means have barred Stalin and the Soviet power from exerting influence over the region. When he sent Randolph, Freddy Birkenhead and Evelyn Waugh there to make contact with Marshal Tito, he was on the brink of a momentous policy decision that affected eastern European political adjustments for another sixty years at least. The British choice to support Tito and his Partisan movement, conceding thereby the quali-fied adhesion of Yugoslavia to the Russian sphere of influence, was the source of much disturbance that ensued.

"Qualified" because Tito insisted from 1944 onwards that his movement should enjoy a certain measure of indepen-dence from Stalinist policies for the postwar development of eastern Europe. In 1943 and 1944 these consequences lay hidden in Clio's womb; the undermanned and undersupplied British and Canadian military formations were left to conduct their own version of the Italian campaign in comfortable obscurity, even though the port cities of the Adriatic especially merited close geopolitical attention. Brindisi, Bari, Ancona, Rimini, even the tiny port of Ravenna, the emperor Augustus's little foundation, and across the narrow shallow sea Dubrov-nik, Split, Trieste; these places have bobbed up in every period since classical antiquity as centres of marine activity of the highest importance for the economic and social history of southeastern Europe.

American policy makers cared nothing for all this. In the light of more recent interpretations of their behaviour it seems that Roosevelt, Marshall, Truman and Eisenhower knew nothing about the hinterland of the eastern coast of the Adriatic and cared even less than nothing about its future. Croatia, Bosnia-Hercegovina, Serbia, Albania, Montenegro have since then paid and paid repeatedly for this ignorance of history. They are still trying to pay down an enrobing deficit of misery and misfortune dating from many centuries ago. Turks, Slavs, the peoples of central Europe have contested power in the Balkans for more than a millennium — closer to two actually — and we learn from this that where three great peoples meet there will always be dreadful perdurable conflict.

This is why Mr. Churchill wanted to mount an end-run that would move northwards from a "liberated" Greece to give the Western allies a foothold in the area during the later 1940s and afterwards. Perhaps his echoing phrase about the iron curtain was already whispering in his head when he persuaded the high command to employ almost exclusively British and Canadian units to pursue the retreating enemy up the line of the railway from Brindisi at the heel of the Italian boot northwards towards the Veneto. All these geopolitical puzzles lay behind the slow difficult advance of the British and Canadian formations along the terrain that lay between the littoral and the first row of the hill towns inland, places such as Iesi or San Marino that commanded an overview of the flats and made the northern advance hazardous.

The Italian peninsula is pure hell for military commanders. It is divided raggedly along its middle from north to south for almost its whole length. The presence of the mountains as a spinal column for most of the distance from the Mediterranean to the Alps and the Dolomites, with brief interruption in the Emilia-Romagna, makes infantry tactics highly problematic. Commanders prefer to deploy their forces on the western side of the mountains, where there is some breadth of room to manoeuvre. The Adriatic coast presents tacticians with peculiar difficulties in moving to the attack; the defenders have things largely their own way there. It is most often a question of movement along a narrow coastal strip, always under the eyes of defenders who naturally select the frowning heights for their defensive posts. The tactics dictated by the geography have not changed since the times of the greatest Caesar, who crossed his Rubicon moving from north to south in this very theatre of war.

In the Italian campaigns of 1943 and 1944, an invading force moving northwards against a defensive position held by battle-tested troops had the option of stressing either the west end of the line of battle, where Naples and Rome lay and the precious objectives of Florence, Siena, Pisa, or the east end, the Adriatic coast. For wide-ranging strategic reasons, Rome had to be taken and the gateway into southern France approached as soon as possible. The Veneto and the Adriatic coast, leading in the eyes of Roosevelt and Marshall into the Balkan quagmire, could best be treated as an ancillary theatre of battle unworthy of the deployment of major forces. It was a kind of irksome necessary evil to be left to the attentions of the Brits and the Canadians, out of the mainstream. Naples, Rome, Florence, Pisa, Genoa were the great objectives. Ancona, Rimini, Ravenna could be left to the mercies of the slowly withdrawing German troops whose defeat was to be obtained only by the use of great force against strong defensive sites, an operation too costly to be risked. Let small forces slowly roll up the eastern end of the line of battle as the Germans gradually fell back northwards for fear of being outflanked. The German defenders in the east had no future and could be expected to contest the advance vigorously; they had no open line of retreat. Very soon, if they gave enough ground, they would find themselves backed up against the Dolomites northeast of Trento, trapped in a position that would allow no line of retreat into Austria. Their senior officers had in any case been ordered to hold their Italian positions to the end. They would not have been welcomed back to the Fatherland; they had no place to go.

The defenders were not numerous but they were in a desperate situation and every man knew that the high command was prepared to let them fall where they stood rather than divert support from the major defensive theatre across the Apennines, where Anzio and Montecassino were held with such energy. The eastern defenders were just as desperate, but their means of defence were much more restricted. Their retreat up the Adriatic coast was distinguished by the intensity of its engagements, which were nevertheless fought by scattered and not very well supplied formations.

A particular characteristic of this campaign was the ferocity of the house-to-house street fighting in each of the port cities, particularly in Bari and Ancona, where Canadian infantry fought with great distinction against some of the bravest and toughest German forces in Italy. Ancona especially is difficult terrain for attacking infantry moving north, lying as it does right down on the coastal flats, while a mile or two to the north and west of the port the ground rises abruptly and dominates the shore below, finally turning into genuinely hilly country looking northwest towards the central *massif* where Iesi lies concealed, and beyond Iesi the fastnesses of the Marche, and then Urbino.

The modest Canadian infantry formations had been introduced to coastal campaigning in their action out on the flats around Bari, some weeks before their assault on Ancona. In both places essential port installations had to be preserved if possible from destruction by retreating German demolitions experts. Densely mined and booby-trapped along every narrow roadway, and in every part of useful warehousing, sheds, cranes, other transport equipment, Ancona was a hornet's nest for inexperienced officers. It was indeed fortunate that junior Canadian commanders here made contact with a roving band of REME personnel with whom they conducted several operations of an improvised and unauthorized kind, farther north along the railway. At Ancona there were already signs of the lapsing of direct contact with the higher command, benign neglect of a kind more in evidence in intense warfare than the civilian supposes. These REME types seemed to spring out of the ground whenever Canadian troops got too near suspicious electrical installations, or were too ready to handle materials — crates of wine, dog kennels, abandoned automobile tires — susceptible to booby-trapping. More than a few Canadian soldiers suffered grievous woundings, even maimings, before the troops picked up from REME the knack of guessing what might be dangerous and what might not. In the event, combined Canadian and British forces of small proportions almost succeeded in their enveloping movement around Ancona, designed to reduce previous heavy losses in the port itself. Most German personnel might have been obliged to surrender had it not been for a relatively low-level Allied Command decision to allow the enemy to effect a withdrawal rather than damage the main rail line. This reluctance to destroy the fittings of normal economic and social life, with a view to the immediate post-hostilities period when the ports and railways would be desperately needed, became characteristic of the campaign along the Adriatic coast, for what precise reasons no military historian can now say soberly and certainly.

This chance to operate independently of the highest levels of command, because of the perceived unimportance of this part of the battle line, and the low rank of the senior officers in command on the Adriatic, made for a less destructive kind of warfare. There was little feeling for the concept of total war or for any kind of revengeful destruction of local architectural treasures or for the wholesale ruin of townsites that produced the shocking condition of Berlin or the firestorming of Dresden in the closing phases of the war. Across the Apennines, both sides were ready to reduce the abbey of Montecassino to rubble or to destroy the Ponte S. Trinità in Florence without regard to their historic or artistic value. Not so in the east. The brigade and battalion commanders at Ancona or Rimini or Ravenna, on the Allied side at least, had no intention of ravaging the culture and economy of a region that they were at such pains to recapture from the Germans.

The retreating Germans themselves were not particularly destructive, barring one or two instances of mined churches. In several disagreeable cases, though, babies were heard dolefully wailing from hunger, then discovered and rescued from booby-trapped houses or other buildings scheduled for automatic demolition as soon as entered by advancing Allied forces. These infants might truly have been lost by their parents; they might have been kidnapped by the retreating Germans and used as living decoys meant to entrap compassionate soldiers. Who can say? Towards the end of the war bizarre incidents such as these became almost routine, acceptable to combatants whose morale had been sapped away by five years of war. Canadian and British troops on the Adriatic coast discovered a few of these infant decoys, and never knew whether others might have died in a general wave of destruction, but on the whole the campaign was fought out in humane terms.

In that hard winter of 1943/44, the landings on the Channel coast of France were plainly the next major development of the war to be expected. The Italian invasion was treated more and more as a stopgap and a sideshow. The almost informal character of the evolutions put into play by both sides, as one government succeeded another in Italy, grew evident. The nation was struggling to extricate itself from the link to the Nazis and to a Germany plainly approaching defeat on three fronts. Senior Allied commanders vied with one another in seeking new appointments to Eisenhower's headquarters or in one or another of the armies that would take the field in Normandy in 1944. Along the main rail line on the Adriatic coast, operations began almost to resemble some sort of private war. It was the moment of Popski's Private Army, to name one of the somewhat irregular formations that operated in the region following that winter.

Pluyshin was very well informed about Popski's Private Army, indeed regarded this collection of odds and sods as exemplary, a kind of model of how wars should be fought. Always ready to mystify by obscure and private reference, she insisted on keeping me perplexed and largely ignorant of the bearing and accuracy of the facts she had to relate about Popski and his cohorts.

"Oh, they remember him in Classe," she murmured. "They've memorialized him publicly for more than fifty-five years. Say sixty."

"Does anybody remember what went on in Italy in 1944?" I said. "The soldiers all are gone, or in their eighties."

"There are a surprising number of them alive," she said, and began to chatter misleadingly about the great antique monuments of the district. "Those mighty tombs," in the words of a writer familiar with Ravenna and Classe. "The Popski memorial comes in the form of a fine metal tablet. I can't tell you how long it's been in place."

I still had no idea where the conversation was leading, or why it had to be carried on in secrecy. These words were spoken at our second meeting, in the coffee shop on Queen Street. Now and then a couple seated at the next table would glance over at us, wondering what this ancient pair were doing in their hangout.

"If you want to be ignored, look bizarre," Pluyshin said. "I often dress as a . . . bag lady, is that the term?"

"It is," I said, "and you've certainly made yourself look the part today. How have you cast me?"

"As an indulgent private benefactor," she said, smart as paint. She often tells the truth, to keep hearers off balance.

"I look like a bum," I said.

"Bum. Bum? Is that not an indecency?"

"Not in current North American English," I said, pleased to set limits to her omniscience. "Here it has the meaning of an itinerant beggar, a tramp or hobo. In British English it refers to the buttocks, and may have mildly indecent associations, but nothing more."

"Then you look like a bum, but you don't really look like a bum."

"Perhaps that's the best evaluation of the situation," I said. The people at the next table were enjoying the tone and contents of our talk; no confidential communication would now be possible. I rose to my feet, not without difficulty, the tables being placed very close to each other, and inclined my head in her direction. "Time to go." I was still waiting for her to unfold the burden of her tale. What had been communicated so far was in the nature of a feeling-out process, like the opening rounds of a championship boxing match. So far no damaging blows had been attempted, a light jab now and then, a feint, a clinch, a break in the action.

"What metal is Popski's little memorial plaque made of? It must have been meant to last if it's out in all weathers." I meant this for a feint, but it drew a useful reply.

"It is not in precious metal. It might be some long-wearing base-metal alloy with much iron in it. It isn't shiny but it hasn't rusted at all; the lettering is perfectly plain and un-corroded. And it isn't out in the weather; it's fastened to the brick wall on your right as you enter the porch."

"And this is Classe you're speaking of?" I wasn't sure of the precise location of the place. My display of ignorance seemed to embolden her to a display of independent spirit not really needed at this stage of our relations. She tossed her head, then moved past me, disrupting certain seating arrangements and making her way out onto Queen Street where she sank quickly into the swirl of remarkable and bizarre types who passed and repassed along the sidewalk. I let her go; she didn't give me a backward look but I knew I'd hear from her again soon. A natural go-between, she most likely passed the intervening weeks in going back and forth between Canada and Europe. From what she said in our first two meetings, I got the impression that she wanted further discussions of Italian affairs as connected with the aims of Canadian diplo-macy. I know that Canadian diplomacy is usually taken to be American diplomacy and water, but this is not really the case; it is simply what the world likes to imagine and it makes a useful cloak for Canadian aims when they happen to diverge, as they often do, from long-term U.S. policy.

Let's take Italy and Italian diplomacy as a start-line. What could Pluyshin have to bring forward through unofficial chan-nels — I now saw myself as an unofficial channel — that might be of vital interest to both Italy and Canada? Where would such a connection take root? It could only be some matter of economic convenience and negotiation over matters of trade and commerce. Canada and Italy were both among the G7 nations, the seven most richly endowed peoples on Earth. Both ranked low among the seven, indeed at the bottom. They might very well have common concerns that were not those of France, Germany, Britain, the U.S. or Japan. What circumstances might unite the two lesser powers, in a smallish bloc of their own, opposed to directions taken by the IMF, a body intrinsically subject to the sway of the truly great world economies? Pluyshin as currency pirate or illicit exchange trader on a grand scale — the notion amused me greatly. Nobody looked less like a manipulator of currency values than Gerda Kotecke Pluyshin. Yet with her, as I was learning, almost anything was possible.

Did she perhaps have the ear of exalted Italian powers, and if so, which ones? What sort of deal did she have in mind? Whatever it was, it must bring her a fortune, something in the order of millions. She would certainly not undertake any protracted function as the international bankers' secret Pandarus. She could not possibly have the ties or links to the ministries of finance and revenue required to support such a role. Her powers of coercion or persuasion operated only in the world of art exhibition, circulation and sale, as far as I knew. She must be trying to sell me — us — something expensive.

Why this talk about the Italian campaign in World War II? Was there some obscure carry-over of gratitude, favours owing, from that distant time? Some debt now to be acknowledged, a promissory note come due after sixty years? As an adolescent safely at home in Toronto in 1944, going to the wrestling bouts at Maple Leaf Gardens with Bea Skaithe (just lately deceased, in obscurity and need), I'd paid no attention to Italian affairs, at that moment incredibly tangled and unpredictable. The Italian soldier, I imagined, was an habitual runaway, Italian life and society at bottom comic and lightweight. I was a fearfully ignorant child, with no awareness of the central importance of Italy in the transition from the social and political forms of classical antiquity to those of the present day. I had not heard the maxim Rome never dies, she only sleeps. Nor did I realize that when you undertake a journey towards some social or political destination of grave importance you always meet some Italian coming back from there. And as for music, painting, architecture . . . what is there to be said?

In the era since 1944 I'd had a few clues about these matters driven into my poor ignorant head. Now I found it fascinating to speculate about Canadian ties to southern Europe through Italy. I've heard that the Italian community in Toronto is the second largest in the world outside Italy, numbering in the area of half a million souls. There must be more Italians around New York, but the ties of mere population growth have made Toronto an Italian city, where it isn't an Oriental city. This reflection gave my perceptions a new angle. I began to imagine all kinds of secret associations between Canada and Italy that might supersede the traditional Canadian links to France, Britain, the U.S., Japan. Could Canada and Italy have things in common that I'd never considered before? I've been ridiculed by certain friends for holding the view that Toronto and Venice have striking resemblances, something I noted when I was in Venice in 1980. But there is much in the idea; the parallels are striking when once you notice them.

When I'm around the Toronto Islands, for example, and their wide tracts of landfill and new harbourage, I always think of the Venetian lagoons and of the way the Queen of the Adriatic rose out of swamp and slime to become the holder-in-fee of the gorgeous East, and I willingly postulate some sort of special relationship between Canada — and particularly central Ontario — and the Veneto. Pluyshin seems to have felt the same way, or at least envisaged a ready market in the Canadian Veneto for her goods. She did not take her project to Montreal or Winnipeg, but to Toronto's Union Station, Queen Street West and the Leslie Street Spit, where she finally unveiled the inner reach of her proposals to me on the day my son quitted the upper atmosphere in search of Mars, or Ares, as the Greeks called the god.

Roosevelt, Marshall and later Truman could arouse no enthusiasm for Adriatic adventures among the American power-brokers of their time. Venetian painting has always taken third place in American eyes to that of Florence and Rome. Titian, for example, hasn't the place in the hearts of the great American curators and art historians that the Florentines have made for themselves. The treasures of Rome are better understood across the Atlantic than the magnificence of the Accademia. Henry James senses something of the American resistance to Venetian enticements, making of the city of the lagoons a perilous environment for the sick; he brings his princess there to perish and it is clear that he is troubled gravely by the Venetian ambiance. It suggests the eternal confused blending of fatality and fortune. Milly Theale, the American princess, the heiress of all the ages, has both the great fortune and the fatal infection. Those who come from the New World, in James's eyes, do well to abstain from ready indulgence in the ambiguous pleasures of Venice, even though this may mean ignorance of the greatest achievements of the Venetian school. School and college classrooms across the U.S. and Canada featured for generations the presence of Raphael's *Madonna of the Chair*, in sepia reproduction, while admitting no representation of the *Assumption* from the Frari, religious painting of equal expressiveness, in the same academic institutions. North Americans know far less about the artistic and cultural distinctions of the Veneto than about those of Rome or Tuscany, hardly surprising but perhaps regrettable.

In the winter of 1943/44, the obscure Canadian infantry formations campaigning along the rail line from Brindisi to Ravenna and beyond found themselves now and then brought into association with the hard-bitten crew of adventurers who professed allegiance to Lieutenant-Colonel Vladimir Peniakoff, commander of what has since become known as Popski's Private Army. This officer had none of the mistrust and half fear of Venetian blandishments felt by the generals at the other end of the battle line. Colonel Peniakoff, a brave and sometimes headstrong officer, was a student of Venetian art and political history, with a knowledge and love of its greatest works shared with few commanders in the theatre. Of relatively low rank, he nevertheless possessed remarkable initiative, and the power to camouflage his intentions and movements from both friend and foe. In the spring of 1944 he was operating almost as his own commander. He cultivated opportunities to lie low, move with stealth, make no excessive logistical demands, in short to draw no attention to his formation from his immediate superiors. What he had in mind as objective was the preservation of the great works of architecture and mosaic that are situated around Ravenna. It is for his success in this undertaking that he is memorialized by the plaque in the porch of the great basilica of S. Apollinare in Classe, where he is identified as Lieutenant-Colonel Vladimir Peniakoff, DSO, MC, the preserver of the basilica from the destructive impulses and acts of the German forces in retreat.

Pluyshin dilated at length on the significance of this plaque, during our meeting on the spit and in later encounters during the tricky negotiations in which we soon found ourselves entangled.

"It's astonishing how the local folk keep it up; they polish it and wipe rain marks and mud from the lettering. It might have been placed there yesterday, but it was put in place soon after the war and the engagements it commemorates."

"Were there more than one?" I had not yet visited Ravenna or Classe. My Venetian adventures had drained my fellow-feeling for the art and the great art cities of the Veneto. Ravenna can't be more than seventy miles south of Venice, easily reachable by rail if you don't care to drive, but I'd never examined its riches. I still felt inclined to confuse the two basilicas dedicated to S. Apollinare, the one in Classe — the greater of the two — and the other in downtown Ravenna, S. Apollinare Nuovo. At first I had not grasped the sense of Pluyshin's repeated references to secret infantry movements in wooded country or shore territory. I had not realized that Classe, though it possesses an architectural gem of global renown, and is of great antiquity, is nevertheless a small village of a few hundred residents with the look of a summer resort like Jackson's Point, Ontario, in the 1930s. I've never found out why the great basilica and its extraordinary interior are located there; no doubt there is some very good reason. The place bears the same relationship to Ravenna as Torcello does to Venice, that of a small first settlement superseded by the unlooked-for development of a neighbouring townstead. The emperor Augustus comes into the picture here; eventually he located his base of Adriatic fleet operations on this coast. Fleet is *classis* in the Latin of the Augustans. Hence the name Classe, the base of the fleet.

There is a massive statue of Augustus, a copy of a well-known Roman work, standing outside the entrance to the basilica, just where the tour buses from Germany and Switzer-land park in their dozens. The emperor points northwards away from the parking lot, as though indicating newly conceived military and naval ambitions. He wears a heavy breastplate and other warlike accoutrements. Augustus had some serious intentions regarding the country to the north and east of Venice, and hoped to make a major port of Ravenna, his plans including port installations at Classe. I'm not well informed about all this or any of the history of the district. The presences of the basilica and the Castello Bianchini in this obscure place are enough to fill the imagination of the visitor with wonder. Either building, if sited in a tiny Ontario village like Pefferlaw or Island Grove, would attract widespread atten-tion, at the same time be something of an embarrassment to local residents.

The people who live in and around Classe seem to find the presence of these treasures quite ordinary, something almost to be taken for granted, at the same time to be loved, reverenced and preserved. The long-cherished gratitude ex-pressed by the continued polishing and cleansing of the commemorative plaque to Colonel Peniakoff seems precisely right for the district, showing quiet but lasting pride in the place and its history and value.

As Pluyshin remarked in the accents of the guidebook, "The Bianchini have made their home in that neighbourhood since before the basilica was erected. They are the magnates, the great family, of the locality."

I tried to remember instances of the greatness of the Bianchini. Mentioned by Ruskin, Henry James, Byron and Browning, though not quite of the fame of the Montefeltro or the Este families, the Bianchini have been the lords of Classe and environs for fifteen hundred years. The Castello Bianchini, their principal seat, includes wings and outbuildings of various dates from the eighth century almost to the present day. The building forms a compendium of architectural history.

The head of the family holds the title of marchese, originally a title of nobility denominating a lord of border country, the marches that always require specially strong defences against cross-border cattle rustlers and banditti. The reigning Marchese di Bianchini at any given date for a thousand years and more has been the principal power in his province; this ascendancy continues at present, though the twentieth Marchese di Bianchini in the direct line of descent, a man of eighty and more, former resistance operative, connoisseur, farmer, seems finally to be at the end of his resources, barring some new and special development.

Federico di Bianchini has never been one of our international playboy aristocrats. What he has done with his life deserves notice. He has remained close to his estates, has kept the Castello Bianchini in as good repair as finances have allowed, dominated local councils discussing every kind of public business from the conservation of the mosaics of S. Apollinare in Classe, to the thwarting of the terrible intentions of the retreating German troops of 1944.

At that time the present Marchese di Bianchini was twenty-one or twenty-two. He had fought briefly in North Africa as a junior officer in the Italian Legion under Marshal Badoglio and later under Graziano. One of a large number of Italian prisoners-of-war taken in the very early African campaign, he was repatriated not long before German forces began to arrive in the desert to form the reputed Afrika Korps under Rommel. The Marchese found himself out of the war, back home, safely ensconced on his own lands, by the beginning of 1942, only to witness the Allied landings and advance up the peninsula of 1943/44. He had been favourably impressed by the conduct of British troops in North Africa and much less favourably impressed by the conduct of German forces in his homeland.

The principal social responsibility of his noble family, in the eyes of the Marchese, was the protection in time of war of the great art treasures of his native district: S. Vitale, S. Apollinaire in Classe, S. Apollinare Nuovo, the tomb of Theodoric, the Arian Baptistery, the Mausoleum of Galla Placidia. "Those mighty tombs," indeed! Last perhaps on any such list, but a legitimate site in any review of the treasures of Ravenna/Classe/Rimini, there was his own home, the Castello di Bianchini, that rambling structure that included some of the finest Venetian Gothic building away from Venice itself, as well as a series of examples of baroque ceilings painted and repainted over two centuries in cunning false perspectives.

The greatest single work of art to be found there, apart from the mosaics of the region, hypothetically moveable but never until now removed from its very private resting place, is the painting universally known as *Priam and Achilles*, a *chef d'oeuvre* even among the extraordinary last works of the master Titiano Vezelli, or Titian. Never photographed, never assessed by scholars, ignored or perhaps overlooked by Napoleon's generals during their sojourn in the Veneto, mentioned with great curiosity by Byron in the fourth book of *Childe Harold*, and treated as legendary, purely imaginary, by Henry James and Browning, this very remarkable creation of Titian's last months on earth has been in the hands of successive Bianchinis since the time of its creation in 1576.

"It is the last Titian," declared Pluyshin when she first mentioned it to me in the delicate discussions that opened out from those first meetings. Maybe I shouldn't say "opened out" because nothing in the series of meetings in Toronto, Ottawa, Montreal, Venice, Classe or Rome that evolved from our private talks was ever open or public. The whole process until its very last stages was conducted in secret or as near to it as possible.

"Never be visibly secretive," said Pluyshin at one point. "Don't act as though you were in disguise. Simply be yourself; then nobody will take any notice of you. It is possible to be open and shut at the same time." When she said this I finally understood her cleverness and her command of the arts of undercover negotiation. The way to stay under cover is to kick the covers off and lie exposed on the mattress; nobody will pay the smallest attention to you. Pluyshin's disguise as a bag lady is a conception of real imaginative power. When wearing this impenetrable cover she was capable of radical frankness, sometimes of insulting simplicity and obviousness.

"I'm not going to teach you the military history of Canada," she said, out on the spit the day John left for Mars. We had had most of our time together and were preparing to hike back to where we'd left our transport.

"What should I know about Canadian military history?"

"Something at least about two fugitive battalions of Canadian infantry from the Fifth Division that were in close liaison with Colonel Peniakoff's force early in 1944."

"What is that to me, or to the people who sent you to me?"

She made that noise that bad writers spell out as "heigh-ho."

This irritated me. "It's all very well to sigh at me, but you'll have to clarify matters if we are to go any further."

Then she said, "Ignorant dupe!"

"No," I said. "I may be idle and ignorant but I'm nobody's dupe and I won't get mixed up in any covert operations. I'm too old and too well off to be bothered."

"There is your country's name to be considered."

She had me there. We walked along the spit road beside the blue waters of Ontario in early April. Looking along the coolly moving lakeshore, I was persuaded all over again of the importance of love of country, love of one's special place, the real patriotism.

"Oh the dickens," I said. "Tell me what you want."

Then she began the opening-out process. "It was the accident of military history that brought the two battalions of Canadian infantry into liaison with Popski's Private Army."

"Are you describing a formation of rangers?" I asked.

"Exactly," she said, coming as near to smiling as she ever does. "A loose association of troops in brigade strength, much like a commando, operating under a commander of low rank and high initiative."

She might almost have been quoting some official history. The Americans had had a series of formations that they described as rangers, perhaps for romantic historical reasons, conforming closely to this description. Popski's Private Army was exactly a commando or team of rangers without covering orders, and the Canadians who had passed under Colonel Peniakoff's command were operating without specific instructions from Canadian GHQ in the theatre. They came upon elements of Popski's force that were deployed in their operational area and cooperated with them spontaneously. These were fluid situations, and the fluidity justified the exercise of initiative. The officer who has to make decisions at platoon, company, even battalion level always has to be ready to seize chances that might be sacrificed if formal authority for every order has to be sought.

In the field you always have to be ready to leave your ass bare, as it were, if a fluid situation is to be exploited fully. In March 1944 Colonel Peniakoff and his Canadian opposite numbers knew from trustworthy reports received from local resistance groups that German engineers had mined the ground around the principal architectural sites of Classe and Ravenna. They had also planted explosives and incendiaries inside S. Apollinare and the Castello Bianchini. They had been observed at their work by resistance forces disguised as farm labourers and estate carpenters. The Castello Bianchini had been occupied by a German headquarters since the Allied landings of 1943, and had been pretty thoroughly converted to military uses. The one object left completely untampered-with was the *Priam and Achilles*, which was high on Marshal Goering's list of art treasures scheduled for removal to Germany and inclusion in his immense private collection of loot. But by early 1944 the Reichsmarschall had too many other things to think about to concern himself with further collecting.

He did, however, issue instructions to his staff that the *Priam and Achilles* and certain other works on a list that came to light after his suicide at Nuremberg during the war-crimes trials were to be destroyed before German forces quitted the area, apparently on the principle that if he couldn't have them, nobody else should either. Engineers were seen to put the destructive instruments in place and to link up the connections for detonation at a distance. It would have been perfectly possible for the retreating forces to leave the area, allow Colonel Peniakoff's troops access to the mined buildings, then touch off the incendiaries and other explosives. This would at once have saddled the Allied command with responsibility for the destruction of great and famous works of art. Colonel Peniakoff and his Canadian associates made a high-priority objective of these electrical installations.

Officers close to Goering had furnished the German forces around Ravenna with specific instructions: they were to proceed with their work of vandalism almost before anything else. They were to destroy the Basilica of S. Apollinare, the Castello Bianchini and most particularly the great *Priam and Achilles*, even if the action resulted in their being taken prisoner or killed. They were to treat their instructions on a last-man, last-round basis. This communication became known, first to local resistance groups and then to Colonel

Peniakoff and his friends, in the early spring of 1944. Protection of these treasures now became their chief military goal, something that would not have been allowed to a more strictly supervised formation. In late March the two battalions of Canadian infantry that by now made up the principal elements of Colonel Peniakoff's ground forces were moving, usually at night, into enveloping positions around German engineering and communications headquarters on the Classe/Ravenna road, where today suburban buses pass peacefully back and forth.

Observation was maintained from positions along the rail line; it soon became obvious that a general withdrawal of German troops was about to be mounted, in a fallback towards Bologna, itself already threatened with Allied capture. The German forces might be put "in the bag" before another two weeks had elapsed. In this position, some act of revengeful destruction might be contemplated by way of final farewell to glory. By night — this was by now the last week in March and the first day or two of April — the Canadians and the British electrical engineers would move in very close to S. Apollinare and the Castello Bianchini to watch for the installation of demolition charges and detonating lines.

As soon as they took up these positions the observers were able to spot the demolition teams and watch them installing the cables for the detonating equipment; these were heavy cables, wrapped closely in thick insulation, difficult to cut without danger to those doing the cutting. These lines, when carrying a charge, could cause electrocution if approached incautiously. They would have to be removed when the current was off. The difficulty was to discern such a moment. Just when the destruction would begin was problematic. It would be some time after the defence teams withdrew, at the same moment perhaps as the advancing forces entered these buildings.

Two platoons of Canadian infantry were told to advance under cover of darkness almost under the walls of the basilica from their positions of deployment along the rail line. This is a distance of perhaps a quarter of a mile, along what was then a muddy track much chewed up by military traffic, under tall pines and some lesser brush.

Under company commander Captain D. G. Walford, MC, this small force, accompanied by REME personnel, was able to go forward towards their objective, the apse of the basilica, easily detected in the spring night because of its bulk. No enemy troops were encountered during this cautious advance; the infantry were able to move right up under the targeted building, into a small copse alive with nesting birds, the soft night calls of wood doves the only sound to be heard above the murmur of the spring breeze. Captain Walford and his platoon commanders had not expected to encounter nesting birds on this dangerous adventure. But there they were, dozens of them roosting in the tall shadowy trees that obscured a view of the apse. The advancing forces found the presence of these birds a lucky break for them; they would surely provide some warning of an impending move by the defences; but no sign of alarm came from the nesting doves.

The advancing forces pressed closer and closer, under the cover provided by the tall trees and their shadows. Soon they were close enough to locate the cable lines. The cables had been led through the walls of the basilica, an act of vandalism still pointed out to tourists who visit the site. Tour guides still refer in their descriptions to the gallant Canadian troops that cut the cables and prevented the destruction of the basilica and the neighbouring Castello Bianchini. They make it sound easy, but it wasn't easy. It was terribly risky, an operation not much remembered or praised in official Canadian military histories, probably because of the informal and independent stance of the participating detachments. That night the cables were cut and capped off at their severed ends, a very tricky thing to do because the power might have come on at any moment. By morning the two buildings were free of the threat of destruction by explosives and fire. The *Priam and Achilles* were later found to be enmeshed in a network of wiring that was plainly meant to insure its destruction by fire at the will, from one hour to the next, of the commander of the retreating forces. The crisscrossings of wire had to be disentangled and removed from the frame and mounting of this very large picture, without marking the pictorial surface.

Some of the incendiary wiring was lying tangled directly on the surface of the masterwork. No *conservateur de musée* was on hand to direct the removal process. Once or twice the wires were allowed to slip across the surface of the work, leaving faint traces of their movements that were detectable six decades later. The tiny scratches don't go below the surface of the topmost layer of pigment. There is no question of a defacing of the wonderful image. Working in his extreme old age, the artist has sometimes left small areas of the surface bare, in a technique more characteristic of some late-twentieth-century painting than of the High Renaissance. The scratches made by wire often occur over bare canvas; the painted surface is there unimpaired.

The work is indeed a very large one, its dimensions considerably exceeding those of the *Pietà* in the Accademia, running to 143 ½ inches by 156 inches, almost exactly twelve feet high by thirteen feet wide. The framing adds considerably to the impression of size; it seems immense in its present setting. In the darkness of the Castello in wartime, this prevailingly sombre image in its heavy mount must have left an impression of gloomy grandeur in the minds of its rescuers. But none was an art historian. When they were debriefed afterwards none gave a clear description of the painting, except to say that it was large and dark. This doesn't take the critic or scholar very far; the painting continued virtually unknown and unappreciated for another half century and more, except to a very small cadre of Italian experts who were at long intervals invited — or better commanded — by the Marchese Bianchini to examine the work with a view to its conservation. Perhaps a dozen experts viewed the last Titian — as it was customarily described in the literature — over the sixty-odd years that followed its preservation from the shock of war by Canadian infantry in 1944.

The painting never travelled. It was never put on display in a gallery or museum. Access to the Castello in order to view it was closely restricted, not from questionable motives of censorship or mistrust of the viewing public, but because the Bianchini had always treated the Castello as their home. So the remarkable picture hung safely in place unthreatened by vandalism, or the rapacity of some high command, for the remainder of the century. The cycle of life in the neighbourhood of Classe continued on its slow round during all that time, until by the end of the 1990s economic life and its premises had been so altered all over the world that continued possession in a private home — never mind its aristocratic proportions and connections — of one of the world's great masterpieces became less and less feasible.

Imagine yourself coming down to breakfast each morning to find your companions gazing across the table towards a vast expanse of wall on which there hung an enormous Titian or Rembrandt. You might feel yourself to be poaching on the rights of the entire world.

The case is somewhat similar to that of an ordinary man married to an extraordinarily beautiful woman, whose looks are so much a part of the world's inheritance of loveliness as to make the poor husband feel shy of having sequestered such a person in the private position of a wife. Some objects and some persons are not meant for private existence. The last Titian could not remain in private hands for much longer. At the end of the second millennium the present Marchese found his position of mentor and protector of the people of his region simply too heavy to be carried on without some form of public assistance. There seemed only one way out of his difficulties that would be both appropriate to his dignity and a sufficient endowment for his traditional undertakings, which comprised large contributions to the maintenance of the treasures of Classe and Ravenna, support of the regional church institutions, their schools and hostels, mounting of seasonal festivals and other observances. The last Titian could no longer remain in private hands. It was worth such a large sum that according to the present state of the money market, international banking and credit, the Bianchini family were losing from four to six million dollars U.S. annually, the interest that investment of the price of the painting would certainly bring.

A Caravaggio rediscovered in the early 1990s, *The Taking of Christ*, not a large picture, four feet high by five and a half feet wide, now hanging on long-term loan in the National Gallery of Ireland, is said to have a current market value of about forty million dollars U.S. There are only about sixty known paintings by that artist, which pushes his valuations up. But forty million for a Caravaggio supplies a guide to the potential selling price of the sole privately held major late work by the greatest master of the Venetian school. This information more or less brings up to the present moment the narrative that Pluyshin delivered to me during our series of meetings that continued for the first ten months of the year. Her last revelation was the determinant one.

"The Marchese wants the picture to come to Canada, not to Britain, where there isn't the money available anyway, nor the U.S., nor above all to France."

"Of course not France," I agreed, "but will the Italian ministry of culture allow for export of the work?" This seemed unlikely to me. The French, to do them justice, would never allow such a move. Even the Brits have become extremely reluctant to allow national treasures to be sold away.

Pluyshin assumed her most mysterious stance and tone.

"All that can certainly be adjusted," she said softly. I realized that she was streets and streets ahead of the rest of us in the unfolding of the affair. "The Marchese feels an infinite gratitude to Canada for her share in the preservation of the work in time of war; that is why he gives Canada the first refusal. The ministry of culture will certainly issue the necessary certificates."

Then she told me the asking price.

III

GOING PUBLIC

"Query from *Visitor I* received and logged. Computer reconstruction delivers message as 'Has it happened yet?' Reply to message is 'Not yet.' Repeat. Reply to query is 'Not yet.' And here we have an example of the intense human drama unfolding around the epic voyage of the spacecraft. Each of the crew has her or his own story to live through, commanders, researchers, medical personnel and scientists. This particular story has caught the attention of the entire world, the marriage of Professor Goderich, and his wife's life in New York City, and their brave wish to have a child.

"It seems to all of us here at Mission Control that this first space child has taken the headlines away from many other elements of this great human story. We all have to acknowledge the essential rightness of this development. We have felt almost from day one of the operation that the birth of a single human child is as important a story, as worthy of attention, as the conception, undertaking and successful conclusion of the Mars flight. Everyone here is deeply interested in Mrs. Goderich's pregnancy and in her baby, about to be born under the eyes of millions upon millions of viewers around the world. On our screens at this moment you can see recent tapes of Mrs. Goderich at her New York home. She has naturally received the most careful medical attention. World opinion has identified her child with the fortunes of the crew of *Visitor I*.

The final complete success of the historical venture seems to be associated with, and even dependent on, the successful termination of this young lady's pregnancy. It is a deeply touching story. As everyone knows, Professor Goderich and his wife, Emily Underwood Goderich, have the good fortune to be first cousins. Here are pictures of them taken last February, when Professor Goderich spent his pre-flight leave with his wife in New York. In appearance they might almost be brother and sister.

"Those of you who have followed the story of the voyage from day one have been quick to point out, in your letters and faxes and e-mail and Internet communications, how closely the narrative of the birth of the Goderiches' child seems to retell the strange tale of life on Earth and its possible relations with life elsewhere in our solar system, perhaps to the ultimate sources of life in the universe. Those of us who have participated in this undertaking have come to see childbirth, and humanity's first strugglings out of the small territory in which our story has until now been acted out, as deeply connected and overseen by fate, providence, call it what you like. Here at Mission Control we are deeply aware of a close link between the nine months of Emily Underwood Goderich's pregnancy and the time that will have elapsed when *Visitor I* completes its investigations of the Martian surface and turns for home.

"On your screens Professor and Mrs. Goderich, as they appeared together last February, both look in excellent health, a vigorous young couple of great charm. The world has taken them to its heart, as Emily and John. And like any extended family, the admirers of this striking couple have been ready and eager to submit long lists of suggested names for the child, boy or girl. The global excitement over the choice of a name for the baby has seemed to our viewers to mirror a traditional aspect of human life. Technical manuals and computer read-outs are the usual reading matter for our staff, but as *Visitor I* prepares to send the Mars lander to the surface of the planet in a few days, books of names for little boys and girls seem as popular reading here as scientific texts and statistical reports. Not simply names in the English tongue, either. John is the most popular choice for males, but it appears in communications received here as Jan, Ian, Johannes, Johan, Giovanni, Gianni, Ivan, Jean, Yannick, Iokanaan and all of the other variants of the name in world language. Emily seems to have fewer variations, but Milly, Mélie, Aemilia, Emilie and Amélie, and some others, have been suggested. Whatever the gender of the space baby, there has been no dearth of suggestions for naming.

"This flood of suggestions has not been passed on to *Visitor I*. The communications link with the spacecraft is at best tenuous. We have chosen not to risk overloading it with information and requests for comment. The prospective mother certainly has her choices already in mind, as will folks all over the world. The name for a newborn prince could not be anticipated more eagerly than the choice of this child's name.

"Space-travel enthusiasts may think that time spent on this subject is time wasted, but they will be in a tiny minority. At the same time, perhaps we should return to coverage of the actualities of the voyage, now virtually half completed at two hundred and twenty-three days out from Earth. In the next thirty minutes *Visitor I* will make its linkage with *CV I*. We hope to have direct television pictures of the event. Meanwhile, you will see on your screens at this moment a very accurate rendering of the positions of the two craft as *Visitor I* moves closer and closer to its target, the cargo vehicle. As you can see from this simulation, the manned vehicle approaches its consort from the rear, advancing on its target like a mating male, rather than attempting the more chancy task of backing into position like the female partner in a mate. The helmsman aboard *Visitor I* has the entry to the cargo vessel constantly in his sights, and can monitor visually the minute adjustments dictated by the onboard computers that will unite the mates in perfect safety. In a few moments we will be going into direct communications mode. The already-positioned cameras on *CV I* will begin to transmit the sight of the rear panels of the unmanned ship as they slide back the protective seal. If viewers will be patient for just a few more moments, they can witness a remarkable first successful undertaking of this kind in the history of space flight."

TV picture goes to black. Screen fills with snow. Commentator's voice is slow to resume. Intermittent flashing of unreadable black-and-white images with occasional flashes of colour. Commentator's voice resumes.

"We are experiencing some difficulty in stabilizing our picture at this distance. We should have something for you in moments."

Suddenly the picture stabilizes in colour. It is like watching an enclosed premises on a surveillance system. The remotest cargo bays of *CV I* come sharply into focus. It is a technical feat of the first magnitude. A clear readable picture sent from Mars orbit and receivable by viewers on Earth without blurring or roll-out. The experience reminds many older viewers of the early days of live network television transmission, over sixty years ago. First the hesitancy, then the assured technical triumph. In a decade that feat will seem commonplace but it is at present wonderful that it should be attempted, never mind realized with such stunning effect. The whole viewing world watches in fascination as the rear seal panels slide to either side of the picture, then are speedily folded against the walls of the cargo vessel, almost disappearing from sight. As they do this, amazed viewers will recognize the familiar figures of four of the astronauts, poised in position in the nose of *Visitor I*, ready to cross into the successfully mated cargo ship. They know already that the artificial gravity system is operating as it should. The ugly surprise of sudden weightlessness will not occur. The astronauts can enter the cargo bay and move around in it as if they were going from one room to another on Earth. This really is a superlative technical accomplishment. More and more it looks like everything will proceed according to plan. The mating of the two vessels has been managed with exact precision; the television picture has been nearly as good as one produced in studios in Paris or London or New York. The accompanying sound transmission fills with the sounds of muted handclappings and quiet cheering. There are some observations from the broadcast crew that are plainly of a congratulatory tone, and the commentator resumes his narrative.

"An unequalled feat of technical performance, under the most rigorous conditions. We have a message in the studio from the president of the United States conferring the Medal of Honour for Space Achievement on all of the voyagers. This is the highest decoration that America confers on its astronauts and their associates; it is very rarely awarded, but today it is the only appropriate award that the American people can offer to the cosmonauts and astronauts. And other awards are being announced as we proceed with the broadcast, from participating members of ISA around the world: from France, from the People's Republic of China, from Canada, two of whose people are present on the flight, from Russia, home of Colonel Lebedev, from everywhere on Earth, medals and letters of commendation are flowing into our headquarters.

"When the next stage of the mission has been completed satisfactorily, the international response will no doubt be even more affectionate and enthusiastic. The space voyagers will arrive on Earth as among the most decorated human beings in history. Offers of employment, offers of publication of personal accounts of their experiences, film and television offers, proposals for the free education of their children, all these and many many more are coming into headquarters in generous profusion. The Underwood–Goderich baby will be equipped with the most extensive infant's wardrobe ever assembled. We may come naked into the world, but the space baby will not be naked for very long.

"On your screens now you can see four of the voyagers setting up the components of the Mars lander and its adjunct, the surface life-support module, or LSM. The parts of the lander and the LSM clip and snap into place like the familiar toys of childhood. They fasten together simply, sequentially, speedily and securely, with a minimum of time required for assembly. And yet the Mars lander and the LSM are immensely strong in structure, perfectly safe for use in these conditions. Now we can see the form of the Mars lander beginning to take shape, although its instruments haven't yet been fitted.

"Perhaps we should now call over the names and functions of the four Mars walkers who will descend to the surface of the planet in a few days. Colonel Serge Lebedev, the Russian representative among the crew and the distinguished co-commandant of the entire operation, will lead the quartet who will perform the crowning act of the entire voyage, the actual landing. If Colonel Kinnick has seemed to take the lead as between the co-commanders on the mission, Colonel Lebedev has been selected as leader of the landing team, a sharing-out of honours that has been very well conceived. Colonel Lebedev will be the first crew member to step onto the surface of Mars.

"He will be followed by Captain Céline Hervieu, CAF, first woman in history to set foot on the surface of another planet in our solar system. You will see Captain Hervieu kneel, gather some material from the planetary surface and deposit it in a specially prepared cup or trophy. This first handful of dust from across interplanetary space will be carefully preserved for historical record. The trophy has been designed in material that forms a shield against radioactivity, in case the surface dust should prove to be 'hot' in radiological terms. Present opinion in technical circles is that the material will prove quite safe to handle, non-radioactive. No risk will be taken, however; no unsafe sources of radioactivity will be returned to Earth. Captain Hervieu is charged with the responsibility to lodge and protect these precious historical samples, at the same time making certain that they contain no harmful elements that could possibly deliver contagion to Earth.

"Next among the Mars walkers comes Professor John Sleaford Goderich, like Captain Hervieu a native of Canada, although the support and experimental equipment for his crucial researches into the creation of artificial gravity have largely been funded by the Cambridge research groups in Britain. That is where Professor Goderich took his first degree and his advanced degrees, and first proposed his solutions to the problems of gravity creation. He will occupy himself during the Mars walk with observations of the gravitational conditions on the planet's surface and their effect on human activity there. He will also take notes on the qualities displayed by small objects in motion at the surface, with a view to later calculation of the planet's weight. This will be a determinant, and fundamental item of information from the surface, for physicists on Earth. The orbital path of Mars has always seemed to observers on Earth to be irregular. Onsite calculations made by Professor Goderich may perhaps allow final solutions of the puzzles surrounding the path and velocity of Mars and certain other planets and regularly observed comets.

"Fourth of the Mars walkers will be Commandant Hubert de Barny, a native of France, one of the two experts in space medicine on the voyage, who will act as medical advisor to his companions on the surface. He will also make records of temperature, chill factors, possibilities of effective rest and health-preservation, and in general he will supervise the measures taken by his companions on the Mars walk to defend their biological systems against unexpected conditions that may be encountered during the weeks spent on the surface. Some space experts consider the task of Commandant de Barny to be the most important of all for the evolution of our occupation of this strange and foreign environment. And there they are on your screens, the quartet of Mars walkers, in conference at home on Earth some weeks before this flight was launched.

"Our latest information suggests that the Mars lander will be ready for launch within four days. We may expect the landing to take place about November fifteenth. This will remain a significant date in the personal histories of all humankind, a day that nobody who lives through it will ever forget. And at about the same time Emily Underwood Goderich is expected to deliver her firstborn child; this may occur at the same time as Professor Goderich's first steps on the surface of Mars. What a remarkable happening! It underlines more perhaps than anything else could do the close solidarity of humankind: the father walking on the distant planet as the child begins the long voyage of a human lifetime. Every one of us at Mission Control, and the crew of our permanent manned space station *Wayfarer*, and the engineering staff at the landing site on Earth at the Utah salt flats, indeed the entire organization of the International Space Administration, all of us are joined in our hopes and good wishes for the child and its parents as emblems of human progress and development. We end our production today with a friendly inquiry for Emily Underwood Goderich. What are we going to call the baby?"

—————

"No, I'm not letting her in here," the deputy minister said. "Not now. Not yet. Five minutes in the room and she'd have my socks and my bridgework in that carryall of hers. And any budgetary surplus that happened to be going. Let her wait! Do her good!"

"I've put nothing in writing," I said, "neither to you nor to her. But you know the rough dimensions of her proposal. You passed her to me, after all. You must have allowed her some credibility. Is she in the country legally?"

The two so-far silent watchers in the room began to shudder

at this explicitness. It was blatantly obvious to me that no clear-cut reply was to be expected; they were boggling at the inquiry, if "boggling" is the word I want. The dictionary links "boggle" to "bogey," a scary monster, so I guess I've got the right word. They were ready to turn nervously aside from any plain discussion of the woman who sat in the anteroom waiting to see us. Fortunately a stout pair of oak doors barred the entryway to this inner sanctum, and likewise muffled any speech within. They were very stout doors indeed and they made me uneasy; they had the look of prison doors. There is a sense in which a senior civil servant is the prisoner of his ministry. There was no other way out of the room, barring a narrow window that opened on the fire escape. I would not have wanted to be caught in the room in the event of a fire. But at least I could be certain that anything I said inside would not be heard outside.

"Well, is she?" I tried again, and again the three officials pretended not to grasp the drift of my question. "I'd like to know in case of any later discussions that might call my judgment into question."

"Nobody is going to question your judgment," said the deputy minister agitatedly, "but this is a proposal of some magnitude."

"Oh no, it isn't at all. It's a tiny sum of money in the context of the budget of the nation. The federal government will not be responsible for any sum exceeding a few millions of dollars."

"It's a tiny sum if we're thinking about the Defence budget or the costs of the foreign service. Twenty-nine grand pianos kept in perpetual tune at whatever cost to the taxpayer . . ." The deputy minister snorted irritably. "And nobody to play on them except the children of the embassies. Disgraceful."

"You can't charge off those pianos for Cultural Affairs services. That would be deceitful; they exist only to impress embassy visitors. They're not kept in very good tune, either. The one in Kuala Lumpur, a Yamaha —"

I was interrupted by one of the listeners, the security man.

"All right. She has no legal status with Immigration; she just stepped off the jet and sauntered through the gates. Nobody stopped her or looked carefully at her papers. She appeared as a casual vacationer."

"A casual vacationer," I repeated. "Sounds like the title of a forgotten novel of the eighteen-nineties, perhaps by Howells. I don't suppose that at this time of day anybody reads or remembers Howells —"

I was interrupted again.

"Will you kindly stop that?" said the deputy minister. "As a very young man I was able to observe your father in action. He had a great gift for digression."

"First I'd heard of it," I said. "I prefer to remember him as an activist."

"Well, please don't set up for to imitate him. We don't hold the possibility of deportation over her head. Where would we send her? Nobody knows."

One of the listening onlookers — not the security man — leaned forward and said, "Do you know what she lists as her native tongue?"

This was a bit of a stunner. "Magyar? Finno-Ugric?"

"English!"

"Surely not!"

"It's what she claims on any papers served up as documents. She makes no claim to citizenship of any English-speaking nation."

"Then how . . . ?"

The deputy minister got halfway to his feet. "There! You see? She isn't even in the room and she's dominating the discussion. What strange hold does she have over us, that she can rule at a distance? She who must be obeyed!"

It seems fair to note that he said these things in the accents of comedy and parody.

"Are you quoting Rider Haggard or John Mortimer?" I asked.

"Both. What's good enough for old Rumpole is good enough for me."

"Do you still have those books on your shelves?" I said. "I haven't thought of them for years. Is Mortimer still living?"

"I'm sure I couldn't say," said the deputy minister, "but in their day those stories gave pleasure to millions. And look, see? We're still locked into discussion of this woman's literary sources. Let's move forward, gentlemen. What precisely does she have in mind?"

"A whacking great finder's fee," I said, "and in my opinion worth every cent."

"Then you would approve her proposal?"

"I can approve it," I said, "without binding myself to anything. I have no spending authority, and I'm not responsible to the electorate, but since you ask me direct, I can say that if the work of art is what she describes it as being we'd be getting a bargain. I'm ready to examine it for you, and I can claim to have a qualified expertise in the field. More purely technical evaluations would have to be made at the present site of the painting, evaluations of the physical condition of the surface, the chemistry of the pigment, the possibility of reframing and of transporting the work. Some of these matters would have to be gone into before making a formal response. But if the work is what it professes to be, then I would say that the offer has to be taken very seriously."

"Over fifty-five million dollars Canadian?" said the fourth man in the room, a high-level finance officer. We made a well-suited quartet, a security man, a finance man, a deputy minister and an independent observer. "It's a middle-sized amount," I said. "Immense when considered as the price of a single work of art, but very small when compared to the price of a major missile or a jet fighter. I believe that the money can be found." I sensed that the matter of Pluyshin's fee was about to be tabled.

"What does she do for her five million?" the security man asked.

"Nothing very special. It's simply that the transaction can't go ahead without her. She's the essential catalyst; there is nobody else I know of that can produce this sensational effect."

"We didn't approach her; she came to us," said the deputy minister. "There we were, snoring happily in our little beds in dreamless sleep, when suddenly she swam in image into our nights."

Pluyshin and her extraordinary proposals had certainly made a profound impression on him. "Proposals" in the plural. The Titian proposal was not the only element in her game-strategy, not by any means. It happened to be the only one that she had made clear to me. I was dashed and even miffed to discover how many were the consequences of the notions she had first brought to my attention. In essence they ran like this.

The Bianchini family were now in financial straits that kept them from exercising their traditional functions as arbiters of behaviour and protectors of their dependants. The aristocratic principle is by no means dead in Italy. Governments there have recognized the social use of the aristocracy without wishing to subsidize it. If one of the great families, over the last half century or so, has wished to dispose of its personal property — medals, coins, rare books, furniture, tapestries, minor works of art, letters and similar documents — in an effort to maintain an inherited social ascendancy, then local and even national governments have usually not prevented such sales, sometimes even turning a blind eye to the re-searches of tax collectors. Governments have been reluctant to interfere with the doings of families like the Bianchini, partly from some sense of their value to Italian culture and society, partly from an awareness that they have provided certain social services at less cost than any official form of relief agency would require. So the great families have been allowed to sell off their treasures without strict policing of the financial yield. Probably wisest not to strip a culture of its traditional pillars of allegiance, cohesion, support. Even administrations of the far left have not been slow to allow to the great families some of their privileges in return for the encouragement of social peace.

In extreme cases, such as the sale of the last Titian to a non-Italian buyer, this sound working principle might not readily be applied. Italian opinion, rarely unanimous on any subject, might coalesce around opposition to the export of a magnificent and unique work of art. A Ministry of Culture that issued an export licence in such a case might drag a government to defeat. Two or three points seem to come naturally out of this discussion. Why Canada? Why should the Bianchini family restore their fortunes by the sale of the *Priam and Achilles* to a Canadian gallery or consortium of buyers acting in the interests of Canadian cultural life? Did any Italian/Canadian link exist that would mollify wounded public opinion and explain to Italians the bearings of such a tie? The presence in Canada of a large Italian/Canadian population provided one fine talking point in this connection. The stated wish of the Marchese Bianchini to commemorate Canadian military achievement in his region towards the close of World War II provided a second. Other debating points lurked behind these, some of them very pressing and not at all food for the public in their implications. It is true that secrecy can no longer be maintained in diplomacy or other momentous negotiation among national powers, but at the least, a decent obscurity may be a legitimate goal of those agents of the public interest who would just as soon find that nobody was watching them too closely.

"It's very important that we all approach this matter with clean hands," said the deputy minister, "and with nothing on our sheets that could compromise us. My other guests this afternoon" — he indicated the money man and the spy — "have had no traceable connection with arts funding. No more have I. None of us was around when the Dürer drawing was bought. *Nude Woman with a Staff.* So we can't be tied to it and the circumstances of its purchase."

This riled me a little bit. "The purchase was made in daylight, and strictly in accord with the practices of the day," I said. "If the acquisitions officers erred, it was by excessive enthusiasm for the qualities and reputation of the work. Another drawing from the same series was acquired by the Metropolitan Museum staff at the same time; nobody now questions their wisdom in having made the purchase. Both buys were made perfectly publicly and nobody questioned them at the time."

"You mean that nobody paid any attention," said the money man. "Art purchases by major institutions weren't big news then, the way they are now."

"A decent obscurity," I said, voicing my reflections of a moment before. "The great thing to remember is that nobody is paying any attention to you. Hide nothing but do nothing to call attention to yourself, do nothing by stealth, and Bob's your uncle."

The security man looked puzzled at times, as now. I offered a rough translation. "*Robert, c'est le frère de ton père.*" Now he looked still more puzzled. "It's simply a silly English idiom," I said. "It has no coded contents. I really could just as well have said *C'est un fait accompli.*"

"Robert is my uncle," he said slowly, then relapsed into glum taciturnity. I saw that he was someone to be watched.

I said, looking directly at him, "In the case of the Dürer drawing, acquired from the Lubomirski collection when it was sold up in the 1950s, the ugly word 'loot' has sometimes surfaced. Putting aside the fact of Prince Lubomirski's legitimate ownership of the materials, the National Gallery bought the drawing on the open market in London from a reputable dealer at what was then a good price. There was no question in anyone's mind of the gallery's having stolen or looted the work clandestinely. What makes the purchase at all worth referring to is the enormous increase in the market value of the drawing. I think it was bought for under twenty thousand dollars, a considerable sum for the times. This afternoon, at an open auction, it might fetch as much as a hundred times that amount, say two million U.S. That sounds enormous. But there is no question of our gallery officials having looted or stolen a work that was worth two million at that time. The rise in art prices is the only factor that makes the sale noticeable."

"All the same, we've got to tread very carefully," said the deputy minister. "We can issue bulletins — trial balloons — serially, making it clear that the matter is being well ventilated in the media, without seeming to court an actual outburst of publicity. That's something you should know about, Matthew."

"Just wait till you've sampled it," I said. "It's like nothing else on earth. It's crueller than being buried alive. Let's keep this one as decently free from publicity as we can, at least until the sale has been completed. If there is to be a sale."

"I have no authority over arts funding, and no contact with those who do," the deputy minister said, "but I can tell you that there will be no repetition of the Newman and Rothko affairs, which are still hashed over in administrative circles as examples of how not to involve the public in discussions of funding for the arts."

I felt bound to register an objection. "But this same tendency for art prices to rise has justified those purchases at what were even then very modest amounts. I think the Newman was bought at one million four. Am I right?"

I expected the finance man to have the figure in his notes, and of course he did. "That's about it," he said, without even looking at his documents. I guess the figure is written on their hearts. When they open up this fellow for his postmortem, the names Rothko and Newman will be found on either ventricle. I thought it wise to go on defending those earlier ventures. "Both works are now worth ten times what was paid for them in real dollars. I call that a sound acquisitions policy, and I think the cultural agencies have a pretty solid record in that respect."

Naturally they guessed that I was about to plead a special case.

"What do you look for from us?"

"Support in the private arena of culture diplomacy."

They all winced at this. "We don't know what that means," the deputy minister said. "We're not foreign affairs specialists."

"Perhaps not, but every government department has diplomatic links and policies, isn't that so? Are you in favour of closer ties with Italy, within the overall bounds and structure of the G7 agreements?"

I saw that I had gone too far and too fast. From their exchange of cool stares it seemed that they were going to deny all knowledge of the existence of the G7 structures, of the annual meetings of these nations, of their preponderance in global monetary and fiscal activities. They might never have heard of the sacred word "Mitsubishi." Perhaps a shaking-up would do them good and advance my aims. Maybe not. It was hard to estimate at this juncture. I decided to risk everything on a single roll of the dice.

"We've been drawn progressively closer to Italy over the last decade, in every new alignment of G7 power relationships. Our traditional ties to the U.S. or to France, or to Britain, have long since ceased to have real consequences, as far as liberating ourselves from our trading bind goes. We're the least populous and usually the least productive of the seven. Italy comes next. I think that once or twice in recent times our national production has almost equalled that of Italy, but we have never topped them. The population of Italy exceeds ours by fifteen million."

The finance man nodded in approval.

I went on. "Even combined, our joint annual production does not surpass that of Britain or France, nor does it begin to rival the immense economic leverage exerted by any of Germany, Japan and the U.S. In effect, G7 is a three-tiered edifice. The great world economic powers are Germany, Japan, and the U.S. France and Britain occupy the middle tier, and we and the Italians come last, in the third tier. It seems clear to every analyst in the finance press that Italy and Canada are the poor relations of the bloc."

The deputy minister gave me an encouraging smile. I felt like a lively graduate student who has pleased his professor. "There are many very good reasons why Italy and Canada ought to pursue related, articulated policies to defend the integrity of their currencies and credit. An obvious one comes to view as soon as you give the matter close attention. Why shouldn't individual members of EU or NAFTA act independently of the unions to which they belong, so as to link the two blocs? I can readily imagine France kindly offering her hand to Mexico, as she has done in the past. The French feel no special love for Quebec or for the whole of Canada, as they have shown in the past. And they have a history of intervention in Mexican affairs. I would be surprised to learn that no official at the Quai d'Orsay has ever made some such proposal to his or her masters. The French might well be eager to intervene in Mexican financial policy-making and trading activity, if only to embarrass the U.S. They like nothing better than any move that goes counter to real American policy."

The deputy minister received my remarks sourly. "I don't see how you can put forward these remarks publicly."

"We four aren't exactly the public. Or are we?"

I had not meant to embarrass my companions, and was surprised to see the security man blush violently. You'd think that with his age and field experience he'd be able to maintain an unaltered expression in face of surprise. But no!

I said, "You've just told me something I didn't know before. I was simply speculating idly. Now I can see that an Italian/Canadian link, which would give NAFTA a keyhole view of EU affairs, and vice versa, is an obvious motive for action. I expect now to be told that this is an aspect of the affair that you had hoped to conceal from me. Am I right? Am I simply being asked to lend my expertise in the vonderble vorld of art while remaining strictly out of anything that lies behind high matters of art dealing?" Light was breaking in on me. "We get the last Titian, and they get this surreptitious merging of policies. Perhaps not so surreptitious. Knock three zeroes off the lira values, and an Italian/Canadian currency peg is already matter of economic fact. We could have a pair of maverick currencies trading reciprocally, out of the bounds of the economic unions to which each is supposed to belong. Pluyshin is sent to us — to you — with a proposal to waive the export regulations on major works of art. Otherwise we'd never get the painting out of Italy. In return Canada agrees to begin discussions of a tie-up of the two moneys, with direct convertibility an ultimate aim. Native-born Italians, of whom there are well over a million resident in Canada, are enabled to transfer payments to the homeland — from one trading bloc to the other — with an ease unparalleled elsewhere in either bloc. It's rich. It's a very good idea. Everybody in on the transaction gets something. They get convertibility, and they get to knock those embarrassing three zeros off the lira, so that a hundred dollars Canadian is worth a hundred new lire, not a hundred thousand old ones. We get free and ready export of the great work of art, which the Italian officials represent as a lofty diplomatic stroke, cementing our cherished and traditional cultural ties. The National Gallery gets *Priam and Achilles* and leaps into the ranks of the top ten galleries in the world. Pluyshin gets her fingering fee and lives happily ever after. The Marchese Bianchini is refinanced in splendour and richness of appearance. He invests his fifty million Canadian very safely, and remains the magnate of his region. All fine! All exemplary! But I can foresee a snag."

The finance man's knee jerked convulsively when I said this, and I could swear he gave a quiet sigh of relief. Fifty-five million for a hundred and fifty-six square feet of old, dirty canvas? Absurd!

Perhaps I may have been giving him sturdy philistine opinions that he didn't really hold. He might have been a connoisseur for all I knew. The recesses of financial administration in the federal government are closed to me. I've now and then been on a federal payroll, always on short-term contract. I've never yet had to meet a budget or fire anybody to meet a budget cut.

That makes me the philistine, at least in that area of action. I don't know about finance and budgets, and could scarcely expect the finance people to know about Titian and the cash value of his final works. The figure of fifty-five million had been arrived at God knows how. In an open market, with the Americans and Japanese bidding, the price might go much higher, might exceed the previous record for an indifferent Van Gogh acquired by Japanese interests over a decade ago.

But on Pluyshin's showing, *Priam and Achilles* wasn't about to be put up for bidding. The stipulated price had been put forward by the Marchese Bianchini, through Pluyshin, as a definitive price; no negotiation would be permitted. We were in a take-it-or-leave-it situation. The Bianchini family obviously considered — with good reason — that they were doing Canada and Canadians a great favour by conceding them this first-look option. As I understood the matter, the work wasn't to be offered for sale on the international art market until the Canadians had had their chance to consider the proposal. The Marchese showed in this a nice sense of his own dignity, and that of the Canadians who might take up his offer. No concealment and no publicity; these were meant to be the hallmarks of the transaction. But the big snag might remain in place no matter how discreetly the matter was handled. Fifty-five million for a hundred and fifty-six square feet of old and dirty canvas? Five million as *commission on its sale* to be passed to some mystery woman who never got her picture in the papers and never appeared on television? This was expecting a lot from the Canadian public. On the face of things, at first look, I simply couldn't see the federal government putting up the money for the purchase.

"Where's the money coming from?" the security man asked. That this hard question came from him first rather surprised me. Perhaps he represented a legitimate element of Canadian opinion. Security staff can only guard information that somebody wants to keep secure; they are the servants of public opinion as much as the rest of us. They tell themselves:

this is what Canadians want kept secret. They don't say to themselves: this is what we are going to keep from Canadians in the interests of national security.

I may be wrong about this, but I don't think so. The security folks I've met have invariably seen themselves as public servants, acting always in the nation's best interests. So when a security man asked the key question, I saw that he was expressing the knee-jerk reaction of the populace. Where indeed was the money to come from? There could be no question of lobbing the ball back into the Marchese's court. He was a man, as I soon discovered, of inflexible will. He simply would not bargain. If we couldn't meet his terms, he would go elsewhere and doubtless do better. He was trying to honour us, and we could hardly ask him to reduce the price of the honour. We might quite legitimately ask him to let our expert (myself, as it turned out) verify the state of the work; that would be an acceptable request, but the price could not be pegged to the condition of the work.

I said, "I think the money simply has to be found. I'd never forgive myself if we let this chance slip." I didn't know what I was saying, but my instincts took me in the right direction. "If my son can go to Mars at the constant risk of his life, I can go to Ravenna for my country," I said. This was a showy statement, but I saw that I had hit the right note. And afterwards there was an unspoken agreement from almost everybody who dealt with me in the matter that the link between the actions of the Canadian space voyagers and the acquisition of the last Titian wasn't simply factitious. Wise diplomatic behaviour might make of Italy a participating member in the space voyage by way of the connection between me and my son. Our son.

Edie would have to be involved in any trade-off involving us. I didn't quite grasp this during the first conferences with the deputy minister, but as the complexities of the project unfolded before us I came to understand that the two of us would have to be full participants in this final game. The money had to be found, the concessions from governments concerning export and import of major works of art had to be exacted, the funds made available to the purchasing agent. Me? Ancillary injections of funding to install and maintain the picture, to arrange for its public display and for its protection, the consent of the officers of the National Gallery to house the painting, either as part of their permanent holdings or as being on permanent loan, these and many other matters had to be dealt with. The technicalities of stock-issue, for example, became a pressing matter for my consideration; here various government offices were of immense use in cutting through red tape for the sake of speed. You don't simply advertise in the financial papers that you are prepared to sell shares in your company to anybody who may wish to buy them. It's a more closely supervised operation than that. "Where's the money to come from?" and "I think the money has to be found" were like choral refrains accompanying the early stages of the developing project, finally becoming the cue of the whole affair. Without foreseeing them, I had very early accepted the responsibilities of the fundraiser. I had more or less declared that the fifty-five million dollars would be forthcoming. The lesser, ancillary sums were not going to be my responsibility. Let agents of the three ministries involved and the officials of the National Gallery worry about that. Transport and mounting charges might in the end run these additional costs through the roof. I wasn't to worry about that. My business was to find the purchase price.

Once that was in hand, government officials could go ahead and pay out the ancillary charges without fear of inflamed public opinion. They could avow to an inquisitive public that the work was a *gift to the Canadian people!* They could adduce the goodwill of the Marchese Bianchini and his lovely Marchesa (his third, as it happens, and much younger) towards all Canadians. It could truthfully be said that only a very small part of the purchase price would be furnished from public funds. All the arrangements for the acquisition and mounting of the work had to be made quickly, against a deadline that suddenly imposed itself on us.

"I think we can have her in now," the deputy minister said. Then Pluyshin appeared between the double doors of the big office, shedding the light of one of her rare smiles upon us.

"This lady will be proud and happy to put you in contact with the Marchese Bianchini," the deputy minister declared, as though everything had been settled amongst us. The security man and the finance man now vanished without uttering additional words. The three of us who stayed put now began an exercise in connivance that led to my flying to Milan on the next day but one. Malpensa is an airport that I really dislike — too near the foothills of the Alps. I like an airport to lie well out on a flat plain, so that its approaches needn't seem too abrupt. I had minor Milanese business to attend to. I wanted to take another look around the Brera, for once not *in restauro*, a condition that afflicts all the great galleries from time to time. Half of the Brera collection had been inaccessible during my last visit. I was glad to have a brief stopover before proceeding to Ravenna by rail. Pluyshin, as arranged, went ahead of me, and had two solid days with the Marchese before I arrived. This was just at Christmas time, when an air of bonhomie pervaded the Italian scene. Allegiance to Christian practice has attenuated itself in that country, but deep religious associations remain in place. Ravenna towards the time of the Nativity wears a cloak of slightly embarrassed festivity. The city has preserved tacit allegiances out of loyalty to the extraordinary specimens of high art that Christian culture has left it. The site of S. Vitale can never become wholly secularized.

I spent a first night in the tomblike Jolly Hotel, much more funereal in its aspect than any of the city's mighty tombs. The next morning, December 24th, the Marchese's car called for me, a stylish Lancia sports sedan, and whisked me away to Classe, and from there across the fields and low ridges southwest of S. Apollinaire to the site of the ancestral home of the Bianchini.

I've seen many similar houses in northern Italy; none has this one's peculiar mixture of shaggy disrepair and radical grandeur. Its linked buildings sprawl over nearly half a mile of ground without ever showing a plain front elevation. There isn't one. The Castello Bianchini seems more like a collection of village offices, carpenters' shops, stables, a chapel, than a single building's unified whole. "Shaggy" is certainly the right word to describe the overall impression you receive as you approach along the main drive. There is a famous set of wrought-iron gates, showing the beasts of the Bianchini family emblems: greyhounds, lions, bears, a fox. These gates, six hundred years old, are wholly free of rust, having been scoured and scraped free of corrosion once a week during that period of time. A family of retainers has existed for the whole time with its sole employment the cleaning of the famous gates. Some part of the purchase price of the Titian would no doubt go towards the preservation of these people in their customary place and duties. I hoped so anyway.

An even more valuable family connection, amongst the host of retainers clustered around the great house, was that of the much-ramified family of Battaglia, museum officers to the Marchese Bianchini for many centuries. The successive sons of the family have acted as *conservateurs* of the innumerable works of art deposited in the Castello over the generations: paintings, sculptures, jewellery, every imaginable sort of work in metal or wood or cloth. The building — or buildings — houses a collection that in any other country would long since have passed into the care of the national museums. In Italy these works have remained in private hands to be cared for by the family that owned them and the dependent families that conserved them. Not our contemporary way of maintaining a superb collection of works of art, but a viable alternative, not to be despised.

I had very little contact with the Marchese on my first visit.

He was far too grand a personage to be approached by an emissary in my humble position, and besides was not in residence at that moment. The flag of his marquisate was not to be seen above the tower that rose above the main entry to the Castello. This banner, or gonfalon, which was flown immediately upon the return of the Marchese a few days afterwards, is a remarkable example of late medieval heraldic design, telling the tale of the rise of power of the Bianchini family in economical and explicit symbolism. There are lots of foxes depicted on its large rich folds, perhaps a hint from its designers concerning the mental powers of the successive heads of the house. In fact the banner shows two lions and five foxes; there may be more to the symbolism than I grasped at first look.

If the Bianchini are a foxy stock, their retainers the Battaglia (in English, Battle) are equally cunning and perceptive. I was escorted around the Castello's various libraries, galleries, muniment-rooms and storehouses, by Marcello Battaglia, the eldest member of his clan, now perhaps in his early seventies. He had grown up on the Bianchini estates and had lived nowhere else during his long and useful life. He had received no formal training in the historiography of art; he just knew where everything was and what it was and where they had gotten it. He had lived with this abundance of masterworks, and lesser works too, from infancy. Each piece was as familiar to him as the rarities in the collection of some renowned bibliophile are to their owner.

He knew the collections far better than their nominal owner. I had known Marcello Battaglia by reputation although he had published nothing, not being that way inclined. He was best known among museum officials as the man in charge of *Priam and Achilles*. He was known to possess an impressive expertise in the care and handling of the masterworks of the Venetian school. Sometimes he would be invited by the officials of the Accademia to contribute an opinion about some proposed program of restoration, or perhaps about the authenticity of a work by a minor master from the southern Veneto. He had a knowledge that is simply not buyable, not to be found in museum catalogues or specialized monographs. He treated the works under his care as a jockey does the thoroughbred under him, as they approach the starting gate. He had an instinctive, unpurchasable awareness of the nature and structure of the pieces entrusted to his care by his forefathers unto the fifteenth generation.

I grew to reverence this aging trickster, who never tried to teach me anything. He simply stated facts and allowed me to draw my own conclusions. It was evident that the proposed sale of *Priam and Achilles* had wounded him deeply, but he never complained about it. He could not have breached the traditional rubrics of aristocratic possession and servitor's obedience. He must have hated me, and never showed it by any sign.

He even lodged me in a fine little suite, bedroom and sitting room, somewhere on an upper floor of the central mass of the Castello. For the life of me I couldn't tell you exactly where it was. I found it hard to get back to it and more than once had to be led from the nearest bathroom to my own quarters by giggling maidservants. What a house! I knew that the Marchese and his consort were somewhere in the building the week after Christmas, but I was not invited to join in the festivities. There was of course a chapel adjacent to the central parts of the building, and the masses for the season were duly celebrated with some choral accompaniment, not of the first quality but not bad either.

It wasn't till the second day after Christmas that Marcello Battaglia invited me to join him in the great gallery that lay along the left front of the building on what the Brits would call the first floor, and we the second floor, a confusion that slightly riles me. It ought to be cleared up one of these days. Anyway, the gallery was up one flight of the grand staircase, off to the left, and there, carefully shielded from excessive light, hung Titian's *King Priam Before the Tent of Achilles, Begging the Body of Hector from the Hero, for Burial.*

The work carried the evidence of its authenticity on its surface. It could have been nothing but a product of the master's very last years, comparable to no other of his works but the wonderful *Pietà* in the Accademia. I mustn't let my enthusiasm run away with me, but when I came up to the painting and stood there gazing at it all my misgivings fled away. I saw that by whatever means short of outright theft this thing had to come to us. Just having one object like this in the country would make Canadians citizens of a great world. A masterpiece ennobles its possessors. As I stood there my imagination began to busy itself with specific plans for the transport of the painting to Ottawa. In my mind we had already taken possession; there could be no turning back.

I saw as I stood there in the modified light that I had been joined by Signor Battaglia and another man, a slender spruce gentleman of something over medium height, perhaps five years older than me, which made him old enough to have served with the resistance. This was certainly the Marchese Bianchini. I was overcome, wholly mollified, by the first thing he said to me.

"I congratulate you on the arrival of your first grandchild. Andrea, isn't it?"

Like everybody else in the world with access to a television set, he'd been following the adventures of John and Emily and waiting for the arrival of their child. I was slightly confused by his mention of the baby's name because Andrea is a feminine name in English, my daughter's name, as it happens. In Italian it's masculine, indeed the name of one of the great heroes of Italian naval campaigning.

I said, "Andrea is given in English as Andrew, sir, if it is the name of a boy. His parents had only one name on their list for a boy, it seems. He was Andrew before anybody else in the world was told of it."

"I believe not the first Andrea Goderich," said the Marchese, with refined politeness. "He must be the great-grandchild of the author of *Sin Quantified*."

"It's kind of you to remember a work almost sixty years old."

"But who could ignore the humanity of Andrew Goderich?" said the Marchese. This put us on a footing of the utmost cordiality and shared confidence. I wondered where the Marchese had met my father. Surely not during the war. As far as I knew, the Marchese, then barely out of his teens, had confined his anti-Nazi operations to his home province. My father had never been on Italian soil in wartime. They might have met at any time in the later 1940s, during the time preceding the publication of *Sin Quantified*. It was a point worth clearing up, but so far I've never gotten around to it. It seemed enough that the Marchese knew about my father, his writings and his Nobel Prize; this awareness made our conversations more informal and more productive. The descendant of a twelve-hundred-years-old house can never see himself as existing on quite the same level as ordinary people. At best he can approximate the levelling attitude. But the Marchese has always been perfectly charming to me, though inflexible about the market value of his great possessions.

"We shall not bargain, my dear Goderich. You have only to see the work to understand that the naming of a price is a pure formality; the object is in itself priceless. The notion of a price collapses when faced with something like this.

"Did you know that the Germans had already made preparations for the removal of *Priam and Achilles*?"

I had not known that.

"But yes, it is true. Do you see those faint marks on the wall, between the two great windows? They are plastered over from time to time but they invariably resurface. They are traces of the opening in the wall made by German engineers in 1944, in preparation for the removal of our Titian. Only prevented by the providential arrival of the Canadian forces that drove the Nazis off. The Titian should belong to them and to their inheritors. Do you not agree?"

If it was a sales pitch, it was a most refined one, and much more, and I could not have resisted it in any terms. It seemed to me a heaven-sent opportunity freighted with historic necessity for Canada and Canadians. As I stood there in front of the Titian, I was completely and overwhelmingly persuaded that I must do everything in my power to bring the work to Ottawa. So that for many years to come, when the exotic name of the city surfaced in polite conversation anywhere in the world, heads would nod and people would say, "Ah yes, that's where they have the last Titian." The name of the city would gradually associate itself with perfection, the absolute and utter best, the finest of its kind that there is to be had.

From the time of that first visit to the Castello Bianchini, God forgive me, I was thinking in round bald terms of a Goderich/Codrington Wing of the National Gallery signalizing the primordial days of the new millennium, the Goderich/Codrington millennium. I saw, standing there between the Marchese and Marcello Battaglia, just how the thing was to be worked. This was my very last ambition; eternity beckoned. Let the deal be decently, even nobly handled. And the name that has recurred so often in these narratives streamed broadly into my consciousness.

Codrington Hardware and Builders' Supplies. Since 1867.

To the social reformer's ancient question, What is to be done? I made the only fitting answer: we will go public with the company, retain some small part of the realized capital for our needs, and turn the remainder into a special fund for the purchase of the Titian and its presentation to the nation. Without having to work it out laboriously, I arrived at a sale price for *Codrington Hardware and Builders' Supplies. Since 1867.* A flourishing retail enterprise with its central outlet in Stoverville and three branches, in Cornwall, Kingston and Smiths Falls, with another projected to open in Belleville next year, the company should be worth well over thirty million at current share prices. If Edie and I were to retain a couple of million from the sale as investment capital for our personal needs, there would still remain a cool thirty million as a contribution to the purchase. I could think at once of two or three potential additional participants in the purchase. Crown Royal Tobacco and Lamp Trust were my first choices, and proved in the event to have been the right ones. The whole organizational structure flashed before my eyes as I confronted the painting. I was ready to make a full commitment.

"We will want to buy the work at your stated price," I said to the Marchese. "That will be the net yield to you. Our committee will arrange for transport of the picture following its removal from this site. It will become part of the permanent collection of the National Gallery of Canada. I can readily predict where it will be displayed."

Perhaps three or four times in a lifetime, a person has to make a command decision that entails grave consequences. Often this has to be done as a leap in the dark. So be it!

"I'm exceeding my present authority in telling you this," I said, "but you will find that I have described the situation accurately."

The Marchese bowed to me, turned, and indicated the shadowy marks on the facing wall. "We will remove the picture through the aperture that the Nazis prepared for us. There is a roadway immediately beneath, created by the German engineers. Transport can draw up very closely just below."

He seemed as eager as I was to put the removal on foot as quickly as possible. That was the tone of the subsequent negotiations. The whole procedure unfolded as quickly as anything that has to do with government departments ever does.

"You will hear from me directly after the beginning of the year," I told them, "and my communication will be specific, exact and binding."

I flew back to Ottawa the next day, the thirtieth of December. There was no time to be wasted. Already a grand scheme for the painting was lining itself out in my imagination. Our thirty million — Edie's and mine — would clearly be enough to get our names on the installation permanently. The store was

Codrington property; the Goderich connection was by marriage only, and a somewhat compromised marriage at that. It would have to be the Codrington/Goderich Wing. I even knew in those first moments just where the Codrington/Goderich Wing should be located in the building for maximum impact on visitors. All the bits of the undertaking fitted together tightly. Even the time available for carrying out these proposals was very, very tight.

It was the beginning of the new year. The voyage to Mars and the return trip would occupy another six months, until mid-June. For the sake of poetry, let's say until Midsummer's Day. Then after a successful return to Earth, the voyagers would be sequestered at some medical centre for thorough physical examination and debriefing. Say ten weeks for all that, most of the summer. My son and his compatriot, Céline Hervieu, might well be available for a grand pubic appearance sometime towards the end of September.

That allowed us the nine months of human gestation in which to go public with the sale of shares in *Codrington Hardware and Builders' Supplies. Since 1867*. Collect the cash yield in a central fund. Deposit moneys retained by us for personal use in a family sinking fund. Bring Crown Royal Tobacco and Lamp Trust into line as associate contributors. Rally public opinion in favour of the great gift. Get a commitment from the feds for that last two million. There was clearly much to be done in this short time. Some financial institution would have to front the purchase price, recovering the money afterwards when the funding should have been brought together. That's what banks are for, aren't they?

It looked like an impossibility during that first week of the new year. But fortunately there was no destructive criticism of the project when it began to be acted upon. The world's attention was too completely focussed on the adventures of the astronauts for any other news story to receive more than cursory attention. This lucky circumstance was a great help to us. We were able to function in the plain view of the generous public at all times. By the point where determined opposition might have been mounted, we could reasonably show that the time for opposition had gone by, that these debating points should have been raised weeks earlier, and so forth. We found ourselves in the best possible debater's stance from the very start. As it turned out, no really harmful criticism of the project was ever put forward. Even the right-wing elements in the federal opposition parties could find no reason to reject a gift of over fifty millions. Quite impossible for them to maintain, as had been said in previous cases of costly purchases of works of art, that a child with a reel of masking tape and a box of acrylics could do as well. It was plain to any viewer that masking tape and acrylic had nothing to do with this particular piece of art.

The sad thing about the acquiring of *Priam and Achilles* as far as the usual philistine opposition was concerned was that they all knew that they liked the work. It convinced everybody of its worth at first sight. The entire arts community, the daily papers, the global webs, the broadcasting media, all were in favour of the acquisition on the publicly stated terms. This helped a lot. There was no sterile debate about art education, the class structure, dead white European males, the legal status of masterpieces as belonging to private owners; none of these hoary questions ever arose. I will declare at once that it was delightful to manage the purchase without having to justify it at the bar of public opinion. It was a master stroke, though I say it who perhaps shouldn't, to propose from the start that the dedicatory ceremonies for the Codrington/ Goderich Wing should take place in the presence of the two returned Canadian astronauts.

So when I put my concrete proposals to the deputy minister in the first week of January, I was astonished to find how ready he was to act on them, ready indeed to take them to his chief, a woman not much noted for an interest in the arts. But she got onside immediately, took the matter into Cabinet and defended it three or four times before her colleagues with maximum effect. Her actions on our behalf may have been motivated by a wish to retain her ministry. A Cabinet shuffle had been impending for some time; this was just the sort of bold move that would impress the PM. When the tie-in to the Mars flight became clear to the minister and the PM, they were all for the acquisition of the painting, especially at such a small cost to the government. The project must have struck the Cabinet as money for jam, one of those can't-lose undertakings that occur sometimes in the life of a government. An election was two years away, and this would be a popular event.

My next move was in the direction of the commitments from the financial donors I had in mind. And I had to persuade my wife to participate. I never feared that Edie would refuse to fall in with these designs, as another person might have done, despite thirty years of estrangement. It amounted, after all, to our giving thirty million dollars to the government in return for our names on a plaque. Give Edie credit; she had a large and ready vision of the project.

She had good personal reasons for supporting the public sale of *Codrington Hardware and Builders' Supplies. Since 1867.* I won't go into them since they were more her business than mine, although I was involved in them. I met with her in London many times during the runup to the acquisition and installation of the Titian, and she gave no trouble in our discussions, which were on a perfectly friendly basis. We'd both arrived at a time in life when wealth begins to seem more of a burden than a blessing. I'd had quite enough of the administrative responsibilities entailed in running the company and was very ready to off-load them on any new management team that a new board of directors might want to name.

The remaining elements of the funding were Crown Royal Tobacco, originally a Montreal company, now based in Toronto, and Lamp Trust, Montreal-based, with close ties to the liquor business and to New York, and the big board. I chose these two organizations because of their immense wealth and the grandiose character of their operations. Eleven or twelve millions wouldn't seem like a large bite to either of them.

I've sometimes been asked why I went first to the tobacco and distilling people. The answer must be obvious. Both groups had again and again shown great readiness to help fund arts programs. A far greater readiness than governments at any level! Certainly they have their own axe to grind; they want to make propaganda against the groups that would like to banish the use of liquor and tobacco from our communities, going on from there to cure us of all our wicked habits.

I have no interest in lobbying for tobacco salesmen, but I'm not certain that the use of tobacco is vicious, as violent crime is vicious. If people wish to inhale tobacco fumes, you can't legally restrain them, as long as their fumes don't inconvenience non-smoking neighbours. You can rightly ban smoking on public conveyances, but you can't make smoking criminal; you can't ban it everywhere. Prohibition didn't work.

The use or abuse of alcohol is something else, probably a much older custom than smoking, found much more widely in human culture and often approved by moral and religious leaders. I approve of the beneficial uses of beer, wine, spirits, only noting that some of us can't deal with them moderately. I don't know why. But we certainly can't banish the use of beer, wine and spirits universally because some of our fellows can't handle them. I believe that the use of tobacco products is on the point of disappearing from human culture, but that the use of alcohol will persist far into the future, perhaps as long as humanity itself. Drinking seems a genial and harmless enjoyment to me; smoking seems less harmless and less genial. In a confined space, in a jet aircraft or a small hotel suite, tobacco smoke can be really offensive and injurious to non-smokers. But neither practice seems immoral or contemptible to me, and I have no objection to cooperating with tobacco or liquor merchants in a project like the one that was now on the table.

Edie and I retained for our personal maintenance considerably less than one-tenth of the yield of the sale of the family
company, the rest of it being vested in the fund that was set
up to direct the spending on the Titian and its transport and
maintenance. The proceeds of the share-issue came in first;
this gave the fund a certain solid authority. Special administrators were appointed — I was one of three — and the actual
deposit was made to a bank close to Parliament Hill. The
interest that the money began to earn as soon as it was
deposited was employed in defraying some incidental costs.
There was a small office, just a reception room and a couple
of meeting rooms that the administrators used. There were
phone service, a fax terminal, which proved extremely useful,
and full computer and Internet services that we used for
research. As yet, we had no special status or federal approval.
We simply acted as receivers of the sums subscribed.

Lamp Trust placed eleven and a half million to our credit
not long after our contribution was made. The Trust must be
the behemoth of arts spending in North America. Its headquarters building in Montreal is an outstanding example of
the modernist architecture of the 1950s and early 1960s. More
Philip Johnson than Mies, it outshines most of what has come
along since in the post-modernist guise. Lamp House must
have cost much more than eleven million. Patronage of the
arts on a grand scale was therefore a family characteristic. It
took no more than two weeks of concentrated discussion to
persuade their board to supply the needed sum. That brought
us to forty-two and a half million. The interest earnings on
these deposits now had to be accounted for rigorously. I found
myself in the unusual position of acting as a public watchdog
over the care of money that had only a moment before been
held privately by me and my wife. Right hand watching left,
or something like that. I had to spend a lot of time in Ottawa
during those first hectic months. I conferred regularly with a
firm of auditors that had been appointed by us as special
administrators' consultants. We were dealing with amounts

of money that were large in one perspective and small in another; this gave the whole undertaking its air of confusion.

But I was determined from the beginning to make it a model of public administration, with every cent accounted for in the clear light of day, and no spending allowed beyond what was absolutely necessary to carry out the scheme. No junkets to Europe to consult experts. No wining and dining in Ravenna or Venice. No socializing with the Marchese for the sake of a free meal or a gala weekend. I think the final statements to the auditors after the project was complete must have surprised them by their accuracy, clarity and completeness; there was not a single cent unaccounted for. Mind you, there were occasional tricky bits, as for example the thorny question of Pluyshin and her entitlements. It was settled from the start that her five-percent finder's fee, five million in Canadian funds, was to be lodged in a Swiss bank. But her tax problems were not our affair, and our administrative committee couldn't bring themselves — ourselves — to pay the money to a Swiss account number. That would have smacked too much of the kind of secret international intrigue of which Canadians must never seem to be a part. In the end the matter was arranged by paying the whole price to the Marchese with the request that he deal with his agent in his own terms. Pluyshin got her money as soon as payment was made to the Marchese.

She then applied for Canadian citizenship! Can you believe it? And the Immigration Board has not been slow to act on her dossier, I don't know on whose advice. Nor where the dossier is now. But I suspect that the application is due for early action; she may even have been accepted already; certainly her finances must have been a solid recommendation to the board, at least as solid as those of any magnate from Hong Kong or Taiwan. It looks as if Pluyshin's fee is about to return to Canada.

For the record, the most recent information I have on Pluyshin suggests that she has bought a small house in the country, somewhere in central Ontario. I have not tried to locate her address. It would be hilariously funny to discover in the end that Gerda Kotecke Pluyshin was a native daughter of York County, born in some village like Aurora or Richmond Hill. Such things don't happen very often, but they do sometimes. Anyway, she got her money up front, so her story ends fairly happily.

Crown Royal Tobacco came third in line among the donors. As the corporate title suggests, Crown Royal is simply the Canadian embodiment of a vast conglomerate with extensive corporate ties worldwide. Based in London, this multinational is now transforming itself from a tobacco company, pure and simple, into a ramified post-industrial organism with bewilderingly multiple interests and holdings: a pharmaceutical house, land holdings on every continent including Antarctica, a shipping line with its own container docking facilities in thirty ports worldwide, several newspapers in many languages, a TV network, four major engineering and construction companies, paper mills and many other enterprises besides cigar and cigarette factories. To such an organization, a gift of eleven million or thereabouts could seem a fleabite. Some fleabite! Receipt of the Crown Royal donation brought our total amount in the bank to over fifty-five million, all of it earning daily compounded interest at a most-favoured-client rate. As well, Crown Royal lent us a trio of veteran public-relations officers who did magnificent work for us.

The final donor stood shivering on the brink for several weeks, then issued payment by cheque from the government's central operating fund of the final two million, bringing the amount in hand to just on fifty-seven million.

In the end, after the purchase was complete and the work safely on display, there remained a very modest surplus in our fund that eventually became a comic embarrassment to our committee and the ministries involved. Whose money was it? Not mine and Edie's. We'd disavowed all claim in the capital sum we'd paid in. Neither Lamp Trust nor Crown Royal would touch any of it. I think the Auditor-General's office finally dictated the solution. The special acquisitions fund was wound up under their supervision and the capital was paid into the operating budget of the National Gallery, where it was used to pay the costs of mounting and preserving the Titian. The nation received a munificent present at no cost whatsoever to itself, and the gallery was put to no special expense on account of the gift. It's surprising how often a gift can embarrass its recipient's resources. I've noticed this time and again; no gift comes entirely free. But in our case, even the transport charges from Classe to Genoa, to Montreal, to Ottawa were met with interest received on the acquisitions fund. Quite a triumph of public administration.

Now it began to be obvious that plans for a grand public festival, to be mounted for the first showing of the painting on its new site, should be prepared and submitted to the appropriate authorities as soon as possible. What we aimed to do was simple and sensible, and calculated to be wonderful publicity for the occasion. Never mind that the Goderich connection with the last Titian was tenuous. John was our son; that seemed connection enough. Various great publicity agencies would be all too ready to maximize the importance of the connection, especially as they would be able to link it to the romantic tale of the hero who meets his son for the first time long after the child's birth. What a story! What a yarn!

When the media got hold of the Codrington/Goderich elements in this great national benefaction, and saw its tie-in with the heroic tale of space conquest, they made a banquet of it such as the world's publicity mills had never seen before. Adam Sinclair's sad story had produced a torrent of publicity that had very nearly driven me past the limits of my nervous endurance. Now for a second time I was to be subjected to this horrid process, on an even grander scale. The government of Italy, for example, was not slow to profit from this tempest of coverage. The Codrington/Goderich acquisition of the final Titian tied Italian Renaissance culture directly to the new cosmography of space exploration. It made possible a double

conquest of Mars: first the Red Planet, and then the shadowy
figure of Ares/Mars as he lurked in anger in the recesses of
Priam and Achilles, the god of war.

Exploration invariably brings responsibilities in its train. I
had hoped for a long time to free myself from the weight of
management of *Codrington Hardware and Builders' Supplies.
Since 1867*, by more or less giving the company away. Then I
learned that you can never walk away from your destiny. The
new management wanted me as board chairman; they offered
substantial fees that I was unable to refuse. But before all
that, there was the business of Tony and his bequests, which
I now have to narrate.

IV

IN FOR TESTS

"Antarctica is as bad or worse as a living site. That is the first lesson the astronauts have drawn from their nearly three weeks of Mars walk. There isn't the snow to reckon with, Mars having a virtually waterless environment. But the eternal winds and low temperatures are conditions found equally at the South Pole and on Mars. Perhaps this is the time, in our series of broadcasts, to pay tribute to the gallant women and men who maintain human presence at the South Pole, where every litre or gallon of fuel, to operate transport or to power the generators that supply light and heat for the camp, has to be flown in to the site in conditions that vary from very hazardous to nearly impossible.

"Women and men can come and go freely in the base buildings of the South Pole, wearing shorts and T-shirts. They can look forward to ice-cold soft drinks with their meals, or to steaming hot coffee. An environment like that of the most temperate climate on Earth has been maintained at the Pole against all the hazards of nature and problems of supply. And what has been managed there, in the worst weather on Earth, is being copied in the long-term plans for permanent manned stations on Mars. During their three weeks on the surface of the planet, the four Mars walkers have gathered essential information about weather conditions, soil and rock textures, the effects of reduced gravitational pull, the problems of resting and sleeping in exotic conditions of existence. More has been learned in these weeks just past about the fundamental demands of existence on Mars than the human species had gathered during its entire previous history. Our understanding of Mars has been deepened, our collection of materials and facts has been multiplied a thousandfold by the incredibly fruitful investigations of these four researchers.

"To Commandant Hubert de Barny particularly must go credit for having predicted the characteristic qualities of existence under these conditions. Commandant de Barny as medical observer on the Mars walk has had to maintain round-the-clock surveillance of himself and his three companions, so as to compile a complete report on the behaviour of human muscle tissue in low-gravity situations. In the highly artificial environment of the Mars walk, precarious and temporary in nature, Commandant de Barny has been able to provide his companions with the stimuli necessary to keep them in top physical shape. None has reported so much as a slight cold during their explorations. All four have become familiar, if rather indistinct, figures on the television screens of Earth. Commandant de Barny, as everybody now knows, is an amateur tennis player of great accomplishment at a high level of competition. His athletic appearance has made him one of the stars of our coverage of the Mars walk. It seems probable that a career as a television personality may open up for this officer as soon as he returns to Earth. Already the world's communications services are bidding for his attention. Considered opinon at Mission Control holds that Commandant de Barny will choose to continue with a career as the world's leading authority on the physiology of human anatomy in space. He has a great future in either field.

"On your screens at this moment you can see Commandant de Barny applying a standard neurological test for muscle strength and tone of the upper arm to Captain Hervieu. The two astronauts are conducting the examination in the medical cubicle of the surface shelter. It is striking to witness this common medical procedure being carried out in an artificial environment millions of miles from Earth.

"One of the most welcome side effects of the success so far of the flight of *Visitor I* has been the global reaffirmation of the basic human values of enterprise, adventurousness and our deeply rooted wish to know the causes and effects of things, science in a word. The last half of the previous century was marred by what scientists must regard as a saddening anti-humanism, a wish to set humanity on all fours with our fellow animals. Yet the other animals have no science, no art, no imagination such as allows undertakings like the Mars walk. Humanity may well rejoice in the results obtained during the flight, and in the sight of human medical science exercising its preventive and healing function at a distance from home of several million miles. It is the same science as on Earth, and the same tests and preventive measures apply. The crew of this flight will benefit largely from the application of creative medical research to its activities. You can now see Commandant de Barny applying electrical contacts to Captain Hervieu's fingers to obtain a modified EMG, or electro-myelogram reading, a test for neural efficiency. All the Mars walkers have been checked twice daily for any diminution of the efficiency of their supply of neurons through the nervous system. No impairment has been reported to this date, an important result for space physiology and neurology, and for medicine in general.

"Those of us on staff here at Mission Control feel very deeply that humanity at large will be the major beneficiary of these explorations. Observe your screens as the medical analyst reads his results on the neurological equipment. As usual he seems to be getting a satisfactory reading on Captain Hervieu's fitness to carry out further assignments on the Mars walk. Now he detaches the electrical contacts and examines the tape of the neural impulses. He smiles at his colleague; the report will be strongly positive. The crew of Mars walkers

must be the most physically fit quartet of human beings alive.
They are in extraordinary condition.

"And here on your screen is the amazingly clear image of
the interior of the space shelter, just as we have been receiving
it for the past three weeks. You can see most of the living area,
the personal sleep cubicles, the eating and daily living quarters and some of the storage bins. The walls have been
coloured in soft tones of blue and green, a calming colour
scheme, praised as such by the Mars walkers. Our sound
pickup doesn't allow us to reproduce for you the noise of the
continual winds at the planet's surface, but our communications from the crew suggest that the noise level does not rise
to Antarctic pitches. Sleep and total relaxation come fairly
readily. And now the team can look forward to the imminent
end of their stay on the surface. There is no critical threat to
the shelter at this time, but departure from the surface should
not be delayed for more than another eight hours at most.
Colonel Lebedev and Professor Goderich are absent from
the surface shelter at this time, making final observations
of the surface weather, preparatory to the return flight of the
Mars lander to its parent spacecraft.

"Some modifications of the flight plan for the return voyage
to Earth may have to be introduced. The extremely favourable
conditions that the Mars walkers have found during their stay
on the planet have caused them to remain there for forty-eight
hours longer than originally planned. Especially useful and
promising has been the astronauts' ability to function in a
gravitational field very different in its effects on human musculature from that of Earth. Professor Goderich has found that
after a three-week stay on the surface the muscle wastage and
deterioration in bone calcium found in prolonged weightlessness have not occurred under the modest gravitational pull
on Mars. Future explorers should be able to live there without
fear of loss of strength and muscle tone, and without damage
to their bone structure, without the necessity of an elaborate
system of artificial gravity such as in place on *Visitor I*. If

the initial Goderich observations are confirmed by later studies, as seems likely, permanent settlement on Mars should prove much easier to mount and maintain than had been predicted."

Here there is an interruption of the broadcast lasting some hours.

"Mission Control back with you again, viewers. We are resuming our broadcast with observation of the departure of the Mars lander from the surface of the planet. Chances for a wholly accident- and trouble-free mission have now risen sharply. The crew of *Visitor I* may now legitimately feel that they have established the normality and legitimacy of a human presence in space. You can now see on your screens the curve of the planet's horizons as the Mars lander lifts off and rises towards its rendezvous with the more and more visible mother spacecraft. What a magnificent picture! We almost see the mass of the entire planet as the cameras pull away from ground zero. The Mars lander is dead on track for its rendezvous, an operation that will be carried out in about twelve hours. We hope to be able to record the reuniting of the two vehicles, as this is of course a critical manoeuvre. After the reuniting has been accomplished, the crew of nine can settle down to the routine tasks of the 165-day return voyage.

"Owing to the extension of the Mars walk by two days, the most favourable flight path for the return has been abandoned; the time for its adoption has gone by. This was a command decision taken jointly by Colonels Kinnick and Lebedev; the opportunities for fruitful surface observations were judged too valuable to be ignored. Alternative flight plans now being prepared make it likely that a direct return to Earth may be advisable, rather than a final linkage of *Visitor I* and *Wayfarer* at the end of the mission. Meanwhile, the results of experiments obtained during the extended Mars walk have more than justified a change in flight planning.

"To sum these results up briefly, we should repeat first of all that the gravitational force exerted by the mass of the planet amounts to about thirty-nine percent that of Earth. Normal human strength allows a subject to walk and run with great ease, but with enough gravitational resistance to preserve muscle tone and exercise the physical frame adequately. A less cumbersome form of space apparel may be allowable in future. Informed debate about these matters must be deferred until Professor Goderich has undergone a thorough debriefing. But it's now seen to be a distinct possibility that a permanent station will not require an artificial gravity system. This may be the answer to a conundrum that has puzzled space scientists from the beginnings of their investigations. If so, it may be the most important finding of the Mars walk.

"And much else has been accomplished. Space medicine has been much advanced by the observations of Commandant de Barny with reference to the preservation of stamina and muscle mass under these special conditions. Yet another significant finding of the three weeks of the Mars walk is the simple fact of its proven feasibility. We have found continually as our investigations progress that the human imagination invariably outruns our technical capacities. This seems an absolutely fundamental realization. When new ventures become technically possible, they invariably turn out to be in accord with the most specific imaginings of space engineers and designers. And the results obtained always justify the investigation. This is a valuable finding indeed! It may hold true from now into the most distant future. We are beginning to realize that human life may extend itself to the remotest regions of our solar system, and even — who can tell? — beyond the physical and temporal limits of our planetary system. Today we can dream of voyages to the stars that may need thousands of years for their completion, whole cultures and histories of space travellers growing up, enduring for generations, and then evolving into other, unimaginable, cultural forms as the voyage proceeds. The voyage of *Visitor I* will seem brief and rudimentary to those later space adventurers who remember it, but it will always have the honour of having been the first such venture.

"Other research findings will doubtless turn out to be highly revelatory. The Mars walkers have found themselves able to move about with perfect ease and little fatigue. They have covered a part of the planetary surface perhaps a hundred square miles in extent, showing considerable variety in its range of formations: hills, plains, moraines, valleys. Abundant photographic material has been collected, together with many soil and rock samples, all of them very useful in the search for the answer to the fascinating question of the presently waterless state of the planet. Is there water hidden somewhere below the surface of the planet? Do the materials for its artificial large-scale manufacture exist ready to hand? An affirmative answer to this question would accelerate the establishment of permanent human settlements on the planet. From preliminary reports submitted by the Mars walkers, it appears that indications of sub-surface ice deposits have been found, and below them, at deep recesses in the mass of the planet, actual warm springs. Discovery of such springs would of course be an incredibly encouraging result of this mission.

"We are going to take a break now from our on-the-spot coverage of the mission. We will return to the air in eight hours, to telecast coverage of the reunion of the Mars lander and the mother spacecraft. We will remain on the air at that time for as long as it takes for the linkage to be completed and for the Mars walkers to re-enter *Visitor I*. Then the entire crew, reunited and triumphant, will prepare for the final two orbits of Mars and the beginning of the return passage. The astronauts and cosmonauts will then quit the spacecraft in a landing module that will bring them directly to Earth. When we return to the air we may have more to reveal about this change in planning. Meanwhile, our sincere congratulations go out to the brave quartet of Mars walkers and to their fellow crew members who have remained aloft during these fateful

three weeks, monitoring the Mars walk from above and readying the mother ship for her return voyage. The love and the
admiration of the entire human family go out to them in our
words tonight. We salute the first Mars voyagers. We will
never forget their great successes."

———

As this message was being transmitted at the turn of the year,
Tony Goderich experienced peace of mind for the last time in
his life. He could almost put a specific date and time to this
ending. It's about time, he would tell himself wryly. I'm
exactly the age at which this process starts. Almost alone.
Haven't made a key move in over a decade. Should get out of
this house; it has too many bad memories attached to it.
Heath Hurst Road, Hampstead. Who wants to waste away
on Heath Hurst Road? Not me! He knew that he had no plans
to move, plenty of cash but no will to move house. Worse than
that, no new ideas. Companionship is the parent of invention,
he thought. Few solitaries write comedy successfully; for
comedy you need to see what's going on. He saw that he was
lapsing into a state of information-underload, and almost
welcomed the state. The fax terminal went unattended; its
spewings of paper coursed serpentlike across his workroom
floor.

It wasn't as though he received no invitations to resume
work. Appeals from publishers — when would there be another book, series idea, script possibility? He didn't know,
couldn't even guess. His modem went unactivated and his
screens were dead. He did not believe in the permanence and
usefulness of Net-text. He might be wrong about that, but
Net-text never felt like real poetry to him, or even moderately
successful prose. Who would care to collect it? Would collections of Net-text form the libraries of the future? There is
nothing to be feared from new technology, he kept telling
himself, feeling frightened all the same. And as the New Year

s0sl00

came and went, and *Visitor I* turned for home, bringing his nephew back, Tony Goderich felt himself shrinking and receding into the past. His gift of comic invention that had given the world *Balancing Act* and *Down Off a Dirty Duck* fifty years ago seemed unsuited to the new age of instant communication, although there were a few critics here and there who remembered his work and tagged it pre-post-modernist.

He never saw Edie any more; they were too old for amorous exchanges. He had a hunch that her departure for her native place would not be long delayed. Her children were in North America. At least two of them were, and the third would eventually be landing there in the whirl of the greatest surge of publicity — or the second greatest — ever associated with a human undertaking.

The only other action to receive this much space, Tony thought, has been the Crucifixion. And it has taken longer to build up. Then he admonished himself for irreverence in his reflections. All the same, there was some truth to them. The death of the hero, or group of heroes, was always a possibility in stories of great human actions. Was the world tuned in to the voyage of *Visitor I* because of the possibility — at any moment — of a disastrous end to the trip? Until the landing module was safely on the ground of the salt flats of Utah a terrible end to the voyage remained a possibility. He believed that he saw the entire human family enveloping the space voyagers in hate-filled suspicion, and even a wish for their destruction; this was the down side of comedy. The whole world knew about Céline and Hubert and suspected them of being in love. Everybody knew John Sleaford Goderich and Serge Lebedev and Miles Kinnick and all the rest of the glorious band of adventurers, and loved them too. And at the same time waited and half hoped that in the next moment *Visitor I* and its crew might fall apart and perish miserably in the emptiness of interplanetary space. Not until the door to the landing module opened and the ramp was lowered to allow the brave men and women, the sacred nine, to alight and try their Earth legs would the universal mixture of hate and hope turn into unalloyed celebration.

He had brooded over this potent mixture for too long, he told himself. He was living alone in his ten-room Heath Hurst, Hampstead, house. Never entertained anyone any more. Wasted the space around him on new shelving for old books, collectibles, rarities, valuables. Never ventured as far as Knightsbridge, although it was an easy ride on the Underground, Northern Line to Leicester Square, Piccadilly Line to Knightsbridge. And it was he, after all, who had arranged John's place at Cambridge, and had therefore been the true source of his nephew's amazing career. If it had not been for him, there would never have been any question of landing a Codrington/Goderich on Mars. The phrase had a farcical sound. He remembered Edie's wounded remarks on the matter during their last conversation a year ago.

She had cried, "It's too terribly risky; it's awfully dangerous. Why should my son John be the one to take such chances? He'd be better off staying safely in Cambridge. I'll tell you what, Tony, this space exploration is a male toy like the Boy Scouts or the army. Merit badges and medals!"

Was this the natural female view of space science?

"What about the celebrated natural human desire to know?"

Edie stared at him. "If you ask me, the celebrated natural human desire to know is a trumped-up tale, especially when it puts nine lives at risk for a year and a half. I don't know . . . it's what John wants to do, I suppose, and now he's come this far . . . but I'm afraid for him. Astronauts' wives and girlfriends get all the publicity. Never a word about the mothers."

"You're an old fraud," Tony said. "Mothers get more favourable publicity than anybody else."

"You're quite wrong there, you know. Motherhood has become very unpopular in the last few years. It's mothers that cause overpopulation. It's an anti-motherhood age. Be a good citizen of Earth and don't give birth to any children." This was said with great bitterness. "Your namesake, out in British Columbia, our Anthony, you take him for an example. Has he gone anti-motherhood all at once? I think that he must have done. Why else would he leave the U.K. for, of all places, northern B.C.?"

This was a familiar complaint. Tony never knew how to respond to it. His nephew's self-exile to one of the remotest regions of North America remained mysterious to him. He could supply motives for such a withdrawal. Contempt for Eurocentric, consumption-oriented society. A wish to begin a new life on a new frontier, perhaps the last frontier. But he could not imagine the gentle, kindly, middle-aged Anthony Earl Goderich possessing such motives and acting on them. Yet there he was in his forties, associate professor of Canadian and Native Literatures at the University of Northern British Columbia. Unmarried, an irregular correspondent, apparently perfectly contented in his life and work, Anthony was deeply mysterious to his uncle. Dawson Creek? Half his nephew's working week was passed there and the remainder in Prince George. Unimaginable, thought Tony. Indecipherable.

He said to Edie, "Now that all three of them are back on the other side, what's going to happen to us?" He was afraid that he knew the answer; if he was right the answer would be very disobliging to himself; fifty years' residence in London had spoiled him for life anywhere else. Certainly Heath Hurst Road was no great cop, but it was all he knew these days. Heath Hurst Road and Beauchamp Place, not much to take away from fifty years. There might be an idea for a novella in that, with some such title as *Between Hampstead and Knightsbridge*. He couldn't see himself tackling it: too double-minded: pre-post-modernist. Nobody took Hampstead or Knightsbridge seriously any more as occasions for comedy or as seats of inadmissible privilege. The blacks had long since infiltrated both districts and Harrods was awash on oil money. You could no longer compose traditional social satire; its bite was gone, teeth drawn, nothing to chew with or on.

Edie was certainly getting ready to return to Canada, and he didn't know that he blamed her.

If she went, his luck would go with her. He sensed this in his most inward self. Early success had made him financially independent; he had not had to worry about his income for many years. But this relief from pressing need had done little to stimulate his creative impulses. His work in the 1960s and 1970s — his middle period — had been even more lucrative and more praised internationally than the early things. *Cross Now, Queen City*, his association with the art of Adam Sinclair and his reliance on the beauty of Linnet Olcott: these had kept his name and his earning capacity fresh and full of power. But then the course of his life and work had begun to move irregularly, had lost significance. Linnet, and then Adam, had died with his brother's kisses on their lips, to speak somewhat dramatically. He was in the drama business, might as well use its language.

Linnet's turn towards his brother twenty years ago in Venice and her dreadful accidental death, alone and unprotected, had shaken Tony badly. He had the sense of his life's chances being fumbled away. And then he, who had given Adam Sinclair his career on a plate, had had to sit and watch from a great distance as his brother lived through the dreadful crisis of Adam's death. They were all in the business of generating publicity, Tony thought, but that was publicity exaggerated beyond desire. Nobody wants the kind of publicity that Adam's death had stirred up for his friends. He, Tony, was well out of that awful nastiness, already more than a decade in the past and still the archetypal case history of the sufferer from AIDS. Many books had been written about it; television documentaries had proliferated concerning the death of Adam Sinclair. His brother Matthew — nobody could ever have predicted this — was now a saint and a hero of the gay community of two continents. Life is full of little surprises.

Banality is a chief side effect of truthfulness. Life *really is* full of little shocks. His long relationship with Edie, who was after all his brother's wife, had borne bitter fruit. No, no, nothing had come of it. No children of their own. How could they have had children of their own, faced with the presence in London of Edie's three children by his brother? As long as Anthony, Andrea and John had been under their uncle's care, the notion of having other children with Edie had been impossible to imagine. He simply could not have done it. Now, thirty years later, he was left holding the bag. Rich and solitary, that was what he was, or was becoming.

Perhaps his physical condition was a function of this moral and psychological shift; certainly there were marked changes in his habits and his health. During his entire previous life he had enjoyed a perfect digestion; he could chew nails and spit tintacks, dine on the pizza with the tackiest cheese in London and process it through his digestive tract with never a belly rumble. Never a pimple or other skin blemish, never any queasiness after the heaviest meal. He had been able to eat what he liked when he liked and had never had the sense (he told himself sadly) to see what a blessing a perfect digestion is.

"John D. Rockefeller would give a cool million to have a stomach like yours."

This vulgar saw had never come home to his breast — or stomach — as it had to the novelist Nathanael West, whose novel *A Cool Million* is an extended play on the truth of the implied joke. The richest man in the world dines on skimmed milk and rusks. Tony was beginning to wake each morning with a distended abdomen and spasms and quakings in his belly. Digestive processing of tricky foods like cheese and chocolate seemed to become problematic, producing overnight the distention and swelling that seemed at first to disappear when he rose and did deep-breathing exercises and some light stretchings, a daily dozen he'd learned in a Toronto high school in the 1940s. These bendings and stretchings probably did little to keep him in good physical shape, but they conferred an agreeable sensation of warmth and muscular looseness. They seemed to banish his abdominal discomforts, at least temporarily.

But there was something else to trouble him physically, a persistent tremor in his hands that had been around for ages and now seemed to be growing more pronounced. Alone at night, reading into the small hours, he began to notice a fluttering in the muscles or tendons — he didn't know which was which — that lay between the thumb and forefinger of each hand. He would put down his book and gaze intently at the hollow in the web between the digits and for a moment would see no vibration. But in a moment, left to themselves without his concentrated attention, the fluttering would start again, sometimes in both hands, more often in the right hand first and then, after some moments, the left.

He found in fact that the whole small world of physical objects was refusing to work efficiently for him. Going through perfectly ordinary doorways, he would bump his shoulder cruelly against the frame. His coordinated judgment of spatial dimensions seemed to be faltering. Pencils fled rolling from him on apparently level surfaces. Curtains hung askew, no matter how carefully he adjusted them. He began to notice that he dropped things or accidentally overturned them with an elbow more frequently than in the past. Something consistent was causing these little lapses. The taut stiffness in his abdomen, just below the navel, was associated with tension and his general psychological state: tense, nervy, anxious, over-motivated.

The abdominal discomfort (he wouldn't exactly call it pain) and the simultaneous tremor, taken together, were suggestive of some specific physical disorder. This was the middle of a peculiarly damp and oppressive winter, the first week in January. Everybody seemed to be complaining about some minor ailment. He had not been to a doctor for over three years, thinking that benign neglect was the correct approach to one's personal health and hygiene. He was terrified of doctors and only went to them when he felt in top form, as one cleans the house from top to bottom before the char arrives.

There had been certain developments in his doctor's career and management of his affairs since he'd last seen him. He had moved his office from relatively humble quarters on the wrong side of Tottenham Court Road, near the university and the medical faculty but scarcely chic or trendy, to the high splendour, professionally speaking, of Harley Street. And he was no longer in purely private practice but had metamorphosed into the directorship of a Centre for Family Medicine, with three junior practitioners on staff.

Tony suspected that "family medicine" meant general practice, and wondered how one could specialize in generalities. If Dr. Brissenden wanted to describe himself as a specialist in general practice that was his affair, but Tony couldn't see how that could be managed. Why not simply bill oneself as a generalist? He finally persuaded himself to go along to the new Centre for Family Medicine, where he tried to interest Dr. Brissenden in his tummy collywobbles.

"Medical science doesn't recognize collywobbles as observable entities," said Dr. Brissenden. "I'll have to ask you to be more circumstantial. What exactly is a collywobble?"

"I know of no medical name for them. Would spasms fit the bill? They seem to come spasmodically. Could I possibly have a spastic duodenal cap?"

The doctor blinked. "Where did you get hold of that term? I haven't heard it since the 1950s."

"A boy in high school in Toronto when I was there had spastic duodenal cap, and the name has stuck in my head. Or how about mucous colitis? That sounds impressive."

"If you had mucous colitis you'd know it," the doctor said. "And likewise, you have not got spastic duodenal cap. Tell you what, we'll try you on Matzeck for two weeks. Here's a prescription, and I think I may have a few sample caps you can take with you. Three daily, to be taken right after meals. Make another appointment for two weeks from today, and keep an eye on the collywobbles, ha ha. The dispensary around the corner will stock Matzeck, or you will find it at any chemist's. And remember, Mr. Goderich, it's very foolish to go more than a year without seeing your doctor."

"I've been foolish," Tony said, "and if you can get me out of this I'll be on your doorstep every six months without failing."

"Every six months would be too frequent," the doctor said defensively. "Once a year would be ample."

"Annually then, without fail," Tony swore. He walked around the corner into Wigmore Street and presented his prescription to a dispensing chemist. There was no wait; the man simply reached behind him and seized a small plastic bottle from a nearby shelf.

"That must be a very popular medicine," Tony said.

"We get them in here for it by the hundreds," said the chemist.

"What's it for, then? What's in it?"

"Ah, that would be telling," the chemist said with a grin. "Have to take that up with your doctor, you would. No business of mine."

"But plenty of people use it?"

"I've just said so, haven't I?"

Tony had to be satisfied with that. Collywobbles, he thought, Matzeck is the indicated medication against collywobbles. Let's hope so anyway. He made his way homewards. He put the bottle of capsules on a shelf in the medicine chest in his bathroom. Then he thought that he might forget to take them if he left them there. He finally placed them on the dining table. Three a day for fourteen days; he ought to have forty-two of them and was chagrined to find that he'd only been given forty. They weren't cheap, either. Little two-coloured caps, one end orange, the other green. He read the label, which revealed nothing. He removed a single capsule from the container and stared at it piercingly as if it concealed some magic secret agent or power to heal. What was the active ingredient? Labels are seldom specific on this point.

He took them faithfully for the prescribed period, checking himself anxiously night and morning for signs of improvement, but there weren't any. His interior continued to broadcast noisy quakings that often resembled musical tones in their accuracy of pitch. As he wasn't seeing many people, his noisy belly wasn't a source of embarrassment, but it worried him. He might as well not have gotten into Matzeck at all; the capsules were ingested and presumably secreted without the least effect on him. In two weeks his supply was exhausted and he returned to Dr. Brissenden full of a need to recount his observations specifically. He made detailed notes on what he'd observed, and handed a copy to the doctor as soon as he was admitted to the consulting room. He noticed then and later that it was idle to prepare these note-sheets; doctors never paid any attention to them. Evidently they preferred to put searching questions *viva voce.*

"No response whatsoever to Matzeck?"

"None that I noticed. I couldn't even taste them."

"Well you wouldn't, would you? They're not meant to have any taste."

"What are they meant to do?"

"They're effective in some esophageal disorders. So we can rule out your esophagus; no problem there. You'd have seen a difference otherwise."

"What sort of difference?"

"Your rumblings would have subsided. I think we'd better try you on a course of istagen. That's the generic name." He wrote out the prescription carefully and handed it across the desk. Tony scanned the slip of paper with admiration. Dr. Brissenden, unlike most medical men, wrote his prescriptions in a beautifully formed and very legible hand. Istagen once daily following the evening meal.

"They may give you Brantigern or Adwell or perhaps Motitek, but they're all Istagen under different hats. The chemist will know what I mean."

"What do these test for?"

"It's a question of ruling things out one after another. You can't make a hurried diagnosis in this area; there are too many related and competing systems involved in the digestive process. We know you're all right from the back of the throat to just above the stomach. Just be patient with us and we'll make a good diagnosis. There may be spastic musculature; it's not unheard of. And by the way, don't take more than a single dose of Istagen at any time. If you miss one, don't vary the dosage in order to catch up."

This sensible counsel impressed Tony powerfully. They only gave him fourteen of the pills this time; he was a little intimidated by them. They were real pills, not capsules, a bright orange that seemed obscurely menacing. Orange for caution? Easy to find in the dark? His Istagen was packaged as Brantigern, a name that had faint echoes of Spenser's *Faerie Queene*. Brantigern was obviously the name of some hero's enchanted and miraculous broadsword, property perhaps of one of Arthur's knights, perhaps belonging to the great prince himself.

What wizard invents the brand names of drugs? They form a new poetic lexicon something like the names of rivers in Spenser, or of pagan deities in Milton. Istagen. Brantigern. Matzeck. Advil. Motrin. Simulcrete. The enchantment of such lists goes back, Tony thought, as far as the Bronze Age and the catalogue of the ships and heroes in Homer, in the second book of *The Iliad*. The spell of the exotic and mysterious. Ibuprofen. Lantigen. Prozac. Hallowed be thy name.

He took only seven of the Brantigern pills, noticed no effect, and took himself off the medication after a week.

"I didn't observe any effect at all. My stomach —"

"Not your stomach. We don't know what the trouble is in your stomach; that's what we are trying to establish. None of the x-rays shows any sign of ulcer or cancerous tissue. The failure to respond to Istagen rules out duodenal problems. That's what Istagen goes to work on. We're making progress, ruling things out, defining the parameters. We're getting there.

Meanwhile, there are one or two other things we need to try. First of all we'll get you onto Simulcrete, twice daily, before breakfast and your evening meal. We may as well go that way at this point; it should relieve the rumblings. And I want you to schedule an appointment at the Radiology Clinic down the street for an x-ray with barium meal. That will give more faithful definition of the picture than we have available at present."

Their fearfully unfamiliar aspect was the worse element of these adventures in radiology. Tony showed up at the clinic three mornings later, fasting, and was asked to quaff a peculiar cocktail compounded of a fear-inspiring, mint-green sludge with an unidentifiable bouquet. Nothing is like a barium meal but itself, he thought. This is a perfectly novel experience. There was a brief interval of repose; then he was placed on a moveable platform something like a giant photographic plate, that tilted and adjusted itself in obedience to a series of messages from the control booth next door. The radiologist and the attendants stayed well out of range of the radiation source. How much of it could safely be borne, he wondered. And the staff didn't tell him about the digestive consequences of the mint-green drink. For three days afterwards, his stool was in texture and colour unlike anything his body had ever produced before, the identical minty hue of the test cocktail. This was a shocking surprise, because so unexpected and so comic/satiric in its overtones. Popean, Tony thought, or even Swiftian.

Dr. Brissenden was offhand and even cavalier about the data obtained by the procedure. He shuffled the reports on his desk and seemed incurious about their findings.

He said slowly, "I often wonder if we are ordering too many tests. There's nothing much here. Is the Simulcrete giving you any relief?"

"I have a relatively quiet time in the evenings. I don't know that the medication is causing it."

"Yes, it's only a palliative at most, and you wouldn't want

to continue with it indefinitely. Come into the examination room for a few moments. I want to look at your hands again. I'm puzzled by something that looks like wasting in the web position next to the thumbs on each hand."

"Good Lord!"

"Not wasting in the layman's sense, nothing like tuberculosis, for example." Dr. Brissenden manoeuvred Tony onto the couch with deft shoulderings. "Now let's look at those hands of yours. What is it you do again? Professionally?"

"I'm a writer."

"Still at the writing, are you? Don't do much work with your hands, I shouldn't guess?"

"Well, actually, I have to do a great deal of work with my hands."

"How's that?" asked the doctor incuriously. He held Tony's hands in his own, squeezing them slowly as with an unenthusiastic handshake.

"I have to do a lot of typing and I never learned the touch system. I've been typing with my forefingers and my two thumbs for fifty years. There's bound to have been a certain amount of wear and tear on the muscles."

"I don't believe we need take that factor into consideration," said the doctor. "That sort of use would not produce the effect I'm observing. Look here now, do you see that vibration, and the hollow place under the skin between the forefinger and thumb? How long have you been having that?"

"It isn't there all the time."

"But you've noticed it more often recently, isn't that so?"

Tony felt that the dialogue was turning into an interrogation. Why should he feel guilt about the hollows in his hands? Should he mention his own theory about them?

"You're sure it can't be from two-fingered typing? After all, fifty years is a long time, and I've been typing with two forefingers hard and fast every day for the whole period. It stands to reason that there would be a bit of breakdown, just from the repeated impact."

"We can dismiss that idea," said Dr. Brissenden. "Mere physical contact of that kind wouldn't produce these effects." He lifted Tony's hands straight out in front of him. "Just hold them like that, palms downwards. Arms straight out in front of you, please. That's right. Now hold the position."
There was a thirty-second silence.

"I see some loss of strength in the shoulders and the upper arms, and I don't like the shrinkage of tissue between the thumbs and the forefingers. It's more pronounced in the left hand and arm. Any discomfort up here?" He put a hand on Tony's left arm and shoulder.

"Only the usual stiffness. Old age coming on, I expect."

"Nonsense. A man of your years has no business to be talking like that. You can put your shirt on, if you like, and come back into the other room."

As he wriggled into his shirt, Tony felt a sharp twinge in his left shoulder. Arthritis? Rheumatism? Bursitis? Inflammation of the bursa sac? Where had he picked up that scrap of information? Had he used it in a play or novel? He could not have pointed out the bursae in his own body, and never afterwards identified them. He shrugged clumsily into his shirt, adjusted his necktie, and sat down facing the doctor in the consulting room.

"I'm sending you along the passage to see Dr. Irwin," said Dr. Brissenden. "We've been associated in many cases. He's a very skilful neurologist."

"A specialist?"

"Not to worry, no immediate problem requiring heroic treatment." The doctor chuckled cheerfully. "That's a little medical joke. We're beginning to get somewhere now. I need to see you again next week, and I'm going to inflict another indignity on you, the barium enema. It's a great nuisance; it involves your participation for most of two days, but we'd better do it, to make certain."

"Certain of what?"

"Just certain." The doctor leaned across his desk and handed

Tony two small sheets of paper. The yellow one was a notice to the adjacent Radiology Clinic ordering the barium enema procedure; the pink sheet was a referral to Dr. Jeffrey Irwin.

"He'll see you in half an hour; we've checked with his office. Just along to the right. And I'll see you next Thursday. You should go round to the Radiology Clinic straightaway when you leave here. We may as well make haste; diagnosis is an important preliminary stage, but it doesn't do to protract it. We're getting there, Mr. Goderich. Goodbye for the present."

Tony clutched his two sheets of paper and left the consulting room, nodding to the receptionist as he reached the office door. She smiled brightly and wiggled some fingers at him.

"The same hour next Thursday," she said brightly.

He halted at the door. "How did you know I needed another appointment?"

She made no answer. She bent her head to the phone snuggled under her ear. "He rang me again last night," she said into the phone. An excited voice squeaked at the other end of the line as Tony passed into the corridor and around to his right. Dr. Irwin's door was inscribed with an impressive list of degrees and appointments, in particular an appointment at Saint Lucy's Institute for Neurology and Neurosurgery. Tony was filled with trepidation. I'm in the hands of a specialist, he thought. The phrase exacted alarm. In good hands. Receiving the best possible care. Resting comfortably. Doing as well as can be hoped. The phrasebook of medical practice, filled with evasion and ambiguity. Naturally Dr. Irwin would be at the top of neurological practice in London; they never send you to a beginner or a bungler. Your specialist is invariably the top man in the field, to hear them tell it. Tony wondered how beginners ever got to do consultations. He pushed open the door and was confronted by a sharp-eyed young woman who might be the twin of the person he'd just seen talking on the telephone next door. Sisters, perhaps?

"Was there something?" she asked briskly.

"They've just sent me round from Dr. Brissenden's . . ."

"Of course. It's Mr. Goderich, isn't it?" She riffled through a fan of dossier cards on her desk. "Yes, here we are. May I see your card, please?" Tony stood silent as his vital stats disappeared into yet another computer bank. There were clicking noises; printout gushed from the maw of a printer. The young woman studied these papers for some time, then spoke with surprising precision.

"Dr. Irwin will see you now."

This unexpected speed put Tony back on his heels. He was destined to remain in a defensive posture during the whole course of his relations with Dr. Irwin, a man in principle committed to rapidity and efficiency of action. The doctor now appeared in a doorway to Tony's left, beckoning him into the next stage of diagnosis like a wizard getting started with some nervous postulant.

"Through here," he said succinctly. They passed into an examination room somewhat larger than Dr. Brissenden's. There was good reason for the extra space. Much of this first neurological examination consisted of short walks around the room on his toes, forwards, backwards, then on his heels, then on one foot, then the other, hopping, standing still while holding one ankle off the floor and balancing. Tricky unfamiliar evolutions.

"The basic preliminary neurological examination," said Dr. Irwin cheerfully. "The most revealing short sequence of tests in the whole of medical practice." He sounded as if he'd invented the routine himself. "Would you strip to the waist, please, and remove your shoes and socks?"

He made Tony repeat the series of walkabouts. The most tricky evolutions were those involving walking on the heels, an action that requires strong and firm ankle musculature and Achilles tendons, and is tiring and difficult to manage if you aren't used to it. Tony felt that he performed badly in his inexpert and ill-balanced swayings back and forth across the room. Once he fetched up against the wall with a sudden lunge that barely prevented him from falling on his face.

He felt humiliated, as though something shameful had been revealed about his body and his lack of self-control.

"Turn around and come here, back on your heels again, that's right. Excellent."

What was he expecting to see? "I'm very nervous," Tony said.

"That's nothing. You should see me in a physician's waiting room," Dr. Irwin remarked cheerfully. Clearly an often-repeated bit of dialogue, used to quiet the uneasy patient, the brief remark was nevertheless encouraging. Tony was glad to be told to sit; his ankles were aching. He perched on the edge of the examination couch, then was instructed to lie on his back. The doctor began to manipulate his toes, but made no remarks about some pigs having roast beef and others none. He simply held the toes in various positions, stretching and bending them apparently at random. Then he ran a finger down the centre of each foot; there was a tickling sensation and Tony felt his toes clench involuntarily.

"The Babinski test?"

"No. Not today. Sit up, please."

There was an interlude with a series of little hammers, all apparently identical in size and shape. The doctor resembled some virtuoso percussionist in stance and in his absorption in the proceedings. He would tap a knee and listen as for some special note, then stand back and try the other knee with another hammer or mallet. This went on for some time. Was there some obscure significance to all this? What was he learning? If the patient knew what was wanted he might be able to produce it at will, from tautened bone or sinew.

One of the characters in a long-since abandoned novel, *Mothers and Daughters*, 1994, had been a woman physician. Watching Dr. Irwin at work Tony saw what it was that he had failed to capture in his portrayal of the medical intelligence at work. Tony's imagined internist had been too deliberate, too attentive to the individual, in short too kind to be credible.

This impurity of characterization had spoiled the novel and he had finally abandoned it. Seeing Dr. Irwin at work supplied an endorsement of his editorial decision. He had been right to give up on *Mothers and Daughters*, even though several hundred pages of manuscript had had to be discarded. He might be able to go back to it now, after watching the doctor, who was now hammering away at the inside of his left elbow joint. The forearm was leaping and quaking without any conscious command from its owner.

"Excellent, admirable," the doctor said again. "Now push against my palm with your forearm. Good, good. Now the other arm. Uh-huh. The left arm is the weaker one."

"I'm very left-handed," Tony said, as if in excuse.

"Marginal difference," said Dr. Irwin, as though generously conceding a trivial debating point. "Give me a left handshake. Squeeze hard! Ouch, there's some power there, all right. Now the right handshake. Good! Fine! That's all, then, get dressed and come into the next room, if you will."

Tony dressed quickly and seated himself in a comfortable chair, watching the doctor as he glanced through his appointment book.

"Have to do an EMG, of course, but when can we get it in?"

Tony felt guilt and shame at his unwarrantable intrusion on the practitioner's time.

"We'll do it at Saint Lucy's next Monday, eight A.M. That suit you?" The doctor scribbled a reminder in his notebook. "You'll sail right through this. How old are you? Late sixties? But good sixties, young sixties, isn't that so? Plenty of vitality."

This observation didn't seem to square with Tony's own judgment of his condition. Still and all, he told himself, there must be something to it. He left the neurologist's rooms more muddled and apprehensive about his feelings and state of health than when he'd entered them. He turned up at Saint Lucy's Institute for Neurology, around the corner in Wigmore Street, exactly on time next Monday morning. This gave solid testimony to his strength of purpose; he seldom rose before ten. Upon arrival he had then to locate the neurological test site to which Dr. Irwin had directed him. This involved following a complex system of coloured lines and arrows painted starkly along cracked plaster walls. These indicators led him to a semi-paralyzed lift, which in turn brought him with glacial slowness to a sub-basement and his place of rendezvous with Dr. Irwin, who came bustling into the electronic testing rooms at the same moment as himself. Quickly exchanging greetings, doctor and patient got swiftly to work. Tony was told to lie on his back, almost wholly unclothed, on the inevitable chilly leather couch. The room was dreadfully cold. Tony felt himself starting to shiver almost uncontrollably.

The neurologist and his woman assistant now began to attach small electrical contacts to various parts of his body; he watched as closely as his awkward position allowed. Head and neck flat against the cold sticky surface of the couch. Deep shivering.

"It's very cold," he said.

The assistant gave him a brief grin. "It's always freezing down here."

"Doesn't that affect the readings you get? Wouldn't shivers like this be recorded in my body impulses?" He knew his terms were inadequate.

"Neurology has no words corresponding to 'body impulse.' We're measuring the strength or weakness of certain electrical currents at specific points in the peripheral nervous system," the doctor said. "But you're quite right about one thing; it's always bloody cold here. I'm trembling a bit from the chill, same as you. These smocks don't give any warmth at all. Of course I'm not stripped for action as you are. Come along now, here we go."

He administered a series of light electric shocks at various points on Tony's body, with particular attention to his fingertips and toes. The sensations produced were mildly unpleasant, suggesting a rehearsal for electrocution. Each time a shock was administered the needle on one or another of a battery of dials leaped spasmodically, and at the same time a reading was recorded on a strip of cash-register tape that gradually emerged from somewhere off to Tony's right. Now and then — the procedure took considerable time — the doctor paused to verify one of these readings, mumbling and chuckling as the session proceeded. At length the business with fingers, thumbs and toes was completed and a further series of points was investigated: just below either nipple, in the hollow of both elbows, behind the knees. The whole session occupied just under one hour, and then there were clarifications and predictions to be dealt with.

"You can get dressed. You must be half perished with cold," the doctor said.

Tony didn't answer; he was too busy shuffling his shirt, trousers, jacket, necktie, shoes back into place. He made some irresolute moves in the direction of an exit, but the doctor held him back.

"Not quite through with you," he said. "Just sit here a moment." His assistant disappeared, wreathed in coils of paper tape, and the doctor eased Tony into a rickety chair.

"Do I pass?" Tony asked, meaning to make a joke of it. "Or is it amyotrophic lateral sclerosis?"

"That's the one neurological disorder that everyone has heard of. Why is that, I wonder?"

Tony said, "One sees it in the medical press; its effects are dramatic, a temptation for reporters. It must be among the ten most-written-about ailments."

"I believe you," said the doctor. "And no, you don't have amyotrophic whatsit. What you do have is problematic, but has to be associated with a poor feed of neurons from the brain, through the spinal column to the nervous system at the extremities. Just look here for a moment." He produced a small notepad from a pocket, and very quickly sketched a crude drawing of the naked human figure without the sexual characteristics, arms and legs extended.

"Here's your spinal column," he said, inking in a tenuous

line down the middle of the sketch, "and here are the peripheral nerve conduits. Now, for whatever reason your electrical
impulses coming along these paths don't have the proper
power, especially in the left arm and wrist and hand. The
muscles of the left thumb and forefinger aren't being properly
stimulated; that's why they show a wasted appearance. I'll tell
you what, we'll do further radiological checks on your spine.
It's an easy thing to do; you'll breeze through it. At the same
time we'll do a CT scan of your neck."

"Why the neck?"

"We may find a stenosis there. I'd be prepared to wager on
it. These two examinations can be done during a one-day
visit. We book you in at ten in the morning and you can leave
in the midafternoon. Better have a companion with you for
conversation; you'll be with us for the better part of five hours.
Do you have anything else scheduled?"

"Barium enema later this week," said Tony through
clenched jaws. "At the place along the street. I'm haunting
the place. Chest, neck, abdomen, esophagus, the lot. Barium
cocktail . . ."

"A little more barium won't kill you," Dr. Irwin said. "They'll
send the results to Brissenden. Would you ask him to fill me
in on his reading? May as well see anything that's going.
I'll make the appointments for the spinal x-ray and the CT
scan. We should be able to take you by the end of the month.
Does that sound all right? You aren't planning to be away
from London?"

"I'll be right here for the foreseeable future."

"That's all right, then. You'll be hearing from us very soon,
probably within a week."

Tony left the neurologist's rooms in a peculiar state of mixed
emotions — feelings of relief at having this medical team on
his side, blended into a wash of anxiety, at moments identifiable as explicit fear. His symptoms were now explained, but
were they being cleared up? Perhaps medical investigation of
our bodies must always be fear-inspiring. We see and under-

stand so little of what goes on inside of us! Humanity, like beauty, seems to lie on our surfaces, soundings of our insides yielding exotic, deeply alarming, appearances. It wasn't that the barium enema was painful or even uncomfortable, although it required an elaborate ritual of preparation a day in advance of the actual treatment. What was troublous and somewhat unmanning about it was its representation of one's interior as entirely foreign country, something like Antarctica, unmapped and weirdly unfamiliar in all its forms, crossed by strange pathways with mountainous protuberances rising here and there on grey horizons.

A more disturbing aspect of these exercises was the cunning machinery they employed. As in the tracing of the barium milkshake he'd consumed earlier, this second test involved his positioning on a flat slab that could be adjusted to any angle. He was fastened to this platform with leather hand and ankle cuffs, tight but not painfully so. Then they began to tilt the slab and he felt that he might go sliding off it headfirst if not for the restraining cuffs. He wished at first that they were a bit tighter. But when the tip of the barium feed was inserted in his rectum he understood why they were left a little loose. He couldn't restrain a reflex jerking pull at his four fastenings as his lower bowel received the fluid.

There wasn't much of it. The administration of the thick liquid occupied only a few seconds and was in no way irritating or distending; it was not like being inflated like a balloon. The only effort asked of him was the momentary struggle to retain the fluid, and this proved easy to manage. The nurse too gave no cause for discomfort or embarrassment; the whole process was carried out considerately and quietly. The attendant — she may not have been a nurse — uncuffed his wrists and ankles gently and helped him off the slab, moving him to his right. As he stood up she handed him a small roll of paper and silently indicated the entrance to a lavatory. He spent some moments in retirement, surprised at the small amount of liquid to be discharged.

That was the last time he visited the Radiological Clinic. Tony felt nothing but admiration for the doctors and technicians he encountered during this period. All these tests seemed to require you to be fastened on a slab or inside a huge drum or in some equally bizarre posture. They were all, he finally guessed, preliminary drafts or sketches of the final and absolute operative procedure, the essential medical table, the one where they open you up and look around inside.

The results of the barium enema were satisfactory. There were some small pockets in the lining of the lower bowel. None of them was malignant or in need of removal. That seemed to be that. Esophagus, okay. Colon, okay. Cards with the note NYD began to turn up on Dr. Brissenden's desk. Tony could read the lettering upside down and the doctor made no attempt to conceal them. *Not yet diagnosed.*

"Irwin's been on to me about Saint Lucy's. They can take you next Monday, if that's all right. It's a matter of half a day; you turn up at ten, on the fifth floor, and they'll show you to your room. They'll ask you to go to bed. I've never understood exactly why. More relaxing, I suppose. There's no special prepping required. First they'll do the spinal picture. This involves the injection of tracer fluid at the base of the spine and —"

"Don't tell me," Tony said. "They place you on a big platform and tilt your head downwards so as to get a gravity feed. The fluid drips down the spinal column towards the neck . . ."

"Got it in one. How did you guess?"

"They're all like that, these investigators."

"Yes, well, it saves any number of exploratory operations. We don't have to risk traumatization of the cord, which is a medical no-no. We can learn much from this examination, and the scan is even more informative. It will interest you to see it done."

"Is this what's called a CAT scan?"

"Yes, but there aren't any felines involved. Let me see, are there any other matters to be cleared up?"

"Weren't there some results from the ultrasound that you were going to pass to me?"

"Yes, I'd almost forgotten that. Here they are: nothing in the spleen; nothing in the liver; nothing in the pancreas or the kidneys. Totally clean. You're a healthy man, Mr. Goderich. Until proved otherwise. Your abdominal discomfort is probably due to muscular spasm. Has it lessened to any appreciable degree?"

"It seems more intermittent than it used to be."

"And your tremor?"

"Continuous but light. I think you said that it was not the onset of Parkinsonism."

"Yes, we're clear about that. I think that nothing remains now but your day at Saint Lucy's. They'll send the results to Dr. Irwin and then we'll confer and inform you about what's happening."

"Thanks very much!" A courteous conversational tone was always to be maintained.

There was nothing extraordinary about the x-ray of his spinal column. The inevitable tilting platform came into play, and the room was even chillier than usual. Fluid was injected at the base of his spine and for the next forty minutes or so pictures were taken that tracked the tracer fluid as it trickled towards his neck; he was placed on the slab with his head well below his hips. There was no special discomfort, only the sense of being treated like an inanimate carcass on a chopping block.

The CT scan was much more interesting in its procedures. He was returned to his room for an interval; then three men appeared at his bedside, wheeling a trolley onto which they eased him with infinite care. Once aboard, he was conducted briskly along the corridor to the wide slow service lift, and down one storey to the CT Scan facility. Here he lay entranced as the medical team shifted him from his trolley onto a powered cot that slid in and out of a large rotating canister or bin, open at each end. This surprising device was surrounded by an apparatus for taking pictures of any part of the body, from just about any imaginable viewpoint. Tony's cot was propelled into the centre of this bin, to a point where pictures could be taken of his neck. Before each shot, said a precise voice over the intercom, he would be asked to inhale and hold his breath, at the same time remaining perfectly still. He would be told when to exhale. The entire process wouldn't take more than about half an hour.

Then they began. "Inhale please; hold it." Brief pause. "Breathe out. Inhale please; hold it." Brief pause. "Breathe out." Forty-eight times.

Writers in general, as a class, hold that absolutely nothing is indescribable. Lying there motionless, vaguely troubled by a need to pee, Tony began to describe this adventure in his head, as if he might afterwards be obliged to write down what all of this looked like. He found it hard to do justice to the scanner, and in the end almost conceded that it was after all indescribable. Anyway, he was in no position to concentrate on problems in aesthetics. The closest he got was to tell himself that the scanner looked like a cement-mixer. The resemblance was not close.

Back in his room, resting comfortably, he was visited by an anonymous doctor, the one who had administered the spinal fluid, who reported on the day's findings in reassuring terms.

"Nothing much in sight, a bit of corrosion in the seventh cervical position, a small disc that shows indications of certain problems. We'll be sending the pictures to Drs. Irwin and . . . let me see, Brissenden, yes. And to our department of neurosurgery."

"Why is that?"

"Customary procedure. We send our pictures everywhere; we're a very popular team, we are. You may get dressed and go home now. I've checked you out. Was your lunch all right?"

"It was surprisingly good. Filling and tasty."

"Excellent. You'll be hearing from your doctors, then. Good day to you."

Tony went home alone, wondering why neurosurgery had been mentioned. He discovered the reason a week later when Dr. Irwin called to discuss the results of these last examinations.

"Now, I'm not in the profession to sell surgeries," he began.

Tony quailed, and the receiver shook in his hand.

The doctor went on. "But you certainly must have this operation, and as soon as possible. There's always a period of waiting, so the sooner we register you on the list the sooner you'll be called in."

"What operation, for goodness' sake?"

"Didn't they say anything to you after the CT scan?"

"Only something about a crumbling disc. I didn't take it in."

"That's the source of the wasting tendency in your upper body, especially in those hollows between thumbs and forefingers. We need to clear out a stenosis that has built up around the cord, in the seventh position. It's classically indicated in these cases. What the surgeon does is called a decompression, simply a little cleanout of corroded matter. Then he'll do a fusion of the two vertebrae that formerly adjoined the disc. There will be some slight loss of mobility in the neck for a fairly extended period afterwards, nothing disfiguring or crippling, I can assure you. Decompression and fusion to relieve spinal stenosis; that's the name of the exercise. Dr. Francis Sherrard will be doing the work, if you consent to the operation. That's an offer we can't refuse. He's perhaps the most skilful neurosurgeon in the U.K. He has a European reputation; you're in the best possible hands with Sherrard. I've booked you in for a preliminary chat with him next week. It's very good of him to see you so quickly. He has an unbelievable schedule."

Here it is, then, Tony thought.

"Are you still there, Mr. Goderich?"

"What? Yes, I'm here."

"Do you want to make a note of the time of the appointment?"

"Certainly, thanks very much."

Details and directions were given, and they exchanged civilities and rang off.

Dr. Sherrard proved to be a man in his early forties with extremely regular features and a shock of silver hair. Almost film-star, leading-man, looks, Tony thought. There was something vaguely disturbing about that, as if the man was unaccountably practising the wrong profession. He knew his business, though; that was beyond doubt. He'd made himself wholly familiar with Tony's dossier, and discussed it with such care that the patient was easily persuaded to consent to surgery.

"I don't seem to have much choice, do I?"

"No, you don't really have a choice," said Dr. Sherrard. His air of confidence was persuasive without salesmanship. "If you should choose not to proceed with surgery the effects of the stenosis will intensify, and this will accelerate with the passage of time. In another eighteen months you would probably find yourself locked into a more and more rapid process of neural and muscular deterioration. But the operation, if it proves successful, will arrest this decline. You will be able to look forward to several years of unimpaired neural function. This is really the only reasonable course of action open to you. You should come in for treatment as soon as we are able to find a bed for you."

"Could you tell me a little more about that you intend to do, and describe how you'll do it? You must work in some very tight places in the neck. Isn't it full of muscles, joints, vertebrae and arteries? How can you get at the disc?"

"This will be microsurgery with the latest equipment. My hands never intrude into your neck; only very small electronically guided instruments are permitted physical contact. There is no risk of infection. The decompression is always monitored by computer analysis, and I follow the process on the scanner. It is not a complex procedure but it could not have been carried out ten years ago."

"Is it risky?"

"The failure rate globally is just under five percent. Here at Saint Lucy's we've never done the procedure without success."

"That sounds all right, then," Tony said. "I don't wish to waste your time in further discussions. I'm ready to sign a form, if that's required. You'll be doing the operation yourself?"

"Yes, I can assure you of that. There will be other persons present in the room: the anaesthetist and his colleague, an assistant for me, who observes the screens at all times, one or two of the residents, as this is a teaching hospital. This is the only way for them to master the technique. Have you any objections to their presence?"

"None at all. I'd be proud to help them learn."

"It is not an unusual case, but every case presents points of interest. You can never see too many cases and the next one may be unusually complex."

"And that's all you need to say to me?"

"Yes. If you'll just sign the consent form and hand it to my secretary as you leave."

"Just one other matter, doctor. Is it a general anaesthetic or will I be conscious in the operating room?"

Dr. Sherrard seemed disconcerted by the question. "General anaesthetic, of course. This is a very delicate intervention requiring complete immobility, or as complete as we can manage. You are allowed to breathe, but more motion than simple respiration would be undesirable. So you'll be right out of things for about five hours. The anaesthetics are highly effective."

"It takes a full five hours?"

"You have to allow the anaesthetist some time. I'll be working on you for perhaps four and a half hours. Might be a shade longer or shorter. That will depend on what the scanners show us, but about five hours should do it."

"Just one final question. What physical improvements can I expect, over the long term?"

"The effects won't be dramatic, but the wasting process will be arrested at once. And over the next months and even years the impulses from the brain will be fed to the periphery with greatly improved efficiency. You may occasionally feel the full effects of this, tinglings, light spasms, twitchings. Our physiotherapists can show you how to handle anything of that kind."

Later on, Tony visited his solicitor's offices and completely revised his will, inserting the generous bequests that afterwards proved so surprising. It took just about eight weeks for them to find a bed for him at Saint Lucy's; he was called in just at the end of February. After that, events seemed to accelerate. He was booked in on a Monday afternoon, about two, and installed in a small but pleasant single room. At three a young neurosurgical resident came in and took a detailed history; at four they took his order for his evening meal and recorded his selections from the menu for the following four days. His stay was expected to last for five or six days. He refused sedation, against the advice of his nurses, but passed a comfortable night, to be awakened just before seven on Tuesday. From this point on he was rapidly transformed into a medical statistic, the first accident to the spinal cord, from a decompression/fusion, in the hospital's history. The under-five-percent failure. When the team went into, and around, his neck, they saw at once that the targeted discs and vertebrae were deeply mired in deposits of calcification. While these deposits were being extracted, the electronic instruments unfortunately traumatized the spinal cord, bruising and then crushing it. The brain impulses were interrupted and then blocked. Death ensued.

So the good Tony Goderich, Big T, whose works of the 1950s and '60s had given pleasure around the world, went into the dark alone. And like those works (*Balancing Act, Down Off a Dirty Duck, Claude and Gertie, Cross Now*), he was soon forgotten by almost everybody.

V

SINCE 1867

"Young Andrew Goderich is five months old today, and his father sends him his best anniversary wishes over the most complex communications system in human history. Now that *Visitor I* is better than halfway home on her return flight path, the form of her home planet shows up more and more clearly in reflected solar radiation, like the evening star, Venus, on a clear summer night. As *Visitor I* comes nearer to Earth this image of the home planet will lose its resemblance to a star and begin to resemble our moon, as it rises and sets nightly, progressing through the phases of the lunar cycle. The voyagers will be able to measure their progress by their observations of Earthrise and Earthset, by their sight of the crescent Earth, the half Earth, then by the glorious sight of the full Earth, as the cycles complete themselves. The home planet will move through two complete sets of phases and a part of a third during the remaining time of the voyage. At latest calculation, the time remaining will amount to about ninety Earth days. Touchdown at the Great Salt Lake flats should occur about July 15th if the present flight path is maintained. As of this morning, April 15th, no major rethinking of the path seems likely to be proposed.

"Now better than halfway home, the crew members tell us that living conditions aboard the spacecraft have almost begun to be taken for granted. But all of us connected with the Mars trip feel that it cannot be taken for granted in any way. The crew must not let themselves be lulled into a false sense of security. Many precise adjustments and revisions of planning still lie ahead. Therefore, we here at Mission Control have worked out a series of informal experiments for the crew to carry out from time to time. The more day-to-day experience of the behaviour of the spacecraft at interplanetary speeds that can be gleaned from these tests, the better, especially for the prospects of later space voyagers. We need to glean every ounce of information and experience that we can from these off-the-cuff tests, partly to justify the enormous cost of the mission, and partly, as Professor Goderich has observed, partly for the hell of it.

"Now onscreen at this moment we see a simulation of the half Earth as it should appear from onboard *Visitor I* tonight at nine Eastern Standard Time. This image, of great beauty, derives ultimately from data obtained during the *Apollo* flights of the late 1960s, close to half a century ago. Those first views of Earth from an almost lunar position have continued to be accepted by two generations of Earth's inhabitants as true impressions of our home planet as it appears among the many planets, satellites and asteroids that patrol the solar system.

"We can now supplement and correct that impression by actual accurate scientific recording equipment.

"This is Day Terminal Minus Ninety. Tonight we are going to try to bring to your home screens as accurately as possible transmissions directly from the interior of the spacecraft, beamed to us in full colour, of Earth as our planet appears from the spacecraft. At this time Earth will look like a tiny half moon just starting to be visible at what is still an enormous distance.

"Almost simultaneously we will start to transmit pictures of Earth as it appears in the astronauts' skies. Here at Mission Control we are eagerly anticipating a striking likeness between our simulation derived from photos of the late 1960s, and the actuality of Earth's appearance in the heavens. This likeness will not be very clear to viewers tonight, but it should grow more and more evident until at about Minus Thirty the image from the 1960s and that of the period in which we are living will seem almost identical. Actuality seems to imitate invention. Our simulations are very close to reality.

"Our earlier transmission of greetings from Professor Goderich to his son was designed as a dry run, a first attempt at a live transmission of this kind. And fortunately the pictures of Professor Goderich that we received earlier were a fine, true representation of his appearance. We are now waiting for a telephone communication from Mrs. Emily Goderich in New York. Later we will try to talk directly to her on live television. Right now I'm advised that we have Mrs. Goderich on our telephone circuit. You will be able to listen to our brief chat.

"Good afternoon, Mrs. Goderich, and hello to young Andrew. Did he see his father just now? And did he know who he was?"

"Well, he couldn't very well, could he? He's never seen his dad."

"Did he respond to the pictures on the screen?"

"Yes, he did. And he reacted when his father said, 'Hello, Andrew.' "

"You must be very proud of your two men?"

"We're proud of all the crew of *Visitor I*, and we just love our little boy. Isn't he lucky to have such a father?"

"Indeed yes, Mrs. Goderich. Thank you for talking to us at such a moment in your life, and please accept our very best wishes for yourself, your little son and your husband."

"Thank you for arranging this birthday surprise, or rather this five-month-anniversary surprise."

"It has been a pleasure and an honour to talk with you. Goodbye, Andrew, and happy anniversary. Goodbye, Mrs. Goderich."

There is a short interruption of sound transmission.

"There you have it, viewers, the voice of Mission Control in conversation with Emily Underwood Goderich in New York

City. Now back to our account of the spacecraft's return trip to Earth. At Day Terminal Minus Ninety the home planet will seem like a bright star about the size of Venus in the terrestrial summer skies. Then as the countdown goes on the voyagers' image of Earth will gradually grow into a likeness of our moon. The weather systems on Earth, the cloud forms and the great windstreams will be plainly visible at Day Terminal Minus Thirty-five. In the last days of the return voyage, the crew will be able to keep a close watch on the phases of Earth in its relation to solar illumination.

"As those of you who have followed space news from the beginning of the return flight will know, the original plan for the homewards flight has been considerably modified, owing to the delayed departure of *Visitor I* from Mars. It has not been possible to impose a Hohmann ellipse path for the return flight; the spacecraft will not be able to proceed directly to the permanent space station *Wayfarer*, arriving finally at the position maintained just before departure, just over one year ago. At headquarters our aim is to make the re-entry and landing procedures as clear-cut as possible, and we have therefore evolved an alternative return procedure.

"At Day Terminal Minus Three a startup firing will take place in the backup landing shuttle that was designed into the spacecraft from the beginning. This method of bringing the crew back to Earth's surface has been projected as a viable alternative from the earliest moments of the planning of the trip.

"What will happen is this. At Day Terminal Minus Two the crew will commence loading operations in the BLS, or Backup Landing Shuttle, whose design had been worked up from the space shuttle vehicles long in use in various national space programs. The BLS of today is big enough to transport the entire crew of nine and their collection of scientific samples and data. By the end of Day Terminal Minus Two this transfer will be complete. Then one of the most exciting evolutions of the whole voyage will take place. Thirty-six hours before the end of the voyage, the entry ports to the BLS will be sealed and the large mass of the spacecraft *Visitor I* will be jettisoned. It will enter permanent orbit around Earth as a new and sizeable satellite, a gift to Earth dwellers of a new heavenly body or second moon. Our projections suggest that this second moon will remain in orbit almost indefinitely, certainly during the passage of many human generations. It is likely that this satellite will be referred to by astronomers as *Visitor I*, as a reminder of the bravery and endurance of its great crew.

"When the mass of this new satellite has been left behind, the BLS will be positioned to begin a manoeuvre that should be relatively free of danger, taking place very near the atmosphere of our home planet. The familiar problems of re-entry will of course be in play. A wedge-shaped space will be open for the BLS entry to the upper atmosphere, a space like a keyhole, three degrees wide in the 360-degree circle that rings Earth. It is imperative that a correct angle of approach be maintained. If BLS makes too shallow an approach to the upper atmosphere, it may flip up like a stone skipping on water and rebound away from the edge of the atmosphere into space, perhaps on an irrecoverable new path. If the angle of approach should prove too acute, BLS could burn up from the effects of friction and excessive heat. Neither of these developments is predicted, however. Colonel Kinnick, with his vast experience of space flight in the space shuttle program, will surely be able to position his BLS very precisely for re-entry.

"But all that lies ninety days in the future. Now the time has arrived for Professor Goderich to scan the skies visible from *Visitor I*. He has his cameras pointed and ready, and in the next moments we should begin observation of the April skies as seen from the spacecraft. Attention, everyone! Here it comes into view. And there we are, a full panoramic view of the heavens as they are scanned in deep space. This is a wonderful achievement, an extraordinary feat of television transmission in full colour, over millions of miles. I believe our planet is about to come into view. Can you hear me, Professor Goderich?"

There is the usual interference. Then suddenly the voice of the astronaut comes through with amazing clarity.

"Yes, Mission Control. We hear you very plainly. Are you reading our picture? Can you see what we see?"

The rest of this exchange is free from serious interference.

"Professor Goderich, can you pick out Earth among the objects visible in our picture at this moment?"

"Earth will be coming into view in about twelve seconds, as our cameras track around to the appropriate quadrant of sky. Careful now." This remark is directed at an onboard assistant. "Steady . . . steady. *There!* There's Earth, plainly visible in the upper left part of our picture. About the size of Venus as seen on an ordinary summer night, brighter and larger than any of the deep-space objects, but not yet as detailed in appearance as the full moon seen from Earth."

"Is there any sign of Earth's moon?"

"No, we're still too far away from home for any such detailed sightings. In the next weeks, as we come closer, the Moon may be visible from our viewing ports. And anyway, we can see our own familiar and much-loved planet as she appears from away out here. We will try to transmit pictures regularly as we approach our home base. By the time we are set to jettison *Visitor I* from the landing shuttle, our last viewing of Earth should just about fill the screen. And now, once again, before we shut down to conserve power, here is a final glimpse of Earth, brighter than the evening star, an object for poetry, in the upper left part of the television picture. The happiest of targets for all of us here on the mission. We are all looking forward to a gradually enlarged sight of home during these closing weeks of our long journey, as one day succeeds another. Until tomorrow night, then, Mission Control, and let's congratulate ourselves on this historic first."

"Thank you, *Visitor I.* That was Professor Goderich speaking from the control centre aboard the spacecraft. The final pictures from *Visitor I* will show us what the astronauts and cosmonauts will see as they go back into weightlessness in the BLS. This return vehicle is not equipped with the Goderich artificial gravity system; the crew from the spacecraft will be coping with unfamiliar environmental conditions during the closing hours of their epic adventure and the conclusion of the voyage, eighty-nine days from now. Tonight we congratulate the crew of the spacecraft for providing us with magnificent broadcasting. Be sure to watch tomorrow at this time for our continuing series of Earth images from space. Goodnight."

I saw this historic telecast while sitting in a deep, comfortable armchair in the studio at 32-A Beauchamp Place in Knightsbridge, the house that Edie had bought thirty years ago, when she and Tony decided to live in separate quarters. Tony may have contributed something towards the purchase price, which, even in those distant days, must have been very high. Somewhere between half a million and a million. Pounds, not dollars. Even though Edie had received large, large payments very regularly — the largest share of the current earnings of *Codrington Hardware and Builders' Supplies. Since 1867 —* no single one of those payments amounted to the capital sum sufficient to cover the cost of this desirable residence, freehold, only a few minutes' walk from Harrods and the V and A.

Yes. Tony must have helped her to buy the place, I concluded as I looked around. The television image faded, the voice of our son John was no longer being transmitted from its distant point of origin. I shivered, thinking of the immense distance that still separated John from his father and mother. She and I, at least, were no longer separated. We sat up very late to watch the telecast that had originated in New York; we had had hours and hours of companionable half silence together in the studio on the second floor of this odd little house in Knightsbridge.

This was our first face-to-face encounter in a little more than thirty years. In the interval our children had matured into middle age. The eldest, Anthony, was now well into his forties. The youngest child had achieved world fame. And the middle child, Andrea, lived in the rich plenitude of marriage, motherhood and greatly deserved happiness as Andrea Goderich Greenwald. Among other things, she was a full partner in the Toronto firm of Goderich, Greenwald and Partners: Urban Design and Architectural Consultancies. Quite a mouthful. Each of our children had travelled long and far in those three decades. Their mother and I had not gone nearly so far; we had remained paralysed for the whole time in a posture of reciprocal enmity. My brother, her lover, had gone farther than the rest of us. Who could guess where he might be at this moment? He had died in the operating theatre, not six weeks before this meeting. Tony. Big T.

I looked around me. You don't acquire houses like 32-A Beauchamp Place in the middle of London for pennies. He had certainly helped her. I sank further into my armchair and took a long gulp of cool mineral water. Nothing alcoholic in this situation, thank you! Conclude no business agreement over any drink stronger than water, a reliable maxim. I thought, let prudence protect me now.

Then she crossed the room to me carrying freshened drinks. I felt my resolution weakening even though my drink was only iced, lemon-flavoured mineral water. Time had altered us grievously. I'm an old man, I thought. I look far older than she does. I felt jealous of her well-preserved exterior, on the threshold of her seventies, and damn her, she doesn't show it, or hardly at all. Where does she get the money to have her hair done so smartly? And the dress! What can that have cost? In Edie's place I'd have cried poor, appeared in a jumper and worn, paint-smeared trousers. For I was adding considerably to her cares, begging her to renounce much the largest part of her fortune, in favour of this mad proposal to fund the purchase of the finest painting now available in Europe, perhaps in the world, as a gift to our homeland and our fellow-citizens.

"I'm fully seized of the situation," she said, grinning down at me sardonically. I thought, my God, she's going to start talking like a Brit, simply to disguise her thoughts and needle me. Maybe the proposal is doomed from the start; maybe she won't in the end agree to it. But this ran counter to everything I knew about her. She was on the side of the arts, of that I felt sure. An artist herself, still moderately active as a painter and maker of assembled objects, a collector in a small way, as evidenced by the walls of the Beauchamp Place dwelling, she must surely be captivated by the proposal. Neither of us had that many years left to us, at most a decade or so. What more generous gesture could we make towards the nation that had permitted us to lead free and secure lives? We had been petted and even indulged by our homeland, and it was time for the reckoning to be paid.

I noticed that she had brought into the room with her a bulging folder that I readily recognized, the dossier prepared by National Gallery officials for our confidential inspection, bearing the wordy title "A National Gallery Special Acquisitions Fund: Facts and Conjectures with respect to the proposed Codrington/Sleaford/Goderich Wing." The imitation leather binding of this plump dossier was tinted a rich combination of plum and blue; it made a handsome show. Edie caught me looking at it, and grimaced expressively.

"You might give me a kiss before we talk about all *that*," she pleaded. Strong emphasis on "that" might indicate disgust and repulsion; on the other hand it could point to warm approval. It was impossible to judge at this moment. I rose awkwardly from my armchair. These days I find it hard to get up from a sitting or lying position without shoving off hard with my forearms, another indication of advancing age. Nothing to be done about that. I saw that she noticed this little awkwardness, putting out a hand encouragingly, as though assisting some old buffer alighting from a bus.

"I'm all right, just a little excited," I said. "It's been a long time since we met in the flesh. Is a kiss appropriate?"

"Kisses are always appropriate between old friends . . . or old enemies, for that matter."

Conciliation was then to be the order of the day, or even reconciliation. I took a final uneasy step forward and threw my arms around her. She smelled quite heavenly.

"I don't remember your using that scent," I said, proud of my memory. "What is it?"

"It's called White Narcissus. I don't think you can get it in America."

"By America I assume you mean Canada, Mexico and the United States?"

"Oh God! I'd forgotten how touchy you are about that. Dear me! Not available in Canada. Does that make you feel better?"

"Well, yes, it does. We get tired of being nameless and invisible."

"Hence this proposal to purchase *Priam and Achilles?*"

She was evidently fully seized of affairs Titianwise. I inhaled more White Narcissus and tightened my embrace. It felt good, a surprisingly familiar feeling.

"I've never really been away," I said.

"Oh yes you have, Mister, but we aren't here to apportion blame. Let the dead past bury its dead."

She stopped, and sat down abruptly. I saw that she was thinking of Tony, and his magnanimous testament. "Oh Matt," she said. I felt absurdly pleased and grateful at this ready use of my name. "Oh Matt, it's so dreadful about Tony. You must have minded terribly. I had the sweetest letter from Amanda Louise. So moving! But nothing from you to me until this very minute. It was all so unexpected, and do you know, they telephoned me first from Saint Lucy's. He was almost completely alone in London, and we hadn't been together for ages. He must have been so solitary . . . and so rich." She spoke quite spontaneously about that. Edie always talks sense about the value of people's property.

"I'm over here for both reasons," I said. "To wind up his affairs, and to go ahead with the Titian purchase."

I took a closer look at her, a slim trim woman of almost seventy, elegantly coiffed, sweet-smelling, even sexy. What did I feel about her after thirty years? Nothing? Everything? A wish for reclamation of lost territory? Could there be further kisses after that first one? Was it wicked of me to glance in her direction? She was still my legal wife, although our marriage had effectively lapsed thirty years ago. Now she was nobody's wife. Up for grabs, as people say.

I said, "The NatGal people put a surprise in the latest version of 'Facts and Conjectures,' something mightily persuasive. Have you spotted it?"

"I suppose you mean the special concessions from the Revenue officials?"

"Exactly!" I felt inexplicably proud of her astuteness, something she'd developed as a young girl, and never lost. "If we assign them the entire yield of the sale of shares, less one million for our personal maintenance, they'll let us spread the tax deduction for thirty-two million over a decade or more. In effect we'd have no income tax to pay during the foreseeable future."

"But what income would we have?"

"*Rem acu tetigisti!*" I said.

"Oh God," she said, "you haven't changed one bit."

"Nor you, my love; you're as sharp as a needle-pointed little knife. We'd have the income from over one million in invested capital from the sale of shares in *CHBS 67.*"

"Anything else?"

"My salary as an executive of the new company. That will continue for some time to come. Add to that the yield from Tony's bequests."

"So you know about that?" she said.

"It's one of the reasons I'm over here. I've already seen Tony's solicitors. They're almost next door to the Soane museum, did you know that?"

"I've been there with Tony when he was making this absurd will. And I've been in close touch with them ever since he died. I was amazed to learn what he'd done."

"Why amazed?"

"Dividing everything equally between us . . . I suppose you understand what he was up to."

"You think he was trying to bring us back together?"

"As a final joke. Yes."

"There's nothing like shared executorship to bring folks together," I said. "I was Uncle Philip's executor for a while, but was asked to withdraw not long before he died. It's a complex story . . ."

"And we're not going to dish it all up tonight, are we? I'm willing to be reconciled to you, Matt, as far as reason and good taste will allow, but no further."

This seemed a hasty declaration. Circumstances might oblige us to act in an even closer association than that. If there was time. "We'll have to see about that," I said. "There's no difficulty about money, if we're talking about some sort of cohabitation."

"My God, what a phrase. So enthusiastic! Do you realize, you chump, that this is our first meeting since that summer night in 1973, the night that Tony and I cleared off with the children? And now he wants us back together. I can feel it. I can hear him laughing about it, the silly old muggins. Then there's this house. It will fetch quite a sum if it goes on the market. Do you like it?"

It was a neat little dwelling. *32-A Beauchamp Place!* What an address! A room and a corridor wide, no more, four storeys high and only two rooms deep, with a tiny oblong of garden behind it that was certainly worth thousands of pounds per square foot, freehold tenure in Knightsbridge costing what it does. The place had been home to a well-known actress and her friend, a celebrated writer of mystery stories, for over thirty years. Then Tony and Edie had acquired it as the base from which they could act in "some sort of cohabitation," a dire expression. They had never lived here together for any extended period, a consequence of various peculiar conditions attached to their quasi-union. Circumstances that in the end had eroded the strength of the tie that had held them together. Tony had bought his place in Hampstead. The slow loosening of these bonds had been signalled by their contrasting houses.

Life between Knightsbridge and Hampstead, I thought. I wondered how my brother had felt about it. The phrase might have given him a book title.

"A million and a half?" I ventured to guess.

"Certainly all of that, in pounds, of course. But this house wasn't part of Tony's estate. It belongs to me. We bought it together, but it's in my name."

"And there's his place in Hampstead; it comes to us jointly as his heirs. We'll have to sell it, of course. We seem to have lumbered ourselves with three houses."

"I make it four. There's the Montreal place, or did we dispose of it some time ago?"

"By no means. It's let on a very good long-term lease to a very desirable tenant."

"We'll get rid of it," she said decisively. "I never really cared for that house."

Bad conscience, I thought. "It wasn't such a bad house. The children liked it."

"We'll sell it," she said again, more forcibly. She was beginning to sit up and take notice. "What about the house in Stoverville? Does that still belong to us?"

"I've written you more than a dozen letters a year since you left me, dealing with all these matters in detail. Haven't you read any of them?"

"Not exactly . . . not closely. I just bung them along to my solicitors. Except for the ones with cheques in them. Those I send to the bank."

"For your further information, then, the house in Stoverville now belongs to the Codrington Colony for the Encouragement of Visionary Art, and has for longer than you've lived in London. We arranged all that when your mother died."

"I remember now. I expect that I could roost there for a longer or shorter time, couldn't I? Is Maura Boston still in charge?"

"Dead these many years, about twenty, to be precise. You'd find the present curator quite a handful. A powerful young woman."

"Oh? One of those?"

"No. Not one of those, just somebody who likes to have her own way."

"We seem to have something in common."

In these tart exchanges there was nevertheless an undercurrent of acceptance of the change in her situation. With all this real estate in hand, she has no place to call home, I thought. Surely she'll want to be in "America" when *Visitor I* touches down. I began to feel a close link between the activities of the astronauts and cosmonauts watched by the whole world, and those of the women and men at the National Gallery who had concocted "Facts and Conjectures" in secret but with the vigour and enthusiasm of voyagers in new spaces. Perhaps all great human undertakings share in the original and basic rational enthusiasm, I mean the motive that drives people like Pluyshin, and the Marchese Bianchini, and me. Is its name ambition? Or a need to endure, to last the course? There was a neat equation to be drawn between the acquisition of the *Priam* and the return flight to Mars; this hadn't been clear to me at first. Great achievement, great linkages, endurance, persistence. Earlier in our weird era these qualities had been humorously described as stick-to-it-iveness. That wasn't a bad name. It might take you to Mars and back again, or from Castello Bianchini to National Gallery, when no other quality would. I think I've got stick-to-it-iveness. I say this with naive pride. If I could persuade Edie to return to what is really her home, and mine, this quality would have proved itself out beyond any questioning. She'd be in herself a trophy, an emblem of persistence. Tony had taken the early rounds but I'd won the match in the end. I understand that it is base to think in such terms but I can't help it. I minded losing my wife to my brother, minded it quite a lot, without shedding tears publicly. The Beauchamp Place house had been furnished and maintained out of money I'd sent on from *CHBS 67*. It was time to dispose of both holdings.

"We need to work fast if you agree to the proposals in 'Facts and Conjectures,'" I said. "We've got less than six months before the dedication ceremony takes place, and we've got to go public with the share-issue. I've lined up a broker to handle the promotion. McKim, Factor and Déneau, one of the biggest houses in Ontario and Quebec. They'll have the OSC onside as soon as we agree to the sale."

"What's the OSC?"

"The Ontario Securities Commission. There are regulations for the management of stock-issues, you know. You can't just print up share certificates on nice crinkly paper and offer them to passersby. McKim, Factor and Déneau are exactly the right house for us. Unimpeachable record, never been associated with anything doubtful."

"In short, you've got the whole thing set up and ready to move, as soon as I say yes. It's as if you were courting me all over again."

"No, it isn't," I said, hoping not to have to explain why it wasn't, "but we do need to make haste. Can you tell me how you feel about the proposal?"

"Let me get it straight in my mind. We convert *CHBS 67* into a publicly-held company, expecting to raise about thirty-three million on the sale."

"Right so far."

"We retain a bit over a million from the sale as investment capital for ourselves, and donate the rest of the yield to a fund for acquiring this work of art for the National Gallery?"

"Right again."

"And the Revenue people allow us to treat our donation as

a tax deduction, spreading it over, say, ten years."

"Exactly!"

"And after ten years, what then?"

"We'll have to pay tax like anybody else, but our incomes will be equal to the tax demands. After all, there are just the two of us."

"In effect, we're giving away a family inheritance. What about Anthony, Andrea and John? Do we have the right to do this without consulting them about it?"

"I've already done that with Andrea and Josh, and with Anthony. I've talked to Emily about it. There's really no difficulty in our way. Josh and Andrea are doing very well. They don't need us, they've told me so. Andrea was a little curt about it. You know how she can be."

"I certainly do, the little hellhound."

"And whenever I've written to Anthony he's replied in set terms that he doesn't want to inherit anything from anybody. He doesn't like the idea of inheritance. I think he sees himself as some sort of monk or contemplative. He minded terribly when Linnet died." I watched to see how she would respond to this mention of an event more than twenty-five years in the past.

"Don't talk about it," she said softly. "He looked like he was bleeding to death internally when it happened. It took him years to recover . . . if he ever did."

I didn't care to discuss Linnet at this stage in our reunion. Later perhaps, but not just now. "And we don't need to discuss John's finances. He can write his own ticket as far as finance is concerned. He's already rich, much more than a millionaire. Or will be as soon as he sets foot on Earth. One of the most celebrated persons alive. Hard to realize, but there it is."

"Those beautiful aerial cars," she said reminiscently. "Forty years on, and I'm an old woman."

"No, you're not. You mustn't think like that."

"And you've got it all worked out, haven't you? If I don't go along with you, I look like an obstructionist."

She was starting to yield. I knew the signs. "I could fax McKim, Factor and Déneau later today, if you agree. Then they can issue the prospectus . . ."

"They've prepared the prospectus?"

"Well, just a little one."

"You've got everything ready! Come on, confess, Matthew! Have you got papers for me to sign? I'll bet you have, there in that attaché case. I wondered why you brought it along."

"Not actually to sign . . . not today anyway . . . just to look at, with a view to giving consent."

The TV was still on, with the sound down. Snow flickered quietly across its screen. "May I turn this thing off?" I asked, fumbling at the remote control. "It bothers my eyes when there's no picture."

"Go ahead, by all means. What time is it now? Around dawn?"

"It's four-thirty."

"You can send them notice that I consent," she said briskly.

I don't know where she found the energy to make such a decision. I was totally strung out and longing for my bed.

"I can give you a bed here, if the prospect doesn't alarm you."

"I accept with thanks," I said, with a flicker of excitement at the notion of spending what remained of the night in my wife's house. She had the temerity to grin at me; she knew what I was thinking and feeling.

"You're a bad man, Matthew Goderich," she said in teasing accents.

"Bad maybe, but efficient."

"I'll show you to your room, and we can go into more precise details tomorrow. You should fax your brokers about nine o'clock their time."

"You have a terminal in the house?"

"Certainly," she said, looking at me scornfully. "I suppose you're terrified of them."

"I don't use fax very much," I admitted. "I prefer to send a letter — not by e-mail — or make a phone call."

"How very like you, my sweet. Here, I'll show you where you can sleep, if you don't mind wearing Tony's pyjamas."

I said, "I didn't bring any of my own."

"They wouldn't have gone into your attaché case. Come on, you're just up one flight, very comfy, guest bedroom, at the rear of the house."

As I was falling asleep, towards five, she put her head around the door and said, "I'll fax McKim, Factor, Déneau for you if you like."

Usually when I go to sleep very late I toss around waiting for the buses and the birds, but this morning was different. I fell asleep immediately and stumbled into a dream-narrative of startling evocative power. The time was some distant year early in our marriage. It seemed as if we were back in our first Toronto home, an apartment over a store frontage on Yonge Street. Edie kept popping in and out of the half-lit room in which I sat; it might have been a breakfast nook, or even the bathroom. Tony was there for some reason, although he rarely came to visit us there before he left for England. Adam was there too. At one point the four of us sat down around a card-table laid for breakfast, with a jar of marmalade and four small glasses of juice. Suddenly the room was lit up brightly with sunshine; it got in my eyes, hurting them and making me shed tears. Then I woke up. The sun had indeed risen and was shining through my back bedroom window, right into my eyes, in waking reality. I sat up abruptly. I'd had about fifty minutes' sleep and I felt dreadful as one does after that sort of brief rest. My mouth was sour and my limbs very stiff. I wondered about the rest of the story begun moments before in my abridged dream. I hoped that it might be continued the following night so that I might dream of a further episode that would finally unite the four of us.

I had a real, wakeful breakfast with Edie later that day, in the kitchen at the bottom of the house, a continental-sized snack. I like the full English breakfast but wasn't to enjoy it that day. She insisted on getting right down to business, in rather a hard-driving style that I remembered from thirty years before. I saw that she wanted to act quickly. For some obscure reason the notion of presenting the nation with a magnificent work of art, as a memorial to all the Codringtons, Sleafords and Goderiches, had captivated her imagination. While I sat at the breakfast table imagining the four of us reunited, she was drawing lines on the checked tablecloth with her fork and giving me my orders.

"We'll want to go straight ahead with this, I mean today. We've only got six months in which to arrange matters."

I felt as I had often felt years before in her presence, as if I were being co-opted for a venture that had been mine to begin with but wasn't mine any longer.

"Whoa, whoa, girl," I said. "Slowly, take it easy. We've got to walk before we can run."

"Nonsense! We already know how to walk and run. You want to hold the dedication ceremonies at the National Gallery on October 15th, a Friday. Now tell me frankly, Matt, what made you choose that day? I mean that specific date. Why a Friday, for example?"

"It's the best weekday for an official gathering in Ottawa. You get lots of diplomatic response, from the embassies and the department." I had other, more private reasons for choosing that date, that I considered my own business. I've never revealed them to anybody and I won't now. But they were good reasons.

She seemed satisfied. I could see her eyes filling with visions of the splendour of a full-dress display of ambassadorial pomp.

"Would the Americans send the president, do you think? I mean if John and Céline and Hubert de Barny were to be there?"

I hadn't thought of that. "They might send her," I said. "She's one travellin' woman. She's been everywhere in the world except, I believe, to Antarctica. I know that she's visited the North Pole."

Edie's eyes were now bright with planning, at seven-thirty A.M. She poured me another cup of decaf and settled the other breakfast dishes in the machine. It was clear that she ran the house alone. She was as alone as me.

"Let's write the fax for McKim, Factor and Déneau," she said. "We'll need to be explicit and precise."

That tone, explicit and precise, marked our relations from then on. No question of the excitingly romantic resumption of an old love. I was foolish to have imagined it. This new tone was perfectly acceptable, might even lead to our living together again, most probably somewhere between Ottawa and Stoverville. I knew that I might not care to cohabit with Edie in our old Crescent Road apartment in Toronto — far too many memories!

My mother, Uncle Philip, Andrea, Amanda Louise and Emily, and most of all Adam. Crescent Road was not the right setting for resumption of relations with my legal wife; in fact we never afterwards stayed there permanently. I kept the place on, an unnecessary expense, for several more years. I had my own motives for going on with it. It was the repository of most of the feelings I'd accumulated through the second half of my life, my long time as an unwilling near-bachelor. I loved that old dump on Crescent Road, and leaving it would have made me dwindle into a husband.

Let me be plain about this. Edie and I never got back on the footing we'd shared in our first years together, when we loved each other. Thirty years' break in our relations had made any such recovery impossible. However, we did finally manage together to work out a relationship with an almost unique tang. I don't know of another case of a married couple who have lived apart for three decades without divorcing, who then go on to re-establish an intimate, confidential association, without very friendly feelings for each other. More than a marriage of convenience or a mere business partnership but less than love or friendship, this qualified union seemed to satisfy, even represent, the social world around us. Very soon after its resumption our acquaintances began to act as if we'd never been separated at all. This was part and parcel of the wrongful readiness of human society to forget our dead, those former agents in our lives whose absence from the scene makes them impotent. I came in time to resent this ready acceptance of our cohabitation on the solid footing of legal marriage and joint holding of valuable property. It ignored the fact of my brother's thirty years as Edie's companion and, for some time at least, her lover. I had not enjoyed the situation when I was part of it. Little to enjoy! All the same, my brother's death was too high a price to pay for its dissolution.

Hang it all, I gradually found myself thinking, I'm not even her friend, not really. I'm really just a joint property-holder. Tony was her real life's partner, and I felt no pleasure or satisfaction in my brother's early departure from the scene. But the world's business has to be carried on, no matter who quits the stage at the end of the second act, or halfway through the third. That first morning we got through an enormous volume of business. It's amazing how much you can dispose of, using contemporary methods of correspondence. I had thought Edie's fax terminal a foolish and wasteful expense, until I saw how it facilitated the exchange of essential messaging. Doing our business at extraordinary speed, we soon advanced far along the road of settlement of most of the problems connected with the issuance of shares in *CHBS 67*, particularly through the Toronto Stock Exchange. There, we were assured by McKim, Factor and Déneau, discriminating investors of the highest type stood poised to oversubscribe the issue. And this proved later on to have been an accurate estimate of the company's standing in the eyes of the investment community. A subject of very long-term growth, never a loser at year-end, a succession of favourable balance sheets, regular expansion, fully computerized inventory, three major outlets, one of them over a hundred and thirty-five years old, an unimpeachable reputation with the buying public. An exemplary midsize retail trader with great prospects for further expansion.

I had brought to the Beauchamp Place house a whole set

of papers for Edie's signature, even down to a waiver that allowed the public company to continue using the name under which we'd been doing business since Confederation; as the major living representative of the Codringtons and their interests Edie was clearly empowered to give such a permission. The company name proved to be a major asset for quite some time, as the principal element of what is known in retail trading as its goodwill. I often thought, all this time, that the almost mystical weight and power of association of the phrase *Since 1867* was decisive in promoting the almost instant success of the share-issue. So far as I'm aware, no other prominent retailer in Canada had used the phrase and the claim it insinuated so widely and publicly for so long. It had a succinct neat feel to it, a claim to be linked to the foundations of the nation, a kind of brave and solid probity that can only be proved out during more than a century of doing business.

It didn't take anything like a century, however, for the transformation into a publicly-owned institution to take place. By the third week of April, McKim, Factor and Déneau had received the documents bearing our signatures authorizing the sale, the number and price of the shares, the residual payment to our joint account in a Stoverville bank, the payment of the rest of the yield to the Special Acquisitions Fund of the National Gallery, subject to supplementary payments from Lamp Trust and Crown Royal Tobacco. By May 3rd the project had assumed the form in which it was afterwards made permanent and enduring, setting a standard for the management of public benefactions that was the first and highest anywhere in the Western world. We were first in that field.

During this period it became clear that one or both of us eventually would have to establish residence somewhere between Ottawa and either Toronto or Stoverville. I retained my pied-à-terre in Toronto and could resume regular occupancy there at any time, but I didn't want to share the place with my legal wife. We both thought it wiser not to share living quarters, at least not for some time to come. A future summer might find us resting together at the cottage on the large lake northwest of Stoverville where our family had enjoyed some of its happiest moments. I envisioned quiet evenings on the west-facing sundeck, moments snatched from the round of commitment to public action, during the unfolding of our eighth decades. At well over seventy I could imagine nothing better than several weeks passed in near-seclusion at the lake. I was not alone in enjoying this dream or fantasy. When she decided definitively to sell her Knightsbridge property, agreeing at the same time to put Tony's Hampstead dwelling on the market as part of our shared inheritance from him, Edie kept referring to the lake country northwest of Stoverville as if it were just as pressing a part of final fantasies of peace for both of us. Peace instead of conflict at the finish.

I found myself recalling incidents from our early times together, and these recollections gave me at first the muted pleasures of idle nostalgia, those of the old family album. Then, surprisingly quickly, this soft-edged quality, faded, sepia, crumpled at the edges, faintly scented like old paper, began to disappear, to be replaced by a brightness of image that surprised me indeed. It was like watching the past become the future. I felt like going out to the lakeside cottage near Athens and taking dozens, perhaps hundreds, of pictures of this blending of the past and future. A new album, a revived past, still filled with possibilities beginning to unfurl after all the years.

And observing her haste to wind up Tony's affairs, her readiness to put her own house on the active London real-estate market, I concluded that Edie too had had enough of residence abroad. She would probably never settle down in Toronto, a place identified with my side of the family. Stoverville seemed the focal point of her plans for whatever was to come. She was still the river girl she had declared herself to be the first time we ever met.

I guessed she might have plans for resuming a river girl's

career on somebody's boat, one of those pleasure craft moored more or less permanently at a riverfront marina. At the same time, such a craft might be well in sight of her *chef d'oeuvre*, the mural "The Genius of Politics . . . ," which she had executed on the south-facing rear wall of Stage Stoverville in the late 1960s.

I remembered, thinking these things over, that the officers of the joint board of management of Stage Stoverville had often, in the intervening thirty-five years, issued invitations to Edie to come back and retouch and repair this celebrated work. Washed down by the weather, bleached by the sun for a generation, scoured and dustblown by the freshening breezes of Octobers now distant history, the famous mural had with the endless succession of the weather lost some of its hard-edged management of forms. Colours had softened, here and there blurred. Naturally, too, the satiric point of the mural's narrative had softened and become more genial, less acrid in its imagery. It seemed appropriate, as *CHBS 67* was emerging from mere local ascendancy into national prominence, that the famous mural should likewise be given new paint, perhaps a whole new interpretation.

Anyway, after rejecting various proposals of that kind at regular intervals over more than thirty years, Edie now found herself inclined to consider one of them seriously. For such an undertaking prolonged Stoverville residence was almost mandatory. So two of the central icons of Stoverville history (Stoverville has its history, like Paris, Vienna, Rome) came back into Edie's attention, and were about to be reanimated by her. She sought a commission to retouch the great mural, and planned to take the next two summers over the project. And she decided to apply to the curator of the Codrington Colony for a lease on one of the small flats housed in the building that, it will be remembered, had been her childhood home.

"Visionart," she exclaimed, one morning just before she left Beauchamp Place for the last time. "Does the colony still promote the production of visionary art? There can't be much demand for it in the new millennium; we may have to wait for another thousand years for the visionary tone to reassert itself in art." She paused, vexed by some intrusive reflection. "The 1990s were times for visions," she said. "I never went in for it myself, but here in London you could flog any old load of rubbish, as long as it had an other-worldly look to it."

I found her turn of phrase highly entertaining. "Any old load of visionary rubbish," I repeated, "with an other-worldly look. I've never seen any work that fits your description exactly, although plenty of the art of the last decade might be described as insightless, or right out of it, or something." I wasn't sure where the discussion was headed.

"*You* know," she said encouragingly, "Mapplethorpe and the guys like him."

"Mapplethorpe's images are about as pornographic as the Rolls-Royce radiator sculpture, which is surprisingly erotic when you examine it, but not arousing. He was a formalist from the start."

"To his fingertips?" she said, with a wry grin.

"Never mind about his fingertips," I said. "They don't come into the argument. You can look at one of Mapplethorpe's explicit forms from across a crowded room, and what you notice first is the poised formal elegance of his shapes, in two dimensions. Flat forms. Then when you move closer you see that it's his famous fountain of urine and you feel foolish at your own surprise. If you then back off, and let the design revert to its original flatness, its non-representational state, you feel sly because you remember the narration that's hidden in it. But that's only a second-level element of the work, just like all the representational mimesis of art. Mapplethorpe was neither a visionary nor a pornographer. Anyway, he was dead before the 1990s, so he isn't a fair example."

"Are you certain of your dates?"

"No, I'm not, but the point isn't relevant."

"It's a point you brought up."

"Well, now I'm revoking it."

"Pornography and the pornographic are the secular world's homage to the visionary," she said disconcertingly. Disconcerting because of the pithiness of the sentence and its convincing, argument-closing, sound. I was silent for a brief time. The only way to counter a genuine aphorism in debate is not to reply to it. Let silence swallow it up; perhaps it will then be forgotten.

At the same time I found her parallel between the visionary and the pornographic an attractive standpoint from which to launch a discussion. Plenty of bad visionary art — especially when it founds itself on some imagining of the infernal — includes elements that can only be considered obscene, shocking. Even some great figures, Bosch, Ensor, Spencer, whose work aims towards the visionary, have willy-nilly shown us the obscene writhings of souls in torment. Perhaps the vision dictates what a poet has called the necessary glory of dung. The vision may require the dung and the flames, just as the heat of the smelting is needed to melt out the pure iron.

I thought about Mrs. Codrington's visionary sequence, soon to be revisited by her daughter a generation after its completion and installation in the upper rooms of the Codrington Colony for the Encouragement of Visionary Art. Those twelve formidable representations contained no explicit likeness of the infernal and the heaps of ordure usually found in pictures of Hell. The nearest approach to Hell in her visionary sequence is to be found in the departure of the damned souls of Stoverville into everlasting fire, in the third and lowest panel of the triptych, "The Population of Stoverville, Ontario, Entering into the New Jerusalem." There the souls and bodies of the damned are treated with an almost comic naturalism that recalls the art of Norman Rockwell. They are perfectly realistic pictures of then-living Stovervillians; some of them were deeply wounded by their inclusion in this plain representation. Lawsuits had been hinted at but in the end none of the damned souls in the panel proceeded to court, perhaps from fear of cross-examination.

Anyway, Mrs. Codrington's depictions of certain of her fellow-citizens as either damnable or damned might have stood up all too well in court, especially the identification of Herod and Judas as good Stovervillians. Nobody ever sued Dante for placing them in the Inferno. Probably they felt pleased and proud to be displayed there; it would have made them feel important.

I remembered very clearly thinking over the Dantean aspects of Mrs. Codrington's dozen masterworks. I never got to the bottom of this matter but I do recall noting that the bodies of the damned were not treated indecently. They were not shown in collections of severed body parts, or buried under mounds of dung; they looked very much as they would if you were to pass them on King Street. I considered this a subtle and highly appropriate solution to the problems of narrating the horrid and disgusting by visual means. Mrs. Codrington's pictures are more convincing than those of Bosch, whose demons are absurd, laughable. Editing out the dung and the rotting body parts was a fine stroke, I saw. Perhaps the visionary in art did not after all require the presence of the horrid to authenticate it. This brought me back to the photography of Robert Mapplethorpe, poor man.

"I believe that Mapplethorpe was raised a Catholic," I said, half to myself, barely audibly. But Edie caught the reference at once.

"That doesn't seem to have done him any harm as a photographer."

"He seems to have been able to slough it off. And he's your visionary pornographer, right enough."

As usual Edie was away ahead of me. "Titian is never a visionary, not in the portraits, not in the evangelical works like the *Assumption* in the Frari. The Blessèd Mother is standing on real clouds that provide her with excellent support. The heavenly world rises out of this one, as an incarnate Heaven, rather than as an invisible pure bliss, mystical, unworldly."

"Yi-yi-yi! Go a bit slower, lady. You can dish all this up with

Irene Berrick in the long winter nights in Stoverville," I said evasively.

"Who is Irene Berrick?" Edie asked.

Ms. Berrick was the current curator of the Codrington Colony, having held the position for over a decade. She was solidly entrenched in the curatorial apartment and would require some budging indeed. I thought with mild malice that my wife might find some difficulty in digging herself back into her childhood home. But as usual where Edie was concerned I was quite mistaken.

I described the terms of Irene's appointment. "A solid well-trained professional with two degrees in art history and more than a decade of professional experience. You'll find her impressive."

And of course they found each other impressive, and got along like a house on fire, or rather two houses on fire. It turned out that Irene Berrick had carefully studied all the creative work done by May-Beth Codrington's associates and descendants; she therefore knew all about Edie's career as a painter and muralist, taking off from her critical study of "The Genius of Politics . . ." that had appeared in *The Burlington Magazine*. Edie rarely looked into such journals, and had missed the essay when it appeared. When Irene Berrick drew it to her attention, its treatment of the artist — highly favour-able — put its friendly author solidly onside with Edie, a position never afterwards forfeited. This meeting took place in the first week in June, just when the precise mechanism for the acquisition of the Titian from the Marchese Bianchini was becoming a matter of public comment and debate.

When it became public that the National Gallery was pre-paring to commit just over a million and a half dollars from its operating funds to the transport, installation and main-tenance of a great European masterwork by a long-dead white male, intense public debate might have been expected, over the amount involved and the nature of the work, its place in art history and its yet-to-be-determined usefulness as a teaching instrument in the formation of young Canadian art historians.

The Canadian art press, at that moment open and ready for discussion of some novel and possibly scandalous matter, attempted perhaps mischievously to stir up controversy about how the work was to be acquired and then cared for. Where would it be displayed? What other works by the master were in Venetian galleries, or in other great museums? Wouldn't *Priam and Achilles* overshadow all the other works of the Venetian school now in Canadian hands? How could you mount a touring show that contained one masterwork and two dozen works of the third order? Surely good sense dictated that such a large expenditure should be laid out in acquiring and displaying several lesser works, perhaps some old-master drawings to develop the gallery's already impressive holdings in that field. Yes? No?

Even the influential and authoritative critic of *The Globe and Mail* failed to generate real controversy over the question. Maybe the general public had grown tired over the years of complaints about government extravagance in arts funding. Either the Canadian public had greatly matured in two decades, or twenty years of steady slow inflation had made the sum in question seem like small potatoes. Perhaps both conditions were in play.

NATGAL COVERUP?

PUBLIC AUDITOR QUERIES TITIAN SLUSH FUND

CHANCE OF A LIFETIME: DIRECTOR

BARGAIN AT FIFTY-FIVE MILLION?

The difficulty in drumming up opposition to the acquisition of the picture lay in the provable fact that almost all of the fifty-five million was coming from innocent private sources. Countervailing headlines started to show up in the press. My own participation in the semi-secret negotiations was at first hinted at and then brought vigorously before the public. In mid-June, the spacecraft only thirty days from home, my family relationship to one of the most celebrated people now living, Professor Goderich of Cambridge and Mars, went a long way towards convincing Canadians of every age and both genders that there could be nothing underhanded or ill-judged about the purchase. It came to seem in the eyes of the great public as though the voyage of *Visitor I* and its imminent finish were somehow linked essentially to Titian, the National Gallery of Canada, the Marchese Bianchini, Canada's participation in the Italian campaign of World War II, the glories of Venetian painting in the High Renaissance, and the open-handedness of Crown Royal Tobacco, Lamp Trust and Matthew and Edie Goderich.

Or better: Edie *Codrington* Goderich.

Plans for an officially approved Codrington/Sleaford/Goderich Wing in the superb gallery building were now leaked to the press with the predictable result. *Visitor I* was drawing ever closer to Earth. The great and glorious Titian masterwork was about to be shipped to Canada. The two occurrences became connected, then almost merged in public awareness. Here was an almost unique instance of the birth of a myth. In reality the events had little to do with one another. But as the countdown to Day Terminal continued, Canadians began to feel proud of the Canadian initiatives in great parallel undertakings, the Mars flight and the purchase of the last masterwork to be allowed out of Europe.

Here my old friend Pluyshin came into her own. I remember revealing publicly at least once or twice that a finder's fee had been included in the fundraising for the Titian. The finder was never identified by name. Pluyshin worked her connections with the Italian Cultural Property Review Board to their absolute limit. A small part of her fee went on entertainments and very modest gifts — not cash gifts — to certain middle-level officials. Nobody of ministerial rank was ever consulted for the record about the issuance of an export certificate. The Italian arts press maintained a dignified, wholly inexplicable silence about the matter, something almost unheard of. When it was mentioned in the Italian press it was invariably immersed in a bath of putative high-level international diplomacy, as a gesture of thanks from Italy to Canada for our nation's exemplary conduct of military operations along the Adriatic coast in 1944 and 1945.

Then there would be a mention of the large Italian colony in Toronto and the smaller but still considerable Italian population of Montreal. Pluyshin was simply a master, or mistress, of this type of stage management, never appearing in the negotiations under her own or any name. In the press of either country she would be identified as a well-informed source, or as a usually reliable spokesperson, something along those lines.

At her promptings the journalistic accounts of the export of the last Titian always stressed the strengthening of the cultural, political and economic ties that bound our two countries together. Most often cited was the pending decision by joint fiscal and monetary managers to link their currencies in a fixed common rate of exchange that greatly encouraged trade relations between them, at the same time floating the new rate in respect of the other, more powerful and populous G7 nations. This move was designed to transform Italy and Canada into a mini-bloc with its own ends in view, apart from those of the rest of the world's chief economic community.

Naturally these moves had been cloaked in the deepest secrecy, but of course all secret negotiations imply the inevitability of leaks. If there were no attempts at concealment where would the media be?

Pluyshin came and went between Ravenna, Rome and Ottawa all through the crowded weeks before the final sale of the painting, all of her travel documentation under her own name. A smallish, bent, grey creature without obvious ties to diplomacy, finance or economic policy, she had no official function of any kind. Her name appeared on passenger manifests and airlines reservations lists, sometimes as G. Kotecke, sometimes as M.G. Kotecke-Pluyshin, occasionally as Pluyshin pure and simple, without gender specification. She was a supremely persuasive dealer, making the cards fall where she pleased. The notion of a mini-trading-bloc within the EC had been mooted before this, sometimes in Scandinavia, once or twice by Portugal and Spain, never by a pair of nations, one of them not a member of the EC at all.

What was disturbing about the Pluyshin proposals was just this binding together of two countries, one from the EC, the other from NAFTA. Once allow reciprocal collaboration between nations in either community and you were well on your way to postulating world economic union, a concept previously put forward by the most airy theorists. But now here were the two stepchildren of EC and NAFTA proposing to unite themselves currencywise, tradewise, culturewise. The passage of the Titian from the Veneto to Ottawa was the single most significant step in the whole complex process of Italo-Canadian cooperation. It united a land-poor, highly inventive, culturally mature community, somewhat underpopulated to support its ancient preponderance in the arts and sciences, and an enormous landmass, likewise underpopulated, resources-rich, relatively poor in the apparatus of human culture. Imagine a nation like Canada as rich in cultural inheritance as Italy! Then imagine an Italy as spacious and as physically well-endowed and as empty as Canada! Imagine the Medici or the Borgias — or the Bianchini — plunked down in Ottawa at the height of their powers! And then figure for yourself Mackenzie King or Pierre Trudeau pacing across the seven Roman hills! No wonder that the sale, under lax import/export rules, passed without review by middle-grade functionaries on either side of the Atlantic.

Mind you, sometime later the French, who rule the culture kingdom with a whim of iron, raised objections in the European Parliament about the disappearance of the great work of art from the sorrowing European culture community and its relocation in perhaps — in French eyes — the most barbarous political entity of the entire English-speaking Western bloc. Canada! *Canada?* What could a Titian be doing in Canada? Might as well be in Timbuktu or Port Stanley. If that painting was not to be housed in the Accademia, or perhaps the Villa Borghese, then certainly its proper resting place was the Louvre.

Not the National Gallery of Canada! It was in French official eyes a kind of circus-booth hung with dubious attributions vended to callow hosts by the dregs of the European art-trading community. The French moved to have the sale by the Marchese Bianchini nullified by parliamentary fiat, the picture returned to Europe. Nothing ever came of this initiative. Quebec disapproved of it, so it fell to the ground. Meanwhile Pluyshin, realizing that her work — the great achievement of her life — was wound up, moved to collect her entrepreneurial fee, received it in very sizeable instalments, and paid off the small overhead she had incurred, none of it identifiable as bribe or payoff. She then purchased a modest retirement home somewhere in south-central Ontario, or so I've been told. She was given accelerated citizenship, despite being unable to show that she had ever been born anywhere. I seem to recall that soon after the National Gallery mounted the Titian and dedicated the Codrington/Sleaford/Goderich Wing, Pluyshin was named an Officer of the Order of Canada, retiring from the public scene with her honours, as it were, thick upon her. I've never seen her since, but I have associates who claim to have spotted her moving obscurely between the Kawartha Lakes and downtown Toronto, on a GO train or boarding VIA Rail at Cobourg. In any case she is still in southern Ontario somewhere, living quietly, out of the eyes of other agents.

Italo/Canadian *rapprochement*, especially in face of *métropolitain* French opposition, could not have been bettered as an element in persuading Canadians, including Quebeckers, that gift of the picture to the National Gallery was a triumph for emergent Canadian culture. It went far towards doing down opposition to donations to the acquisitions fund by the liquor and tobacco "interests." Canadians still, in the new millennium, need to give lip-service to the goddess of public propriety, voicing at least token opposition to the use and sale of wines and spirits, sometimes even of beer and ale. Tobacco producers receive far more than token resistance.

Certain PR types, hired enemies of the tobacco lobby, strove to make it clear that eleven or twelve million dollars wasn't such a big sum, was in fact a trivial, almost insulting tip or gratuity in return for invaluable publicity. Crown Royal, part of an enormous international consortium, was at some pains to refute this argument. It was maintained that eleven or twelve million could not be dismissed by anybody as a trivial amount; even in the new age, to count your benefactions in seven figures was to be truly generous. And this money was an outright gift with no strings attached. People could not help being impressed by that fact. In the end the tobacco interests did well out of the deal, but so did the National Gallery and the Codrington/Sleaford/Goderich Wing.

It should perhaps be noted that public appeals in the form of collection boxes with slits in their lids, placed in banks, museums and other appropriate locations, yielded very little in the form of spontaneous support. When the boxes were emptied they invariably turned out to contain pennies, nickels and dimes. One- and two-dollar coins were conspicuous by their absence; the appeal to the public fell flat, realizing in the end a little more than seven thousand. It would be interesting to know precisely how many put their small change in these boxes. We seem as a people to be content in these matters to sit back and allow the large social institutions to advance the common good: banks, the government, the major corporations, the universities and the professions, medicine, the law. When a tobacco and liquor company came forward to push the Special Acquisitions Fund over the top, there was no serious opposition to acceptance of these rather Greek gifts. People seemed to feel that liquor and tobacco money was legal tender the same as yours and mine except that there was more of it.

Largeness of conception was wanting. Maybe it is too much to expect magnanimity from you and me. But Edie and I felt that we had been prompted by fatality to come forward with the grand gesture, giving up to public uses a family concern that had always before been strictly private. *Codrington Hardware and Builders' Supplies. Since 1867* had started out very small and had evolved into a unique symbol of Canadian life. During the entire period of my association with the company, really no more than a local emporium at the start, I watched it gradually change into a store with some claim to regional influence and celebrity. When Mrs. Codrington died I deliberately threw in my lot with the company's growth. Many, many times in those forty years I was asked by inquisitive associates how I could reconcile a career as an art historian and writer on somewhat obscure subjects with my position as the executive head of a hardware store and automotive supplies dealer.

Sometimes I would give a pragmatic reply to these quizzings, explaining that our stores carried builders' supplies, cottage outfittings, sporting goods appropriate for our shortish summers, lifejackets, paddles, fishing gear, tents and a wide range of other goods peculiarly expressive of the tone of Canadian life.

I always mentioned, in these discussions, that we also carried in each store a line of artists' supplies of the very highest quality, a commodity seldom found elsewhere in the districts served by us. This service was the product of the initiative of the celebrated May-Beth Codrington; it often deflected the tendency to make fun of me as a ridiculous figure because I spent half my time managing, of all things, a hardware store, devoting the rest of my working hours to art history and art criticism. It appeared to many that the two activities could hardly be carried on together. But I tell you that they can, that they have been. The humblest daily needs for hammers, screwdrivers, ballcocks, washers, piping, for 6B pencils and fine drawing paper, for watercolours in sixty tones, for inks and oils and acrylics, can finally merge into an ideal of retail service that has a serious claim on our attention and our feelings.

In making this service available for a hundred and forty years and more, beginning in obscurity in a small town (now a small city) in the very year that birthed our nation, *Codrington Hardware and Builders' Supplies. Since 1867* seems to have been ordained as an emblem of Canada as enduring as the red maple leaf on the flag. Very small, almost hidden beginnings, of no importance outside of an obscure locality, ignored by the great world of the capitals, Tokyo, Moscow, Rome, Vienna, Paris, London, Washington, joked about and almost sneered at when mentioned at all in these famous places. All this could be said of Canada, as much as of our small retail company.

Quiet internal evolution away from prying foreign eyes, silence in the oppressive presence of the great and celebrated, contentment in the face of apparent failures while long and deep roots are taking shape in the thin deposit of soil over rock. Long and deep roots, ladies and gents. Canadian history!

Then after a century of struggle to survive, the beginnings of visible growth. A branch devoted to roof-trusses and other building materials on the outskirts of town, first stretch of the limbs. Then some evidence of a wish to become a player in a larger game. A second store and then a third, all three stores doing solid business, making the company a valuable mid-sized unit in the board game. And finally, after a century and a half, an effective actor on the scene of the great world. The accumulated earnings of the little hardware store are spent in one heady swoop on the purchase of a great European masterpiece that even the French consider worthy of their jealous surveillance. The masterwork is transported to the Canadian capital and there sited permanently as the centrepiece of the nation's holdings in fine art. As *CHBS 67* goes, so goes Canada, a Hector among the nations.

As Day Terminal approached, and the return to Earth grew imminent, Canadian presence on the stage of the nations grew daily more evident. John's grandmother was first a Sleaford and then a Codrington. His mother was a Codrington and afterwards a Goderich, completing the corners of the Codrington/Sleaford/Goderich Wing.

Edie and I arrived back in Canada for good and all by Day Terminal Minus Thirty.

VI

THE GREAT VANE

"Any moment now . . . any moment . . . the sky here on the salt flats is clear blue without a trace of cloud, just as it was over sixteen months ago when *Visitor I* set out on her epoch-making voyage. This is Day Terminal, July 16th, and re-entry of the BLS is under way. We received a final signal from Colonel Kinnick just before the backup landing shuttle entered Earth's atmosphere. Since that moment we have received no further information from the shuttle, but we know that all her systems are in good operating condition. Computerized tracking of the shuttle until this moment shows that the vehicle will appear in the sky almost immediately. Everyone here on the salt flats is on tiptoe to try to be the first to spot the shuttle as it comes into view, a speeding black dot against the background of blue. Visual contact may be obscured by the sun, very bright this morning at 10:58 Mountain Daylight Time. The first sight of her should be located high in the east central sky close to the sun but not completely lost in sunlight. Hold it . . . keep your eyes on your screens . . . and catch the historic moment . . . just a second . . . 10:59 and thirty seconds . . . thirty-one . . . thirty-two . . . thirty-three . . . THERE SHE IS . . . THERE SHE IS, EVERYBODY . . . THERE SHE IS RIGHT NEAR THE SUN . . . ALL LIT UP AND SHINING . . . HERE SHE COMES."

The voice of Mission Control is temporarily covered by tumult, almost hysterical excitement of the staff at the broadcast centre. The TV picture goes wiggly, then clears, and the speeding shuttle is now clearly in view near the sun, shining like the Archangel in the morning. Mission Control is audible again.

"Oh, thank God they're all right . . . It's all over . . . It's over . . . They've made it back . . . This is a great moment in human history, everyone, a great moment . . . Here they come . . . We'll have visual observation of the first retro-burn . . . Just a minute . . . Should be right now . . . There, there she is . . . Vapour trails from the burning emissions, like fleecy clouds . . . The only vapour in today's sky . . . Hooray! . . . My God! They're going to be all right, they're okay . . . Here they come and just listen to that music . . ."

The band of the Seventh Regiment U.S. Marine Corps, stationed at Fort Lycoming, Salt Lake City, is playing loudly. The tune slowly becomes recognizable as "Happy Days Are Here Again." The band plays the chorus of the song over and over until it becomes very clear that nobody is listening. The bandmaster lets his arm drop, and Mission Control resumes speech.

"We have a fine picture for you, viewers. The object in the centre of your screens, still too distant to be seen clearly, is our BLS, readying for her second retro-burn, which will slow her down and alter her course towards the west end of the long runway, along the hard-baked mud of the flats. We should have easy visual confirmation of this burn. Yes! There it is, around the midpoint of your screens, two puffs of white vapour soon left behind by the speeding BLS, which almost threatens to fly out of the centre of our screens into the middle of everybody's viewing room. What a picture. What a sight, never seen before in the history of humanity, just a great, great day!

"We now have transmission contact with the astronauts and cosmonauts, and will try to bring you audible commands from

Colonel Kinnick as he swings the shuttle around to the west. Altitude approximately forty-eight miles, speed twelve hundred miles per hour and slowing rapidly. Touchdown will occur at about two hundred and forty miles per hour, and rapid braking will follow, a final moment of great danger to conclude sixteen months of heroic endurance. Now we'll try to go to radio transmission of the colonel's orders to his wonderful crew. Hello . . . hello . . ."

Forty-five seconds of noisy interference, then the voice of Colonel Kinnick.

"Don't interrupt us, please! This is very dicey."

More noisy radio signals, whistlings and a series of rhythmic beats suggesting paired signals on closely neighbouring frequencies. The image of the BLS grows larger on a billion screens from Central Asia to Utah and back. At twenty-five miles the tail assembly is easily distinguishable. At twenty-three miles the stubby wings are visible, growing more visible as the craft rounds into final approach path, at what seems to viewers a very steep angle of descent, almost as if the craft were dropping like a stone, almost free curving fall. But the computers are reading off the path correctly, alert to the smallest deviation from the plotted course. Once the little shuttle seems to waver from the steady flight pattern, and a billion viewers catch their breath. Then she steadies out, and at ten miles out markings on her fuselage can clearly be distinguished as burn scars. From this point on observers follow the shuttle as she comes into a flatter path, an unpowered, still very rapid glide. Now the diminishing distance allows a more accurate judgment of her velocity, just as a jet aircraft at touchdown suddenly seems to speed up. Now the BLS seems to accelerate, a highly inadvisable manoeuvre. Mission Control is confused by it.

"Take it easy, Colonel! Slowly . . . slowly . . ."

This is the only moment in the voyage when Mission Control offers advice to Colonel Kinnick; in retrospect it seems comic, and it has passed into the mythology of space flight. It is often afterwards repeated as typical, well-intended but completely useless advice offered by bystanders to the woman or man on the spot. "Take it easy, Colonel! Slowly . . . slowly . . ." Words inappropriate for almost any difficult situation, from saving a drowning man or woman at sea, or taking a show jumper over a wet course, to landing a BLS at the end of a space flight. Well-meant useless counsel, strangely fitting on this historic occasion.

"We have good radio contact with the shuttle," says Mission Control, unembarrassed by the intrusiveness of his previous comment. His listeners gasp. Should Control interrupt Colonel Kinnick at this crucial moment? But no! Even Control feels obliged to observe silence as the BLS swoops into a flat path two miles out that brings her onto the lip of the runway NOW! NOW! NOW!

"We have touchdown. WE HAVE TOUCHDOWN . . . IT'S OVER . . . Finished . . . They're home, everybody. They're home. Home."

Now for the first time since the space voyage began the clipped, authoritative voice of Mission Control is superseded by the competitive accents, on competing commercial networks, of professional trained broadcasters. Their technical smoothness of presentation comes as slightly unwelcome after the disciplined voice of Mission Control. Perhaps this is the place to reveal that this admired familiar tone, unimpassioned, precise, always masculine, has always been an artifact, the creation of a team of six military and naval officers chosen for the sound of their voices. They sound so much alike that listeners worldwide have taken them for a single voice. Needless to name them here, but I should probably note that the senior member and director of the broadcast team was Captain Thomas L. Ritchie, USN, a career seagoing naval officer whose calm, reassuring tones, even at moments of great risk for the space voyagers, have kept the broadcast transmissions clear, lucid and easy to follow. It was Captain Ritchie who narrated the events leading up to the departure of *Visitor I* for Mars sixteen months ago, and it was he who spoke the closing words of the mission that we have just heard.

"They're home, everybody. They're home. Home."

Immediately after touchdown, highly trained teams of nurses under the direction of the faculty for space medicine from the U.S. Military and Naval Hospital, Alexandria, Virginia, were deployed on either side of the runway, as were firefighting and military police personnel. Anti-terrorist elements of the Secret Service were in charge of the deployment, providing protection both for the arriving voyagers and for the high dignitaries assembled on the reception platforms.

The president of the United States and the president of France, the chairman of the Praesidium of the National Assembly of Russia, the prime minister of Great Britain and the prime minister of Canada, the governor of Utah and the governors of four neighbouring western states, the premiers of two of the western provinces of Canada, and remarkably the prime minister of Italy were among the most visible of the throng of officials and space agency functionaries who crowded the platform.

On the ground below, a regiment of communications specialists, interviewers, photographers, cameramen and their assistants swarmed around the arriving BLS like worker bees anticipating their queen. Fifteen minutes after touchdown, the shuttle was manoeuvring into position in front of the reception area and preparing to open its exit ports and lower its collapsible steps. Suddenly one of those comic incidents that often mitigate the tone of moments like these unfolded before the dignitaries. A small brown fox terrier broke through the ranks of security and medical personnel and raced up to the stationary BLS, yapping as the folding steps descended above and then beside it. When the steps were fully lowered and fixed firmly in place, an inner curtain was drawn aside and the forms of the co-commanders of the mission appeared in the exit port. At that moment the small dog paused in its outcries, lifted a leg and did what dogs do in their moments of excitement. An enormous wave of laughter washed across the salt flats. The president of the United States leaned towards her closest companion, the president of France, and made some inaudible comment on the occurrence. There is no great, solemn human occasion without its comic sidelights. The dog remained in place despite the efforts of military police to shoo him away. Meanwhile, Colonels Lebedev and Kinnick stood waiting for the signal to descend.

They seemed to be leaning against one another as if in need of physical support. The medical teams responded to this sign by grouping themselves at the foot of the steps, alert for the least sign of lassitude, the feebleness and paleness often displayed by returning space voyagers of an earlier time. Colonels Lebedev and Kinnick were now seen to be laughing and embracing each other, as they drew their first breaths of the free air of Earth. Colonel Lebedev gestured at the capering terrier and was seen to say something to his colleague. Some professionals who could lip-read in broadcasting situations afterwards put forward their various versions of what the co-commanders said on this occasion, as they stood laughing and smiling at the top of the stairs. There are several versions of what they were saying.

"What?"

"What was that? What did Kinnick say, Bob? Did you get that?"

"Re-run the tape on Auxiliary Two! Hurry it up, guys!"

"Have we got a close shot of his face?"

"Stop it right there. Kinnick looks at Lebedev. They almost kiss. Now Kinnick looks down the steps and sees the little doggie. We all see the little doggie and hope it isn't carrying an explosive device."

"Run it back to Kinnick's face, then forward it. Can you lip-read him?"

"Sure. I make it, 'I'll be a son of a bitch.'"

"Run it back and re-run it."

"That's not what he's saying. He says, 'I see Comrade President Babich.' "

"Hell he does!"

Nobody has ever learned from Colonel Kinnick exactly what he said about the small fox terrier, but his imputed words are part of legend. He and Colonel Lebedev jockey for position for brief seconds, each trying to allow the other to descend the steps first. Neither man wants to take precedence, so they squeeze against one another and come down side by side, to be met at ground level by all the presidents and prime ministers, first among them of course the chief executive of the host nation, who hesitates momentarily as if meditating some question of gender-protocol. Then she casts her arms wide and gathers the two heroes into a wide embrace. The sight of their three heads, hers in the middle and theirs smiling over her shoulders, has been preserved in one of the most famous and most beautifully composed photographs of the new age, worthy of Mapplethorpe at his best. It is a justly celebrated shot. The dark back of the president's coiffure conceals her neck and ears, at the same time showing the fine proportions of her head and shoulders. Her dark suit contrasts starkly with the gleaming fresh white of the two commanders' coveralls. Where did the colonels find those freshly laundered whites, anyway? Who did the laundry on board *Visitor I*? Who gave the colonels their trim, carefully barbered haircuts? What was done with the hair from the voyagers' heads during their long time in space? Does the gravitational field of Mars still support a hazy mist of hair trimmings from nine neatly barbered heads? This is the living summary of space exploration. Barbers in space, stylists in space, laundry in space. Who cuts Colonel Lebedev's hair? These points are not covered in the official protocols.

Surely they must have been discussed at the hundreds of hours of debriefings conducted first of all at the Military and Naval Hospital and then for several months in the hospital facility of the Space Flight Centre in Warm Springs, Georgia.

The presidential embrace, the handsome familiar smiling

faces of the co-commanders, the shining coveralls are all part of pre-post-post-modern historiography; they have become key icons of the united world society that appears to be evolving out of contemporary political life. Gone forever from human social organization, as it seems, is the concept of armed conflict between competing nation-states. Space itself is too small for competition of that outmoded kind. The worldwide reproduction of the three heads — two colonels and a president — is as good a symbol as you could wish for of the new world order. Colonels Lebedev and Kinnick might be brothers or gay partners, wrapped in the embrace of a loving sister, as the trio stand together in the stilled eternal immaterial black and white.

How fortunate it was that the wise photographer had loaded his camera with black-and-white film! Colour photography never confers the feeling of actuality of the black-and-white frame. Never allows itself to be enlarged in a true rendering of its original exactitude. This is a matter for the arts-theorists. Why does black and white enlarge so well when colour goes all fudged and misty in enlargement? The three poised skulls form the most telling and celebrated image from the new age. Now, at some remove from the date of original publication, we sometimes have trouble distinguishing the colonels. Is Colonel Lebedev the one with the upspringing cowlick and the engaging boyish smile? He looks so American! Is that Colonel Kinnick, with his head just above the president's shoulder? His face more solemn than the Russian? You might ask a dozen casual observers of the photo in a midtown lobby or walkway, and defy them to identify the two colonels correctly.

Colonel Lebedev *is* the one with the cowlick. He looks deeply American; but then in another way, so does Colonel Kinnick. Perhaps this only means that the barber on the voyage could only do American stylings. But there may be more to it that will surface as you stare at the photo. You used to be able to identify Russians by their botched and clumsy hair-stylings, but not any more; the Russians have made it into the Sassoon world, and for this we must be thankful. There they stand, the president and her two young men, for all the world to love and admire. The cheering continues.

A reception line assembles at the foot of the staircase to greet each of the voyagers as they descend the staircase one by one. Last three to emerge are the trio of Mars walkers who accompanied Colonel Lebedev to the surface of the planet. Captain Céline Hervieu comes first and we see as she turns her magnificent head in the fresh breezes of Utah that she does her own hair. No amateur barber has touched this coiffure. We are not surprised by Colonel Lebedev's good looks, but we wonder at Captain Hervieu's extraordinary beauty and superb physical condition, and are unprepared for the wonder of her rich auburn tresses.

Directly behind her comes Commandant Hubert de Barny of France; once he puts out a hand to Captain Hervieu's shoulder as she feels with her foot for the next step, and all present seem to sense as a single person the touching affection exhibited in the gesture. Of course all lovers of space myth and space narrative have been hoping and expecting that these two would fall in love, acting out that ancient tale of human care and human union that is the unplanned and free basis of epic. And the fond glance that Captain Hervieu directs at her commandant tells us what we have longed to hear, that those brave two are lovers.

Last to come and the representative of the civilian world of scientific theory and learning that has made the flight possible, not remarkable in physical presence but in perfect health and in full possession of his mental and physical powers, comes Professor John Sleaford Goderich of Britain and Canada, whose theories on artificial gravity have made intellectual history. As he steps to the ground from the final stair, Madam President turns towards a slender figure farther down the reception line. Of course it is the Professor's wife, Emily Underwood Goderich, mother of the first space baby. Madam President urges the couple into each other's arms. As she does so she overhears John's first words to his wife, which Emily later repeats for the world's communications media.

"He said, 'How's little Andy?' "

Then for a brief moment the president of Italy advances to shake hands with Captain Hervieu, Commandant de Barny and Professor Goderich. The group is joined immediately by the prime minister of Canada. The five speak together for about fifteen seconds, then they break apart unwillingly and the scene dissolves into a swirl of partly identifiable figures. The marine band strikes up "Happy Days Are Here Again" and now we can hear them. Perhaps the noise is beginning to die down. A nameless astronaut momentarily displays two of the symptoms of trace-metal loss, then recovers himself and stands erect. Later this lapse is explained by the discovery of a slight defect of the inner channel of the left ear that has nothing to do with calcium or magnesium deficiency. But the phenomenon alarms the attending medical personnel; they start to take over direction of the proceedings, herding the nine crew members towards the nine helicopters — one for each of them — that will deliver them to the nearby Air Force base. There they will be transferred to the jet aircraft that will take them to the hospital in Virginia, and to their first real meal on Earth after their return. Broiled chicken, small peas, potato cakes, gravy. Each of the nine refuses any sedation, and as soon as he or she is given the chance each of them lapses into profound, dreamless sleep.

The scientific, political and social findings of this first interplanetary voyage remain to be calculated; they will be of surpassing importance in human history. Here are listed some of the more pressing results of the mission.

An artificial gravity can be created in a spacecraft that will eliminate the medical consequences of prolonged weightlessness.

The crew of a spacecraft can endure the discomfort
and extraordinary environmental conditions of life
in space for long periods and perhaps for indefinitely
prolonged periods.

Men and women appear to function with equal
effectiveness under these special conditions.

The light gravitational pull at the surface of Mars will
be a positive advantage in manoeuvring on the surface
during future visits.

The Mars surface appears to be readily penetrable
by ordinary mining equipment. Prolonged stays in
sub-surface dwellings appear to be feasible in the
long run.

The Mars walkers appear to have sustained no ill
effects from exposure to daily doses of radiation while
living in a very thin atmosphere penetrated continually
by radiation bombardment of an unfamiliar type.

No surface ice formations were encountered by the
Mars walkers, but they all believe that ice crystals
would be found during further exploration in more
varied locations. They all believe that water in some
form has been present on the planet during its history,
and that ice mines exist below the surface. Ice deposits
may be successfully made use of by later voyagers.

The Mars walkers all believe that permanent peopled
Mars dwellings are not simply likely but are in fact
inevitable in the middle-distant future, and perhaps
much sooner than that.

After full evaluation of the findings of the first voyage,
the united international space agencies should proceed
as soon as possible to pool their belongings, their
equipment added to their data, however secret, in a

single unified program, so as to concentrate efforts and prevent duplication of programs and the consequent waste of available funding.

In larger future spacecraft, provision must be made for an isolation ward or cubicle, so that crew members with temporary viral infections can be prevented from passing them on to other personnel.

Long-term nourishment by means of a very low-bulk diet seems not to trouble crew members. Moderate loss of weight over the duration of the voyage was noted in the cases of seven. Two recorded slight overall weight gain.

For some idiosyncratic reason, two of the male crew members saw their progressive baldness develop much more rapidly in their time aboard than at other times. Both men are in their middle to late thirties.

More varied and sophisticated dental equipment is essential on future flights. At least one crew member should have had practical training in dentistry, including a knowledge of denturology.

Deprivation of ordinary regular sexual activity was conceded by all of the crew members to be a factor in problems associated with the maintenance of crew morale.

Future planning should perhaps stress conjugal relations and their practicability for flight crews. Bonded couples possessing other qualifications for flight training might be given priority in the selection of operational personnel.

Crew members greatly missed their life partners. Relations that developed between Captain Hervieu and Commandant de Barny were an object of stressful reactions among certain crew members, although no loss of operational competence was the result.

Captain Hervieu and Commandant de Barny behaved
with praiseworthy discretion throughout the voyage,
especially during its closing stages when their bonding
was becoming obvious and tight.

The division of command authority between the two
commanders had been a possible source of confusion
and dissatisfaction among crew members, but no such
problem developed. As each crew member possessed
authority in a given field, this special expertness
reinforced a sense of independent self-worth. The
division of command works well when crew members
have a strong sense of their value to the mission,
perhaps less well with more numerous crews where
junior members have little autonomy.

These were the first findings at the Warm Springs debriefings to be released for public information all over the world,
in almost every known language. They are of course preliminary formulations of decisions and policies that have yet to
be firmed up. They will provide a basis for planning of missions as yet inconceivable. Some of these conclusions and
recommendations are elementary and obvious; some remain
hypothetical in nature. Some allowance for "courtship"
behaviour will have to be made if undesirable inflight ten-
sions are to be avoided. Very interesting indeed were the
attitudes of his eight associates to the parenting by Professor
Goderich of a son during the mission. The crew seems to have
been able to put aside personal jealousies, in a really congratulatory attitude towards their colleague. Professor Goderich
commented repeatedly during the debriefing sessions on the
exremely loyal and supportive kindness and care shown to
him by his associates. They were ready to sacrifice time
available to them for exchanges with their families and friends
on Earth to allow Professor Goderich more opportunity to
communicate with his wife at the time of the birth of their son
and afterwards.

The common, sometimes undervalued, human qualities of loyalty and friendship seem to have been strongly present and effective in the preservation of an equable social climate during the flight.

This is not to say that no discontents showed themselves during the voyage. Some problems of overlapping jurisdiction or inadequate pre-flight training were commented on repeatedly by crew members. The officer responsible for medical services, a physician with advanced degrees in internal medicine and an extensive knowledge of family medicine, testifies that his ignorance of dental procedures went some way to undermine the crew's respect for his purely medical training. "Couldn't do anything for a simple toothache" was a common and certainly unfair reaction. The medical officer's provision of treatment in other areas was generally praised, and he himself underlined the necessity of providing his successors with an effective range of dental equipment. Only two crew members were found to have suffered damage to their dentition as a consequence of this absence of treatment; only one lost a tooth as a result of flight conditions. On the whole, therefore, the medical and dental services available to the crew of *Visitor I* were almost completely satisfactory.

Finally, after more than ten weeks of highly concentrated conferences and discussions, sometimes with all nine crew members, sometimes with selected smaller groups, often in one-on-one situations, the Centre for Space Medicine declared itself ready to allow the magic nine to resume ordinary daily life, the regular round of duty.

Most of them took advantage of offers of extended leave. Colonel Lebedev announced that he would now retire from military service in favour of a program of public appearances at home and abroad. His opposite number, Colonel Kinnick, chose to remain in the service. Under much pressure from demands on his time by media agencies, he accepted promotion to the rank of major-general, and it is as General Kinnick that the media now refer to him. He leads a determinedly

private personal life when he is allowed to. Still a compara-
tively young officer, General Kinnick is expected to rise much
higher in the service, perhaps to the highest post of all. That
is of course a matter for speculation; certainly after a long
leave and a program of extensive rest and complete relaxation
the general appears ready to take up a role as a public figure,
spokesman for the nation's military institutions, ready to
become a familiar presence before Congressional appropria-
tions committees as an advocate of further proposals for
space exploration. He is also expected to become a principal
resource person in the design and construction of space
vehicles. He will also assist in the development of the proposed permanent or temporary/permanent dwellings on Mars.
A full lifetime could not exhaust the possible contribution of
General Kinnick to future exploration. It is sometimes hinted
in the media that the general may have political ambitions
that cause him to keep his name as much as possible before
the public, but this is perhaps a profitless speculation that
future events may finally justify.

Not long after their departure from Warm Springs, Captain
Hervieu and Commandant de Barny announced their intention to marry, a decision welcomed all over the globe with
pleasure, and even rejoicing. It seems to be felt everywhere
that the two officers merit happiness for life in each other's
company. The enormous amount of press and television
coverage devoted to Céline and Hubert sometimes seems to
confer on them the status of media creations, like that of some
other personalities who have enjoyed a transient celebrity,
then faded from sight after their moment has passed. Such a
development could hardly be less appropriate. These officers
deserve much more from their fans.

Ten or twelve ridiculous proposals have been put to them,
always with some sort of stardom as a dreadful temptation.
In America and in France this sort of celebrity status has been
conferred on them without the friendly formality of consultation. No day passed for many months after the conclusion

of the voyage that did not give us a new Céline and Hubert news break. They were secretly married; they were going to be married tomorrow or next week. They had been married by the two colonels aboard *Visitor I*. A lot of tasteless speculation came out of this idle invention. None of the crew members dignified this rumour by commenting on it.

Their actual wedding ceremony, as everybody knows, took place in Ottawa during the gala celebrations that preceded and accompanied the arrival of the *Priam and Achilles* and its siting in the newly designed Codrington/Sleaford/Goderich Wing of the National Gallery. It seemed as though the mass-communications network found the names Sleaford and Codrington and Goderich a sufficient bait to draw their attention, fully focussed, for a period of several months, from mid-July through the October 15th date of the ceremonial dedication at the National Gallery, and the subsequent marriage and honeymoon of Céline and Hubert in the Gatineau Hills district northeast of the Canadian capital.

"Uproar" isn't too strong a word for the intense accompaniment of publicity that rose up like oceanic surf around the first North American exhibition of the Titian, the wedding of the two Mars walkers and the media discovery that Professor John Sleaford Goderich was a grandchild of May-Beth Codrington. The three family names united in the wing's title seemed to fuse together the two most exciting stories of the early twenty-first century, the lodging in the National Gallery of the last Titian and the splendid achievements of the leading space scientist. Media researchers began to make hay with Professor Goderich's personal history. He was the grandchild of a famous visionary artist who was by birth a Sleaford and by marriage a Codrington, and he was the grandchild of the winner of the Nobel Peace Prize for 1950, Andrew Goderich. His new little son carried these three names into new areas of celebrity; the professor was on three grounds the designated recipient of this deluge of publicity, and three times entitled to be among those present at the opening ceremonies. A week-long grand round of dinners, diplomatic teas and other assemblies, balls, press conferences, private receptions, the official presentation of the highest Canadian decoration for military gallantry to Céline and Hubert, the Order of Military Merit, and the parallel award of the Companion of the Order of Canada to the civilian Professor Goderich.

It seemed to some of us at the time that the distinction between military and civilian achievement in space exploration was a meaningless one. Céline and Hubert, and Professor Goderich, had undergone exactly the same hardships and risks, done the Mars walk in each other's company. They had shown the same degree and kind of merit in their undertakings. Why the Order of Military Merit for Céline and Hubert, and the Order of Canada for the professor? Were professors — and all civilians — ineligible for the military order?

Not long after the stirring times of mid-October were behind us, towards Christmas of that year, the Canadian government created a new order, in a single grade, that of Companion, for extraordinary achievement in space science and planetary exploration. The Order of Merit in Space confers the right to the terminal initials OMS, and has only been awarded to nine persons, the crew of *Visitor I*. It will be some time before more such awards are made.

As these events and many many others began to gather together and rise to a crest in August, September and early October, a kind of race developed among the participants and organizers of the mammoth celebration. We in Canada were charged with the extra-heavy responsibility of concluding the financial arrangements for the purchase of the painting and its final deposit in its new home. The drawing-together of all the funds that had been made available, in a single repository, the appointment of a funding board and signing officers to oversee the spending of these moneys, preparation of the exhibition site in the National Gallery, the testing from day to day of the electric motors designed to power the turntable on which the painting was to be displayed almost around the clock, all these matters and the other lesser affairs that came up from day to day for attention had to be dealt with immediately as they developed.

We were not permitted to proceed at the leisurely pace of most government undertakings. Under ordinary conditions the purchase and mounting of an immeasurably valuable and celebrated work of art, by a gallery not usually ranked among the world's top ten, would have taken anywhere up to five years from first to last. We managed the whole matter in about ten months, from the time that Pluyshin first surfaced in Ottawa at the end of the previous year until the night of the gala dedication on October 15th. Unseemly haste? The phrase was used by more than one journalist, not just by staid Canadian journalists either. I don't call it that, and I don't admit that we stole a free ride on the astronauts' coattails. Captain Hervieu was a Canadian by birth and upbringing; my son was Canadian by birth, if not by upbringing and education. Two of the most admirable of Canadian initiatives in history occurred at almost the same time. It seemed right to bring them together in wonderful festivity. Anyway, that's how it happened. I don't regret my own involvement in the event for a minute.

I saw more than ever how an obscure local institution like *CHBS 67* might by steady growth and final participation in a great historical moment represent some deep hidden truth about life in Canada. I think of the parable of the mustard seed when I contemplate such an unexpected growth to maturity. The smallest of seeds that yet grows up and becomes a tree so that the birds of the air come and nest in its branches. Very Canadian!

While we were racing to complete our preparations in Ottawa, a group of immensely skilful art historians and archaeologists was working on the transport of the painting from its resting place in the Castello Bianchini. Movement near the work had to be controlled with the greatest care. Should the ancient framing be replaced? Should the work be cleaned? Should the cleaning be done in Italy or deferred until after its arrival in its new home? The scene depicted on the canvas is very dark, heavy shadowy forms dominant in the composition. The painter had perhaps meant to allow his work to darken and, as it were, ripen with the passage of the centuries. A clean fresh brightness might alter the narrative and dramatic qualities of the work quite unpredictably.

It was decided to defer cleaning the painting until the new owners had had an opportunity to see how it looked in its new site. To date, no cleaning has been undertaken. Studies by the most sophisticated radiological photography suggest that the present state of the picture deviates widely from the artist's conception. At least two figures in the original design have been painted over during the evolution of the composition towards its present state. These might be grand allegorical shapes suggesting Conflict and Tranquillity, perhaps simply War and Peace. Or again perhaps Love and Hatred, or Gods and Men. Historians and scholars have continually suggested that the artist, working against time in his extreme old age, not in very good health, deliberately chose to simplify his statement, confining it to the representation of fewer than twenty personages. The available studies from the radiological material seem to dictate that no attempt to return the work to some hypothetical first state would be effective or convincing. This notion is the subject of endless energetic debate among professionals in the field. What is the definitive state of a work of art? Is it the earliest finished state, or the condition of the work at some special point in its evolution? Or what it looked like the last time the artist put his hand to it?

I'm glad that so far no restorer has been permitted to work on the surface of Canada's great Titian. Our caution and hesitation, and our ignorance of the technical aspects of such work, may accidentally have served us well in restraining the restorers from getting at the work with the intention of giving it a thorough cleaning.

Other technical matters of this kind were continually being brought forward by the technicians working at the Castello. The temperature of the great gallery in the Bianchini had been kept for many many years at about eighteen degrees Celsius, just slightly below a comfortable room temperature. What might happen to the painting upon being exposed suddenly to outdoors conditions? This would happen when it was lowered from the interior of the Castello to the waiting transportation below. In the end, certain risks had to be taken gallantly, none of them proving harmful to the work.

I was present at the time the painting was removed from its centuries-old position on the wall that faced across the gallery to the range of windows that gave on a westwards view. These windows had at some time in the early nineteenth century been recurtained so as to allow the surface of the Titian, and some lesser works that hung nearby, to be shielded from the late-afternoon sunshine. The surface of the paint showed no bleaching or cracking, such as might result from too-long exposure to sunlight.

I vividly recall the stir of emotion we all felt when the work was eased away from the wall; something of great historical significance was taking place. But at the same time the operation was just what you expect to find when you move an old picture from a wall that has not been dusted for a long time. It left a huge blank space behind it, its light grey tone contrasting sharply with the dark, dirty greyish-black of the adjoining surfaces. The size of the four spikes from which the canvas had been suspended surprised us by their smallness. Two or three mildly indecent graffiti were faintly revealed behind the painting, probably put there by the workmen who first put the work in its place. And there was the dust of four centuries. We all coughed, and the Marchese made a joke about disturbing the dust of his ancestors. He seemed in good enough spirits about it, as well he might. Fifty million dollars Canadian does not represent wealth of the highest magnitude these days, but it is still a lot of dough.

The present Marchese will probably be Italy's next ambassador to Canada, and this without previous service as a diplomat. As M. de Norpois might have observed, in diplomacy position means everything.

Removal of the painting from the long gallery in the Castello was proceeding at a very deliberate pace as the space voyagers were being debriefed in Warm Springs. It began to look more and more like a race between two historical developments, neither one fully meaningful without the other. Professor Goderich simply must be available at the dedication ceremonies, if only to press the button that would set in motion the turntable on which the painting was placed. That would be right at the centre of the Codrington/Sleaford/ Goderich Wing.

And if the painting should require some sort of special restorative technique, the dedication ceremonies would be pointless. I kept careful notes on the condition of the work, its original frame and especially its wooden backing. This proved to be in remarkable condition, the wood dry and as hard as iron, not decayed nor filled with worm holes. Considered as a stretcher, the original mount had served remarkably well. It was not easy to remove it in order to restretch the painting on its new, tough and long-wearing black plastic stretcher. I watched while this was done. A dehumidifying spray was applied to the back of the canvas and to the facing surface of the new stretcher and backing. The interfacing surfaces had to be perfectly dry and impermeable to new moisture; the painting would remain permanently in its smooth, unwrinkled position against the new backing. The outer edges of the new backing had to be grooved in such a way as to allow a sheath of frontal packing to be slid along the grooves into a position that matched the painted surface in dimensions. The edges were then sealed off with strong adhesive tape and the work was easily transported in this state.

We went by motor transport from Classe to Genoa, and sailed from Genoa to Montreal. I acted as supercargo on behalf of the National Gallery. I passed the last half of

August aboard ship, in transit from Genoa to the east coast of Canada, up the Saint Lawrence to Montreal. The shipment arrived, in perfect condition, at Pier 55 and was allowed through Customs on behalf of the gallery on the basis of my sworn statement that it had not been interfered with in transit. It might, under some other supervision, have been packed full of drugs intended for distribution in Montreal. Not under my eyes. The first officer and I used to examine the shipment three times daily, at different times of day. We would examine the seals carefully to make sure that they hadn't been touched. Nothing came into Canada in that shipment but a work of art valued at fifty-six million dollars.

Not the highest price dispensed for a single work up till that time, the third highest, I think. As a gift/acquisition of the National Gallery, the import duties were waived, or did not apply. I saw the shipment transferred to a special railway car and rode with it inside the car to Ottawa. By the time we got there I was beginning to feel my age a little bit. I had not slept well on the last nights of the voyage up the Saint Lawrence. Too much excitement. Getting near the end of the long road.

On the next day, a Sunday, we faced up to the difficulties of moving the crated painting from the railway yards on the outskirts of Ottawa to the National Gallery in the centre of the city, not at all a simple task. A number of streets had to be closed off for several hours while Canadian Forces personnel officially received the shipment, loaded it into a wide-based vehicle and moved off under close escort, on the alert to ward off any attempt to damage the cargo. This was considered a real possibility by the gallery staff, though not by me.

We proceeded carefully along the quiet Sabbath streets to the receiving platform of the gallery, where the chief of the Special Acquisitions Committee signed for the painting, after hearing my assurance that this was the shipment that had left the Castello Bianchini under my observation. I had to sign or initial a stack of bills of lading, invoices and vouchers, until the gallery people and the Armed Forces were satisfied. Then the crated painting was set on end on specially designed dollies and wedged into a vertical position, to be trundled along to the gallery's labs and accession area. That was my last glimpse of it before the dedication ceremonies. I was naturally curious to see how the staff would site the work for permanent display. I knew more or less how they planned to situate it; powerful electric motors had had to be installed at the top of the long entrance ramp that is such an outstanding feature of the building.

The level, approximately circular space at the top of this ramp sits up off ground level at a considerable height. It is enclosed by transparent panels giving the exterior of the structure a form suggesting a crown; this suggestion of imperial power and magnificence is deliberate and insistent. Across the mouth of the Rideau River, just where it enters Ottawa, the form of the Parliamentary Library likewise recalls an enormous crown. The two buildings, separated by a century in their design and execution, echo one another in their imperial references, though of an unpolitical empire.

Seen from a distance, in the glittering frosty twilight of an Ottawa midwinter, the two crowns, twinned and comically similar in form, make a wonderfully pleasing architectural statement. It was an excellent notion of the director of the institution to install the Titian under the crystal-crowned top of the ramp, for display around the clock. In fact, owing to its extreme visibility in this spot the Titian has become one of the principal sights of the capital, very often displayed on postcards and tourism brochures and sometimes handed out in travel agencies. I should now describe the work as mounted as the chief cultural possession of Canada, apart from the body of work in the arts produced collectively by Canadian painters, musicians and writers. A foreign import like the plays of Shakespeare or a masterwork by Titian, or European music, even when performed by native Canadians, can't be ranked as a cultural possession according to the same standards as the indigenous product. The paintings of Borduas and Pellan come home to our hearts with tremendous force, with nearer and greater effect than even the *Priam and Achilles*.

But judged by the canons of world art, the European masterwork may achieve a status in the literature of art history that the Group of Seven, or Borduas and Pellan, can never approach. This doesn't mean that the greatest work in the arts has all been done by European masters. What it does mean is that the apparatus of publicity and propaganda in the world of art is solidly in the grasp of an international community of historiographers, critics, dealers who all have an interest in constructing and preserving a received order of values and valuations in the arts. To have *Priam and Achilles* in its permanent collection at once gives the National Gallery credibility and status in this international community that it could not have acquired in any other way. And around this central nubbin of credibility whole satellite rings of international acceptance can arrange themselves; Canadian arts institutions will have a name and value that they never had before. The institutions defend and protect the working artist with a spin-off effect that develops from our ownership of an unqualified masterwork. The academic and critical bodies make propaganda for the working artists, who then have a better climate to work in.

That, anyway, is the theoretical view of the link between the arts, the artists and the academic institutions. It is a privileged view. Perhaps it only exists to defend museum culture and its organization of the arts. It's better to have an academic view of the arts than no view at all. We still need bodies to defend and protect the arts and their makers and spokesmen and spokeswomen. Otherwise we would have at best some small struggling clumps of arts-workers, working in loneliness in a very inhospitable social structure. If I had not taken an indulgent view of museum culture I would not have cooperated in the purchase of the Titian, which after all belongs to the world, not to the Bianchini family or the National Gallery of Canada. I would have instructed Pluyshin to peddle her

Titians elsewhere — Japan, perhaps — and to tell the Marchese that Canada wasn't interested.

We'd have been a poorer country in the long run if we hadn't taken up his offer. Canada comes out of the affair looking pretty good, if you ask me. I have no regrets about the purchase, although I know that many arts administrators have lately been grumbling that our money should have gone into bursary and scholarship funding for young artists. What's Titian to us? What are we to him? That's their point, within certain limits a good one. But it is precisely a limited and blinkered viewpoint, one that I'm glad to reject publicly. Dead white male European artists still have much to give to the rest of the world, exactly as living black female African artists do. There needn't be an official agenda that favours either sect in the great game.

That's why I urged the director and his officials to avoid all appearance of a museum exhibit when they were preparing the décor for the background setting for their treasure. Everything should be kept as simple as possible, the attention of viewers focussed on the painting. The work was to be freestanding, in the exact centre of the Codrington/Sleaford/Goderich Wing, on a turntable that turned a complete circle every ninety minutes. The huge, superb painted image moved almost imperceptibly, at the same time obliging the viewer to move very slowly with it so as to maintain a certain consistency of viewpoint, or to stand still and allow the composition of the work to adjust itself as the painted surface shifts slowly in her or his eyes. So far as I'm aware, this was the first time a great work was mounted in this way. The slow speed of rotation allows multiple viewpoints to the student, scholar or critic; indeed it almost obliges one to keep on adjusting one's stance. It is precisely a moving picture.

The turntable rotates clockwise. This has been criticized, I think with some justice, but the spatial layout of the work, in relation to its narrative element, more or less commands that the figures on the left side — Priam and his suite — be viewed first. Then the figure of Achilles should move slowly into a central position, moving very deliberately, but as though he were alive, to preoccupy viewers with the figure of the legendary hero, the central figure of the epic tradition. There is some sense in which the wrath of Achilles, and the appeasement of that wrath, are the subjects of all epic narrative. It is a subject of such power and grandeur that it scarcely asks for accompanying illustration or explanation.

Acting largely on my advice, I'm proud to say, the director and his staff chose to mount the painting unencumbered by the kind of journalistic documentation usually to be seen in public exhibitions at the major galleries. No photographs of the Castello Bianchini. No looped tape recordings lecturing visitors on the epic cycle and its iconography as depicted by this and other of the greatest artists. No potted museum culture. The only element of décor to intrude on our contemplation of this great product of the human spirit is the battery of lighting fixtures that has been arranged around and above it. These fixtures, not all the same size and shape, are controlled by automatic dimmers so that the light on the painting's surface is very soft in the hours of daylight, slightly more insistent as twilight comes on, distinctly brighter as full night unfolds, but never blinding or brilliant. This smoothness of effect, and the absolute quietness of the electrically powered turntable, give the work on its mount the appearance of some great aileron or vane, cutting its way through a mythic universe whose skies are eternal and humane.

Under this soft light the work merges into Homeric legend, the endlessly meaningful and personal qualities of heroic narrative. The wrath of Achilles arises from his loss of Briseis as much as from the slaying of his favourite, Patroclus. He wants his girl back in his tent and his young man alive at his side, ready to receive his embraces. Common motives, yes. But epic actions spring from common motives; we see this around us daily. The wish to visit Mars has elements of tourism in it, and much to do with our desire to motor to the

Grand Canyon or Banff. Soon enough travel agencies will be advertising special excursions to the surface of Mars. Take eighteen months off and visit our alternative world. Book now, before the seasonal rush!

Tourism remains humanity's most favoured recreation; no reason why it shouldn't extend itself to Mars and eventually to the other planets. Curiosity is the principal motive that makes folk long to go on pilgrimages. Greed might be a secondary motive, a teasing need to go there and see what there might be in it for us. It is from this second motive that colonialism comes; the impulse to possess certainly lay behind our first efforts at the colonization of near-space, the Moon landings and the first Mars voyage. But the imperialism in play was not, at least, a nationalistic thrust towards empire; it was internationalistic in character and scope.

This internationalism was the principal and very edifying quality to mark the dedication ceremonies at the gallery on that storied October 15th, the climax of the week of festivity that followed the Canadian Thanksgiving weekend. Thanksgiving in Canada develops early; the specific date being that of the second Monday of October, in that year on Monday the eleventh. It seemed appropriate to the organizers of the celebrations that they should begin with observances of the autumn festival, turkey dinners, pumpkin pies, infrequent accompanying prayers. From Tuesday on, the round of secular thanksgiving grew more and more dizzying. Guests of the highest distinction arrived at the airport almost hourly during the runup to Friday. Presidents and prime ministers. Chiefs of military staff. High officials of the International Space Administration. The chief voice of Mission Control, a voice that made you jump nervously when you heard it in the mouth of the man sitting across the table.

"You must be Captain Ritchie."

"Why yes, I am, sir, and may I ask your name?" I was clearly far too old to be active in the space program in any way.

"I'm Professor Goderich's father."

"Aha! Then you must be among the principal donors to the Titian fund. Isn't that so?"

"That's correct, but it doesn't give me any official rank or title. Plain Mister will have to do."

"Mr. Goderich it is, sir. Son of a Nobel Prize winner and father of one of the Mars walkers. You must be a proud man."

"Yes, I am. I've got something to ask you, Captain Ritchie, a small favour. Would you just say 'This is Mission Control speaking,' in your broadcasting voice? Just to please those of us around you at this table."

He gave an engaging grin. Why do those Americans always seem so youthful? Is it because they prize youth above all things? He shielded his mouth with a napkin, and spoke in low but unmistakable tones.

"This is Mission Control speaking."

Perhaps the words came out louder than intended. There was a wave of approving laughter, some applause, even a muted cheer or two, so that Captain Ritchie almost seemed to blush. And this was a person who only weeks before had held the whole human family attentive to his every word. A strange development. Having enjoyed such an audience, how could even the most modest of men retire into private life?

I asked him, "What are your plans, Captain? Will you remain at your service post?"

"Well, Mr. Goderich, that's hard to say right now. Let's just say that I'm open to all offers."

I suppose that the most-listened-to voice on Earth is always open to offers. After this particular dinner was over and the guests were settled over coffee and brandy in one of the embassy lounges, I spotted several people staring curiously at Captain Ritchie, people who had not been seated near us at the dinner table. How long would it be, I wondered, before his vocal qualities of pitch, timbre and pronunciation followed him into private life? Would his voice prove unforgettable, permanently merged with our notions of the really newsworthy?

There were greater persons than Captain Ritchie or myself to be heard or overheard during this succession of parties, banquets and balls. The two great events, the transit of a masterwork from the Old World to the New, and the first step towards colonization of a sister planet, had become inextricably connected in these last days. That Madam President should leave Washington for a five-day state visit to Ottawa seemed to fit the occasion exactly; she was perhaps the first American statesperson to grasp that Canadians celebrate Thanksgiving in October. In her short address upon arrival at the airport, she spoke of this fact, and was even able to crack a joke about it.

"Canadians give thanks sooner than Americans," she said, and the quip — was it really extemporaneous? — was snatched at by Canadian listeners, as always grateful for any morsel of attention and praise from our great neighbour, and became a kind of anthem on the events of the week.

I think it really was spoken ad lib, but the speechwriters of seven heads of state and prime ministers grasped its nuances; readiness to give praise became a central notion of the week of celebration. And the crush of assembled great ones grew more and more suffocating as the time rushed by us. It was a week of bewildering rumours; the Queen was going to fly in for a surprise visit in honour of the celebrated Cambridge physicist. She never appeared, but the high commissioner conferred the Order of Merit on my son during a state reception on the Thursday afternoon of that glorious week. At least I think it was Thursday. I'm getting a bit vague on some of the details by now. Yes, here it is in my notes: *John, OM. Thurs.* I don't know how he'll find room on his dinner jacket for all his decorations and medals. Mind you, formal occasions where decorations are to be worn don't happen every week. I'm entitled to wear four medals myself, and I've only ever worn them once, miniatures pinned to the lapel of my dinner jacket. That was on the night of Friday, October 15th. I couldn't quite bring myself to display the full-sized medals.

I enjoy having them, and quite like taking them out of their cases to admire them. Four is quite enough, however. John has close to fifty of them, many from places I never expect to see, not even from a great height. Places more remote than the surface of Mars, like Andorra, San Marino and the Cook Islands.

My four medals have no nonsense about military glory associated with them. Three of them are commemorative "jubilee" medals and the fourth is the badge of an Officer of the Order of Canada. Here my son outranks me, as a Companion of the Order of Canada, the most elevated grade of three. These subtle distinctions have little place in Canadian society, but John looks like a Christmas tree when all lit up with signs of glory, as during that hectic week of ceremonies. He'd somewhere or other acquired a handsome dinner jacket, secondhand, as he admitted to me in private. I think it had its origins, at least for John, in the secondhand formal wear department of Moss Bros., the London suppliers of just about anything a person might need to wear.

Academic robes, military and naval uniforms, clerical attire, some diplomatic regalia like ambassadorial dress, and more simply the colourful uniforms worn by various sports organizations such as baseball and hockey teams, all seem to testify to our wish to preserve these badges of distinction and honour, some of them dating back to the late Middle Ages. You can't have a week of ceremonial festivity without a lavish display of these trappings of hierarchical society. I saw an immense variety of robes, sashes, bonnets, orders, medals and decorations, all in the most brilliant hues, during that week. Some of us even devised a game, of which the point was to see how many of the ribbons displayed on some celebrated chest could be correctly identified by the player. This got to be quite an enjoyable pastime; the eye was constantly being assailed by bright contrasting colours. At last count John had in his possession the breast badges of thirty-seven orders, including that strange one shaped like a dead sheep — the Order, I believe, of the Golden Fleece!

Poor Emily Underwood Goderich had for the longest time no decoration to wear. Of course it was the Brits who first noticed this. The command that Emily be given something came apparently from the very highest level. Result: membership in the Royal Victorian Order, or MVO. Honorary, as Emily was not a British subject, but at least it gave her some letters to go after her name; some of her correspondence is now signed with those initials. She keeps the leather case with her MVO badge on a handy shelf in their New York apartment, ready for display at any moment as required.

Of all these immensely distinguished people, hung all over with glittering stars like Christmas trees, the most spectacular in my eyes was Captain Céline Hervieu. In absolutely perfect physical condition, slender as a wand and well muscled with it, she was the cynosure of all eyes at any formal function that she attended. I remember her appearance vividly. She was to be married the following week to Commandant de Barny, himself an extraordinary figure in his various uniforms and hats. But Captain Hervieu surpassed even her fiancé in grace and personal beauty. On the last night there was a formal dinner at Rideau Hall, not very far from the National Gallery. There must have been a hundred and fifty guests, maybe more. Some clever protocol chief from the Governor General's staff had arranged the seating with consummate tact. But sometimes perfect arrangements can be a shade too perfect, if you know what I mean. This was clear to me when I saw that I had no formal grade or title, and must therefore go in to dinner last in the "taking in" procession, which took time. Hard indeed to persuade over a hundred diners to process formally in to dinner in the correct order of precedence; these affairs require practice.

Imagine a state wedding or a coronation without any rehearsal! The guests at Rideau Hall showed an alarming tendency to wander off on their own, out of the correct order of precedence. Who goes in to dinner first, an ambassador or a cardinal? Somebody must know, because the question was satisfactorily resolved that night.

Outside of Rideau Hall, after dinner, stood a fleet of five yellow schoolbuses, each capable of transporting more than thirty passengers plus security. In under ten minutes after dinner the guests clambered aboard, engines came to life, and the guests rolled off towards the National Gallery, looking exactly like a gang of high-schoolers being taken to a football playoff to root for their team. What a cheerleader Céline Hervieu would have made at any time in her life prior to her incarnation as a Mars walker!

The parade of yellow buses took just five minutes to reach the red carpet at the National Gallery and the long graceful rise of the ramp leading towards the Codrington/Sleaford/Goderich Wing, the jewel in the crown of the building, now illuminated under a lowering fall sky, like a crystalline head-piece swathed in a burnous of rich indigo wool.

And as the list of precedence placed me at the tail-end of the procession, I felt liberated from the need to remain in line, trailing up the ramp as the last guest of all. *Number one fifty-five!* I mean, why bother? As soon as the magnificent dignitaries at the head of the line had made their slow way part way up the ramp, I dropped off the tailgate, so to speak, and sidled slowly along beside the slow-moving marchers. I wanted to see my son arrive at the top of the rise and take his place after many adventures at the centre of the official function registering his exploits and the place of his family inheritance in this festival. Presidents, prime ministers, ambassadors and state secretaries should now give pride of place to John Sleaford Goderich, who united our three family histories in his own life and person.

Now I had penetrated right to the top of the ramp, where it levelled off and widened out into a grand exhibition room surrounded by broad high windows looking out at the Parliamentary Library, with the waters of the Rideau and the Ottawa perpetually renewing themselves at one's feet.

Here, shrouded in a smooth off-white cotton wrapping that

was arranged so as to allow for its removal by a single yank of a convenient cord, stood the masterwork, *King Priam Before the Tent of Achilles, Begging the Body of Hector from the Hero, for Burial.* This is one of the versions of the painting's title. There are some others but this is the closest to the Italian original.

Their meeting at the close of *The Iliad* is one of the very greatest and most moving incidents among the narratives of the West, a test of one's capacity to feel.

Now the director of the National Gallery addressed the assembly, reading their names and titles from a long list, a list that took minutes to read, but finally he was free to name three of the four Mars walkers, whose presence here tonight was such a radical honour, and such a source of gratification to the nation. Captain Hervieu and the just-promoted Colonel de Barny would now come forward and together seize the cord that would unveil Titian's masterpiece. Professor John Sleaford Goderich would kindly take in his hands the switch that would activate the turntable and the lighting. Would the three astronauts please take up their positions?

Here they came, a goddess flanked by demi-gods, moving out in front of the presidents and ambassadors, where a ring of red cord ran around the display area. Here they were greeted lovingly by the director. Now he places the cord of unveiling in the clasped hands of colonel and captain. Then he hands the professor a small black object like the remote control on your VCR. The director steps away from the trio of Mars walkers. There is a pause for press photographers and television staffers to do their dire work.

"Now, please!" says the director.

Céline and Hubert yank at the cord. The soft smooth swath of fine cotton parts gracefully, then slides in a rush down from the top edge of the painting. Two teenaged girls — daughters of the director, as it happens — scamper forward, feeling for the cotton wrapping, bundling it up and carrying it away. At the same moment John presses his hand control and the display lights come on. It is at once clear how cleverly they have been placed. The picture tells its story with fully achieved clarity.

The glittering assembly gives a long sigh, like any audience gathered at the circus to witness some extraordinary feat of courage and daring. The painter might as well be a tightrope walker.

The ranks of the dignitaries begin to group themselves in trios and quartets. The president of Italy throws his arms around the shoulders of the Marchese Bianchini and explains to the crowd at large what a great benefaction the Old World is conferring on the New. Most of his words go unheard, for champagne is being poured. The cheerful sound of ice-cubes rattling against bottles mounts in people's ears. The wine is from France, a fact later on explained to the Ontario Vintners' Association as a vinous tribute to Colonel de Barny and the French head of state.

No drinks for the security people. I tried to count the American Secret Service personnel and RCMP in the big room. There were more of them than there were guests; this is often the case when the president of the United States is on hand. I spotted a number of their agents who were of the female gender, their firearms less well concealed under severely tailored jackets.

Soon the drinks, the superb champagne, the Napoléon and other spirits began to have their usual effect on the emotions of the guests. I found myself gripped tightly in the friendly clutch of the Marchese Bianchini, probably because my face was more familiar to him than that of most of the others present. I was in some sense the author of his astonishing prosperity.

"You come to see me again real soon, no?" he seemed to say.

No, I thought, on the whole, no. I had only had one company to give for my country. Farewell and goodbye to *Codrington Hardware and Builders' Supplies. Since 1867.* This is definitely the final time the name will be mentioned in these pages.

The Marchese turned away; his face was succeeded in my vision by that of the director of the National Gallery, a friend of long standing who pumped my right arm and directed his voice at my ears in a kind of noisy wordless sigh. "Got any more deals for us like this one?" he was thinking. Much the same sentiments from the buyer as from the seller. It must have been a good trade-off. Perhaps I had some future remaining to me as an arts entrepreneur. I wondered what my next move might be. Obviously I should try to cross over towards my son, shake his hand, maybe give him a kiss on the cheek, remind him again of those beautiful aerial cars. Would he remember his words? I thought that he probably would.

Sometimes an entire career, a whole life sums itself up in a predictive phrase spoken without premeditation or reflection. But I was not to draw close enough to my son this evening to ask about the Minirail. The crowd was too thick, simple explanation of a complex fact. Too filled with fame. I couldn't push towards him without perhaps falling over a senator or treading on the silvered toes of an ambassador's wife. I decided to stay where I was, and spent some time in maintaining my position like a trout in an eddying stream, so as to keep my balance and avoid accidental nibbles at hooks. Forty minutes must have gone by when all at once a loud female squeal startled all present. Afterwards there were some who swore that it came from Madam President, a surprised reaction to a silent shift in the painting's position.

"Henry," said the woman's voice shrilly, "the painting. It's moved, Henry. It's *moved!*"

Certainly it had. It was meant to do so.

"Isn't that just the cunningest thing," said the same female voice. It was certainly the president who had spoken.

Now the remaining party-goers, perhaps a hundred people plus security, began to stroll around the base of the mount. A senior diplomat, almost a household word in Canada, took from his pocket a packet of paper matches, tore off one, struck it, let it burn down, blew it out and placed it on the turntable.

I heard him mutter, "Let's see where it is in ten minutes."

A security man stepped up to him and gave a brisk order. "You'll have to remove that object, sir."

"Do you think it's explosive or incendiary?" demanded the diplomat.

"You'll have to remove the match, sir."

The diplomat shrugged, picked up the innocent bit of paper. We are in the care but also in the grip of our security staff, who have a greater authority than our own. Madam President does what they tell her without question. So do all lesser mortals. The affair of the spent paper match didn't become a diplomatic incident, but only because the diplomat involved behaved sensibly. He smiled at the agent, retrieved his bit of paper and turned away, leaving the building shortly after-wards, not without escort.

The motion of the turntable and the consequent shift in the angle from which you saw the painting focussed the attention of the crowd on the story element of the composition. They began to puzzle out the meaning of the tale — one of the greatest moments in the world's mythologies of contest and rule. Priam, dressed in a sort of toga, with a golden cincture around his waist and a gilt coronet in his scanty hair, stands at the left, his knees slightly bent, part of his right leg placed in the posture of one about to kneel in supplication. His retinue, crowded into the extreme left side of the space, seem to shrink in horror and despair at the sight of their king abasing himself in this way. Is this to be the end of the great war, they seem to ask themselves.

On the bare earth in the centre of the space lies the torn body of their great and magnanimous hero, the gallant and loving Hector, everybody's favourite. Still in warrior's dress, the body is covered with dust and dried blood, executed in the heavy and dull tones of crimson and grey that dominate the work: there is but little light in the paint. Achilles stands to the right, in front of his tent, clad not as a warrior but in the robes of relaxation or sport. Behind him, through the opening that leads to the interior of the big tent, the smooth body of the dead Patroclus can just be seen, stripped of its armour, lovely in youth, pathetic in death. Achilles seems to be looking in two directions at once, responding to Priam's appeal with a releasing gesture. Take up your hero's body and go, he seems to say, while the position of his head and shoulders suggests a glance in the direction of his dead friend. In the implied confusion of these opposed attitudes the painting expresses the nihilism of every kind of human contest. All struggle, war, passionate love and hate, domination of one person by another, all contention is idle. What it leaves behind is desolation, the death of the hero and lover. The great stroke in the narrative of the painting is displayed above the figures of king and heroes, in the upper centre of the work, where a mysterious ashen mist blows and puffs around, just revealing momentarily the figure of Ares, god of warfare, struggle, confusion and hatred. His heavy helmet lowers over the scene; the face under his visor is skeletal. Ares to the Greeks, Mars to the Romans, best known to the contemporary world as the resident god of the Red Planet.

It took another hour for the implications of the turning picture to fasten themselves in the minds of the last viewers at the end of the evening.

The turntable goes around every ninety minutes day or night and the light firms or dims accordingly. The masterwork is clearly visible from any good vantage point outside the gallery. It turns and it turns on its base winter and summer, in and out of light and darkness, like a magnificent vane or wing.

Turns.